NINE LIVES

ANITA WALLER

BLOODHOUND
— BOOKS —

Print ISBN 978-1-913942-40-3

ALSO BY ANITA WALLER

For my awesome beta-reading team: Sarah Hodgson,
Alyson Read, Marnie Harrison, Tina Jackson and Denise Cutler.
My eternally grateful thanks, ladies.
The punches are never pulled...

The last of the flooding, the last of the rain,
The start of the anguish, the start of the pain.
Calmness remains now where once torrents flowed,
Hearts were sore broken, the night of the flood.

Anita Waller, *Aftermath,* 1963

FOREWORD

Sheffield has five rivers: the Don, the Sheaf, the Loxley, the Rivelin and the Porter. This book is about the Porter, the smallest and possibly the prettiest of all five rivers, and a worthy character in its own right for this story.

The city is built on seven hills, and the Porter descends over one thousand feet from its source among the sedge grass on Burbage Moor at Clough Hollow, near the village of Ringinglow on the outskirts of Sheffield. It takes its name from its brackish colour, which is similar to the colour of Porter, a brown discoloration obtained as it passes over iron ore deposits on the way from its source.

It flows eastward through the Mayfield Valley to the first of the remaining mill dams. Beyond Forge Dam the Porter is defined as a main river. It drops down into Sheffield city centre, where it meets the River Sheaf under platform five of Sheffield's Midland Station. They continue on to meet up with the mighty River Don which then flows onwards until it reaches the North Sea.

To reach this point it passes under many culverts, and in

summer is a gentle river. In winter, in heavy rain conditions, it changes...

PROLOGUE

The body was staged carefully under a tree in Ecclesall Woods, positioned so that an early-morning dog walker would find it easily. The thrill was in the kill, and having the work admired; it wasn't in hiding the bodies away and hoping they would never be found. In the moonlight, and with her blonde hair spread out around her, this one looked spectacular. Her small but perfectly formed breasts were framed by her arms as they crossed over her stomach, fingers interlinked, and her long slender legs led the eye to the light brown triangle of hair at the apex of her thighs.

The hope was that as it was almost midnight, late-night dog walkers wouldn't venture into the woods to disturb the scene; it wouldn't look so good in the dark. This was all about cause and effect, the beautiful symmetry of the girl who had said her name was Lilith. The double-barrelled surname was irrelevant; it was all about the Christian name. Lilith, indeed a beautiful one, and for a moment Lilith's killer wondered what such a pretty name meant. Something to explore later when the whole thing was relived in the early hours when sleep wouldn't come.

With the body of the young girl in place, the black-clad

figure stepped back in admiration. A sight for tired eyes; time to leave it, after the final act.

Crouching down, clutching a sharp craft knife, the roman numerals IV were carved with precision into Lilith's right palm. Number four, and the thought in the killer's mind was full of confidence that the police didn't seem to have any idea who had killed the first three.

Snipping off the tip of the little finger on the same hand was easy, and the fingers were once more interlinked. Silently the killer stopped for a moment to fill the backpack with Lilith's clothes and to survey the scene, before moving swiftly out of the woods and back to the entrance. A glance around and the killer morphed into a jogger, running up the road to the posh houses where the car had been hidden in plain sight, false number plates an additional protection.

Fifteen minutes later the evening's entertainment was over, the fingertip had joined three others in the freezer, the cat had been given some milk, and all was right in a murderer's world.

1

K atie Davids held up a hand and waved as she saw Rebecca Charlesworth walk into the pub.

'Over here,' she called, more in hope than belief that Becky would hear her.

Becky clearly didn't as she did a full three hundred and sixty-degree turn before spotting the frantically waving arm of her friend.

Katie watched as she fought her way through the noisy groups of students, and grinned as Becky made it to their table.

Becky ran her hands through her long dark hair and screwed it into a fresh ponytail. 'I'm ready for this. The essay's done, emailed in, and I want to get drunk now. Is this mine?' She held up the glass of Coke.

'It is. It's Coke, with maybe a drop or two of vodka in it.' Katie patted her backpack. 'If there isn't enough, help yourself. I brought a big bottle.'

Becky tasted it, briefly closed her eyes in appreciation and smiled. 'Perfect. So what are we doing?'

'Do you want to go into the city centre or stay in this area so we don't have to fork out for taxis?'

'Stay here, I think. It won't be a late night, I'm knackered. Don't let me do that again, leave something till the last minute.'

Katie laughed. 'I've been nagging you for at least two weeks to get it done. Forget it now, it's over. Susie and Clare said they might look in later, after *Macbeth* finishes.' She took out a small hairbrush and quickly ran it through her drying blonde-streaked hair. She blessed the day she'd cut it short, so much easier to handle when there was rain as torrential as it had been for at least a week. And she felt it emphasised her elfin features instead of hiding them; the other girls had been so supportive of her decision to chop most of it off.

Susanna Roebuck and Clare Vincent shared accommodation with Katie and Becky, and all four had hit it off from day one, respecting each other's privacy, yet enjoying the friendship created by living in such close proximity. Number forty-three Crookesvale Gardens was happy student accommodation, as far as the four girls were concerned. Even their parents felt relief that their daughters had hit on what they would have wanted for them.

There was a flurry of activity as yet more people pushed their way into the pub. 'Looks as though the Drama Studio is out. We'd best watch out for Susie and Clare, they'll never see us tucked away in this corner.'

Katie and Becky sipped at their drinks and waited for their friends to put in an appearance. It was half an hour before they saw Clare, who stood in the doorway, searching.

'I'll go and get her.' Becky stood and pushed through the throng of people, reaching Clare who hadn't moved from the doorway. 'Clare, follow me!'

A hand was lifted in acknowledgement, and the pretty girl with curly blonde hair, blue eyes and a slight frown on her face followed Becky through the crowd. Clare sat on the stool they had been hiding under the table awaiting their arrival, and turned towards the bar. 'Susie not here then?'

'No, we thought you were coming together.'

'We were. *Macbeth* finished, but I needed a wee, so I went to the loo and said I would see her outside, then we'd walk down here together. When I got outside she was nowhere to be seen. I hung around for ages thinking she might have decided to go to the ladies and I'd missed her, but she didn't appear. I tried ringing her phone but we had to turn them off in the theatre, so I'm guessing she's not put it back on yet because it's going straight to voicemail.'

'Was she okay? Not feeling ill or anything?' They were all aware of Susie's type-one diabetes issues, and her checking of her blood sugar levels; Katie sounded anxious as she asked the question.

'She was fine. She didn't say she felt off, and she always does if she needs some medication boost or a quick Mars bar. In fact she had a Mars in her coat pocket just in case, because we had a laugh about not sitting on our coats in the theatre. It's strange...'

'Let me go and get you a Coke, and I suggest you add something from inside Katie's bag,' Becky said and stood to go to the bar. Her five feet eight height gave her a decided advantage as she elbowed her way through to the front.

She kept checking back at the table all the time she was waiting to be served; she didn't want to have to come and queue again for one drink. She ordered three Cokes eventually, and carried them carefully back.

It wasn't easy pouring vodka out of a litre bottle under the table but they managed amidst giggles. For a minute or so it took their minds off the missing Susie. All three of them, without it ever having been a formal discussion, watched out for health signs in Susie, and they felt concern.

'When I've finished this,' Clare said, 'I'm going home. It's where she'll be, but I don't want her to be there and needing medical help.'

'We'll all go. I'm knackered anyway,' Becky said.

'You've finished your essay?'

'I have. Don't sound so surprised. It's a masterpiece.'

All three laughed. They guessed masterpiece was a hyperbole on Becky's part, but fully understood the relief evident in her voice that her 'masterpiece' was off her mind, and with her tutor.

They finished their drinks, and fought their way out of the pub, turning right and heading up the hill towards the house they called home, instead of the places they had lived in for all of their lives up to that point.

Home was a Victorian house that had been converted into four student flats. Each of them had a large bedroom with an en suite, and on the ground floor was a communal kitchen and a lounge. Clare unlocked the door and called her friend's name as soon as they entered the impressive hallway. Susie didn't respond, so Clare ran upstairs.

She knocked on Susie's door, and turned the handle, but it was locked. Clare knocked louder, but there was nothing, no answering call, no movement. The worry for Susie's safety turned to fear.

For what seemed like the millionth time Clare pulled out her mobile phone and rang Susie. Nothing.

'Is she okay?' Katie's anxious voice sounded up the stairs.

'I don't think she's here.'

Clare reached the bottom of the stairs and headed towards the kitchen where she could hear the clatter of cups.

'Not here? Then where the hell is she?' There was worry still in Katie's voice. 'Should we tell the police?'

Becky laughed. 'I don't think so. They'd think we were

crackers. Clare, who were you with in the theatre? Was there a crowd of you, or only you two?'

'We sat with Jenna, the girl in the wheelchair. She'd parked herself at the end of our row, then there was Susie in the first seat, then me. Behind us was that lad from Birmingham on our course, Danny something or other, then Dom Andrews. Also behind us were the twins, Maria and Anya.' Clare paused. 'I can't remember anybody else. The ones in front of us I didn't know.'

'Is she likely to have gone somewhere with any of them? Did she get chatting to somebody and assumed you'd guess where she was?'

'She's not like that.' Clare shook her head as if to emphasise her words. 'I'm worried, girls.'

'So are we, but we can't do anything at this stage. The police would laugh at us. We're students, prone to doing odd things like disappearing for a couple of days on a whim. Because we know how out of character this is for Susie, doesn't mean they'll believe us.' Katie's sensible voice didn't make them feel any better.

'O...kay,' Becky said slowly. 'The first thing we need to do is check she isn't in a diabetic coma in her room. We know she's not downstairs, but if she came home because she felt ill, she'd be in bed.'

'Her door's locked,' Clare said.

'And am I the only one who can open a Yale lock with a credit card?' Becky said.

Clare and Katie looked at each other. 'How did you learn that?' Clare asked.

'I have two older brothers, Clare.' Becky grinned.

. . .

7

The credit card slid down the sliver of a gap, and all three girls held their breath. It didn't work the first time, but it did the second time, and Becky quietly pushed open the door.

The room was tidy, the bed made. Becky crossed the floor to check out the en suite but that was also empty. She smiled at the row of rubber ducks along the bathroom shelf.

'Nothing,' she said as she returned to see Clare and Katie sat on the edge of the bed.

'So what do we do?'

'Not a lot we can do. Don't put your phones on silent tonight in case she's in a situation where she needs help. Other than that, I hope we go to sleep and wake up in the morning to her in a drunken stupor and lying across her bed, with a hangover from hell.' Becky hesitated, thinking *please God, let that be the scenario.*

'She doesn't drink,' Clare reminded them. 'She wouldn't have had vodka in her Coke tonight, would she? I keep thinking that maybe she got talked into going off with some of the others we were sat with in the theatre, to carry on the discussion about the play. That was why we were there, to make notes and stuff. I would never have had her down as being thoughtless. She's one of the nicest people I've ever met, and I can't get over that little nag that she would have let me know. She knew I was only nipping to the ladies.'

'She didn't go anywhere with the lads you mentioned,' Becky said quietly.

'She didn't?'

'No, they came into the pub a good twenty minutes before you did, in a big group, talking about *Macbeth*.'

'Shit.' Clare breathed out the word, almost as a hiss. 'Then I give in. I don't know what to think. In that five minutes I was in the ladies, she vanished. I tell you, if she's not back by seven tomorrow morning, I'm ringing the police.'

2

Erica Cheetham considered staying in bed. For a mere second she considered it, then she put one foot out, quickly bringing it back in. *Bloody cold*, she thought. *Why couldn't I have been a librarian, or something else that's a nice occupation?*

'Call-out?' Frannie muttered, nowhere near the state that could be loosely called wakefulness.

'Yep. Go back to sleep, I'll ring you later and let you know what's happening.'

Frannie didn't respond, so Erica leaned over, brushed back her wife's short dark hair and gave her a quick kiss on what was showing of her forehead. Frannie's deep brown eyes opened momentarily, closed again, and Erica shook her own head to force some degree of awareness.

She swung both legs out and allowed her feet to rest on the fluffy bedside rug before letting them take her towards the bathroom. She didn't have time to shower, so splashed her face with water, gave her teeth a perfunctory twenty-second scrub, and returned to the bedroom to twist her long blonde hair into a ponytail. Her blue eyes stared back at her and she peered closer into the mirror searching for wrinkles. She counted every day as a bonus when she didn't see one. She quickly dressed in jeans and a top before grabbing a breakfast bar and a travel mug of coffee and leaving the house.

It was still raining, and she pulled the hood of her thick winter coat up and over her head, while she unlocked her car. She reversed down the drive and on to the road after a cursory glance to see if anything was travelling towards the rear end of her car, but it was a token nod to the possibility – who the hell was likely to be out at four o'clock on a dismal late October morning, other than her.

The rain was heavy and she switched her wipers to fast. It had been constant rain for the best part of a week, and parts of Sheffield had flooded. It always baffled her that a city built, like Rome, on seven hills could flood. It was an impossible city to cycle in because of the steepness of the hills leading out from the city centre, and yet it flooded. 'Doesn't water naturally go downhill?' she said aloud, but there was nobody to answer her.

The phone call at three fifty-two had told her of a dead body in the River Porter, at Midland Station.

She frowned as she realised she didn't even know the River Porter was at the station, and she wished there had been time to check the internet – her DS, Beth Machin, would know, and Erica would have to be careful how she hid her ignorance until she could get to a computer.

She pulled into the station car park and put a POLICE ON CALL sign in her car, then ran across to where she could see crime scene tape.

'DI Cheetham,' the young PC Sam King said with a smile, and held up the tape for her to duck under. It occurred to Erica every time she saw Sam just how good-looking he was, and yet he never spoke of girlfriends. His deep brown eyes and dark hair were enough to win the hearts of many a fair maiden, but, like her, he always seemed to be at work.

'Thanks, Sam. DS Machin here?'

'She is. She's having a coffee while she's waiting for you.'

Erica nodded without responding. She saw a railway employee waving at her so she headed towards him, guessing he would know what was going on, and would probably have information for her.

'I'll take you to the river when you're all here, ma'am. You might want to get a hot drink first, it's going to be wet and cold down there.' He pointed towards an open office door, and she saw Beth Machin waving from the window to the left of the door.

She headed towards her sergeant. *Down there? So where's this bloody river?*

Beth Machin, looking immaculate as always despite the early hour, nodded as Erica entered the small office, Beth handed her a mug of coffee. Her red hair was in a ponytail and she'd even managed to put on a little lipstick. Just for a moment Erica wanted to punch her in the mouth.

'Morning, boss. This is Graham Carver, the station manager.'

Erica looked at the tall, dark-haired man with the serious expression, and she smiled at him. 'Mr Carver. Have you been called in as well?'

'I have,' he said. 'If I can help...'

'Is there some way we can have refreshments set up for our officers?' Erica asked. 'It's a cold 'un, and they work better when fed and watered.'

'I've already asked our coffee shop lady to come in. We'll get that open for you. I do want to emphasise that you're going to be really wet, but hopefully you won't have to go beyond the Megatron, because you'll need a boat if you do. The water's running high and it's running fast, so you need to take care. We've had hell of a lot of rain.'

'Is the body still in the water?'

'It's wedged apparently. We had night workers on last night, checking everything was okay because of the amount of rain. The body is in the Porter. It meets up with the Sheaf lower down. Under platform five actually.'

The internet was sounding more and more like a good idea to Erica. She had no idea what the Megatron was, and wasn't there walkways she could walk on? Her bed was sounding more inviting by the minute. She could have ignored the phone call... And rivers met under platform five? This was starting to sound a bit Harry Potterish, and she smiled.

'Ian and Mike are here, boss,' Beth said, so Erica handed her half-drunk coffee to Graham Carver, thanked him, and both women left the warmth of his office for the coldness of the station concourse.

Erica led the way to the man who was going to take them to the body, and he looked at the footwear of the two women.

'They expensive trainers?' Callum McNicol, the night manager who had been the first to stumble across the body, shook his head as he spoke.

Beth and Erica looked at each other.

'We need wellingtons, I assume,' Erica said.

'No, DI Cheetham, you need waders.'

Erica took out her phone and spoke to the Forensics team, telling them they were going to see the body in situ, and to bring waders; the river was deep.

DCs Ian Thomas and Mike Nestor groaned. In looks, both men were an almost perfect match for each other. Over six feet in height, both had dark brown hair showing no signs of thinning, and grey-blue eyes almost identical between the two men. Their personalities matched their kindly faces, and Erica knew she was blessed to have snagged these two men as part of her team.

Ian and Mike had decided to change into wellingtons as

they'd exited their cars, but it seemed they would be as useless as the women's trainers. Everyone hung around until Erica and Beth returned from their cars wearing wellingtons even though guessing they wouldn't be adequate, and Callum led them outside to the car park. The rain was still relentless, and the roar of the water was deafening.

Erica tried to squash the feelings of claustrophobia as they descended through the culvert where the river flowed underground, the river that would eventually meet up with the mighty Don, and end up flowing into the North Sea. The noise was awesome, scary, as they heard the roar of the waters pulsing through. Within seconds they felt soaked, and water had ridden over the tops of their ineffective wellingtons.

They could walk part of the way on a ledge, their torch beams waving around as they struggled to maintain some sort of balance, but then had to drop into the water and feel the intensity of the powerful force of the River Porter as it battled its way through to the Megatron, the cathedral-like structure deep under the streets of Sheffield that was home to the River Sheaf, after it had swallowed up the smaller Porter.

They could see a man in the distance, and Callum turned to speak to them. He had to shout over the roar of the water, but they got the gist of what he was saying, that the body was where the man was. He had been left to make sure it didn't dislodge and carry on down to the Sheaf, and ultimately the Don. The speed of the water would have it quickly heading for the coast, and expulsion into the North Sea.

The body was unclothed, her long blonde hair floating on the water. She was young; Erica estimated around nineteen or twenty, and didn't think she had been dead long. She used her torch to look at the woman, and the way she was being held in situ, trapped by two huge stones that jutted out from the walls of this massive underground tunnel. She wanted to shield her. Her nakedness was on show and she somehow felt that this young girl would be mortified if she knew that four men could all see every part of her. There was nothing obvious to indicate cause of death, and Erica sighed as she switched off her torch.

Beth Machin seemed to sense what her boss was thinking. 'We can't,' she said gently, placing her mouth close to Erica's ear. 'We can't cover her. We have nothing to do it with, and it would be swept away within a minute in this torrent.'

They could see five people approaching in the distance, and Erica breathed a sigh of relief. 'It looks as if Ivor is here.'

Ivor Simmonite, his white hair almost acting like a beacon, raised a hand in greeting when he spotted the small group of people, and two minutes later he was surveying the scene. He tried to wipe the water spray from his glasses, but knew it was a losing battle. He waited for the photographer to finish taking photographs, and then instructed his team to prepare the body for removal. There was no point attempting to do anything under the present conditions, any clues to what had happened would have been washed away by the force of the water; he wanted this young girl back in his autopsy suite where he could investigate how and when she had died.

Erica's team were the first to leave; they could do no more. They had given up speaking, the noise from the rushing water was deafening, but slowly their hearing returned as they reached the normality of the station concourse. Crime scene tape had been extended from the concourse to the opening of the culvert, steering passengers away from the area the police needed to use, and the four of them looked a sorry sight as they emerged.

'Tea?' Ian Thomas offered, and they all nodded in gratitude.

The station was quiet; it was still only half past five, and the commuter rush hadn't started.

'I'm frozen,' Beth said. 'Think we can all fit in that little office?'

'We can try,' Erica said, sipping at her drink.

She led them across and Graham Carver looked up in surprise as they all entered. 'I'm so sorry,' he said. 'I wanted to get some extra seats in for when you came back, but it's not taken you as long as I expected.'

'We couldn't do much down there,' Erica explained. 'They're bringing the body up shortly, so thank you for getting the area screened off. We will have to go back down, but we will be better equipped, I promise you. I don't think any of us realised what the conditions were like. In fact I'll lay odds on none of us knew about this world underneath the station. We couldn't really speak to the man who was looking after the body for us until we could get there, but I imagine there must have been someone else who raised the alarm and Jim stayed with her. I need Jim's details, by the way, in case we need to ask him anything.'

'No problem. Callum McNicol, the chap who led you down, is the man who was with Jim. Callum saw the body first. He called the police immediately, then me. He works nights, he's sort of the night manager, but he sees to any maintenance that needs doing, stuff like that. As day manager, I deal more with passenger-related things, and trains. He's still here somewhere. He came back up after he'd taken your Forensic team down. You want to speak to him now? Jim is called James Hardcastle, by the way,' he added as Beth was taking notes.

Erica shook her head. 'No, we need to get home and changed into dry clothes and shoes, I think. I'll ring you later to say what we want, and see where we go from here. I need to requisition waders for us as a priority, because we're going to have to go back to the place she was found, but it's possible we'll have to go in this damn river at some other point when we find out who she is and where she lived.' Erica leaned across his desk and shook his hand. 'Thank you for your co-operation, and for opening up the café. Police officers will be here for a couple of days, and will be grateful for that facility.'

Graham watched as they walked back across the concourse and headed out into the wind and rain of the car park. *Nice smile*, he thought, *nice lady*; he looked forward to seeing her again.

3

Frannie was eating breakfast when she heard Erica's car pull onto the drive, and she quickly clicked on the kettle. The front door opened, and Erica called out, 'Coffee, I need coffee.'

Frannie walked through to the hallway, then stopped. 'You're wet.'

'I'm fucking soaked,' Erica grumbled. 'Look at me. And frozen. I've been in a river.'

'What?'

'A bloody river! I tell you, Fran, I've seen things this morning I didn't even know were there. You know the River Porter?'

'That's the littlest one of the five, isn't it?'

'I have no idea, but it's not little at the moment. Look at me!' Erica paused dramatically with her arms outstretched. 'Look at me! It covered my boobs!'

'And nice boobs they are too,' Frannie said, trying not to laugh at the amateur dramatics going on in the hall. 'Go and have a shower, and I'll do you a bacon buttie and a coffee.'

Erica moved towards the stairs. 'You're a star. Did the

meeting go okay last night? I didn't hear you come in, I was out for the count by about nine.'

'Boring book, was it?' Frannie asked. 'Yes, the meeting went well, but we all went to the pub afterwards. It was gone eleven when I arrived home, so I tried not to wake you. I moved your Kindle off the bed, and even that didn't disturb you.'

Erica waved a hand in acknowledgement, and Frannie returned to the kitchen, wondering if she should have a bacon sandwich also, despite having finished her toast. She'd lost two pounds the previous week, and she had been trying really hard to not eat rubbish... Her brain took no persuasion and she placed six rashers on the grill.

Erica, in dry clothes, stood and watched as Ivor Simmonite began the post-mortem. The girl's head was resting on a block, her long blonde hair hanging over the edge of the table.

Ivor seemed to spend an inordinate amount of time inspecting her upper arms and instructing his colleague to take photographs, particularly of the tiny butterfly at the top of the right arm, and of the palm of her right hand. He was clearly not going to be rushed into anything, despite there being nothing that could help with identification. Her fingerprints hadn't been on their database, so it would mean much more detailed research to find out who she was.

Erica felt her phone vibrate in her jeans pocket, and she quickly read the message before leaning forward to use the intercom. 'Ivor, I have to go. We may have identification for you. Can you let me have the full report of the autopsy as soon as you have it, please?'

Ivor turned his grey eyes towards her, held up a thumb in acknowledgement, and Erica left the viewing platform.

· · ·

Becky Charlesworth and Katie Davids lifted their heads as the interview room door opened.

'DI Erica Cheetham,' Erica said, and held out her hand. They shook it, uncomfortably, clearly not used to shaking hands.

'You're here to report a missing person?'

Becky stared at her. 'We didn't expect to be reporting to a DI. We thought it would be the officer on duty at the front desk.'

Smart young lady, Erica thought.

'Tell me about your friend. When did she go missing?'

'Last night. She went to the university Drama Studio to watch *Macbeth* with our other friend, Clare Vincent. They're both taking the same course. We'd all arranged to meet in the pub later, but only Clare showed up, worried because she couldn't find Susie.'

'Susie?'

'Oh, sorry. Susie is Susanna Roebuck. All four of us share a house.'

Erica was writing. 'Spell Susie's first name, will you?'

Becky obliged.

'Let me get this straight, so it's clear in my mind. Student accommodation?' Becky and Katie nodded. 'And collectively you are Rebecca Charlesworth, Katie Davids, Clare Vincent and Susanna Roebuck?' Again Becky and Katie nodded.

Erica turned to the next page. 'Can you give me a description of Susie, please? And where is Clare?'

'Clare and Susie had a lecture this morning,' Becky confirmed, 'an important one, so Clare's gone to that so they at least both have notes on it, even if Susie, for whatever reason, isn't able to be there. Susie has long blonde hair, usually wears it down, ponytails give her a headache. Pretty, slim, she's twenty. Blue eyes, but not bright blue, bluish-grey, I'd say. About five feet four. Certainly smaller than me.'

Erica took a deep breath. 'Any identifying features? Tattoos, piercings?'

'She has pierced ears, wears gold studs during the week, but she might have changed them last night for going to the theatre. No other piercings that I know about.' Becky turned to Katie as she finished speaking. 'Which arm is her butterfly on?'

Katie thought for a moment, then pushed forward her right shoulder. 'It's here, at the top of her arm.'

Erica gave a slight nod. 'And do you know her parents' address?'

Becky fished around inside her bag, producing a small diary. She looked in the back, then passed it across to the DI. Erica wrote down the address, noting that it was in Bridlington, on the east coast.

'Are her parents elderly?'

Becky looked puzzled, and turned to Katie. 'No. Mid-forties, Katie?'

Katie agreed. 'If that, actually. Why?'

'It's me jumping to conclusions,' Erica said. 'I kind of assumed they'd retired to the coast.'

Katie gave a half smile. 'No, Susie's lived there all her life. She was glad to get a place at Sheffield, but she loves the coast. All four of us camped in their back garden in the summer. They live in a massive house. We haven't checked if she's there...'

'Why not?'

'We didn't want to worry them. Harry and Olivia are so lovely – we're always getting food parcels and other stuff from them. And Susie can't have decided in a few seconds that she wasn't going to wait for Claire to go to the ladies, she was going home to Brid. She's not like that. I have some pictures on my phone from that camp in the back garden, so I can show you what she looks like.' Katie scrolled through her phone and handed it to Erica.

Susie was wearing a strappy top, her right arm raised to her eyes, shielding them from the bright sunshine. Her tattoo was clearly visible, and Erica used her fingers to enlarge the butterfly.

'What is she like, your Susie?'

'Generous, pretty, clever – cleverer than me, anyway,' Becky said. 'Which is why we don't understand her not contacting us. She knows we'll be going out of our minds with worry. One other thing is that she has type-one diabetes, and we're really concerned because she'll be needing her insulin.'

Erica gave a brief nod. 'Does she have a boyfriend?'

'She has a friend. I'm not convinced it's a love thing, they've been boyfriend and girlfriend since they were about six, but he lives in Bridlington, a couple of doors away from her parents' home. They're close, but Susie's going to have a career that will take her away from Bridlington, so... His name is Brandon Eyre.'

'I know what you mean,' Erica said, again with a slight affirmative nod. 'And the rest of you? Do you have boyfriends?'

'No. We've had a couple of dates, but nothing that would make us think boyfriends. DI Cheetham, is there something you're not telling us?' Worry flashed across Becky's face as she spoke.

Erica stood. 'Give me a couple of minutes, girls. I'll get back to you. Would you like a drink?'

They asked for water, and Erica left the room heading towards the machine. She gathered together three cups of water, then texted Ivor Simmonite, asking for the tattoo picture to be forwarded to her phone.

She returned to the family interview room, and handed out the paper cups of water. 'Sorry, we don't provide glasses, but the water is beautifully cold.'

The two girls thanked her and took sips as Erica's phone

pinged. She opened the picture, and stared at it. It was the same as the picture she had seen on Katie's phone.

Erica waited until they had placed their drinks on the table, then lowered her voice. 'I do have something to tell you. In the early hours of this morning we found the body of a young woman. She matches the description of Susie...'

'No!' came from both girls, simultaneously.

Erica continued. 'And furthermore she has a butterfly tattoo on her right shoulder which is a match for the tattoo on the picture on your phone, Katie.'

At first the girls seemed unable to speak but eventually Becky stumbled through asking where they had found the body.

'In the river?' Katie gasped. 'But she was an amazing swimmer.'

'I think it's highly likely she was killed, then dumped in the river,' Erica explained as gently as she could, given the horrific visions she was conjuring up for the two students. 'The River Porter is in full spate at the moment with all this rain, and if Susie hadn't become trapped as the river passed through underneath the Midland Station, we might never have known what happened to her, as it goes out to the North Sea eventually. I have to go to Bridlington to tell Susie's parents, but we also need to speak to...' Erica glanced down at her notes, 'Clare. I'm going to ask my DS to take you home, and to take statements from all three of you about what happened last night. Please don't contact Susie's parents until I've had time to talk to them, and I imagine they'll be heading to Sheffield quickly to assist us with the identification.'

'Can I see the picture on your phone of the tattoo?' Katie asked, still unwilling to accept her friend was dead. It was clear she thought the tattoo might not be a match.

Erica passed it to her, and she stifled a sob. 'It is the same tattoo,' Katie said. 'The top two wings have a sort of curly S on the edges, for Susie. I was with her when she discussed the design with the tattooist.'

'Had Susie fallen out with anyone in the recent past?'

'No, she wasn't like that.' Becky shook her head in denial as she spoke. 'In fact I've never heard Susie so much as swear, or say a wrong word about anybody. Why would somebody want to kill her? She was so lovely. Her parents will be devastated. She's... was an only child.'

Becky let the tears flow, remembering the week of nights spent under canvas, all four of them joined each evening by Brandon and Susie's mum and dad, Olivia and Harry; the songs they had sung accompanied by Harry's guitar playing. And she remembered the way Brandon hadn't been able to take his eyes away from Susie. She suspected it was a case of absence making the heart grow fonder from Brandon's point of view, but she knew Susie didn't feel the same.

If Becky was ever pushed to talk about the subject, she would have to say that Susie's feelings were more directed towards Clare than they were towards Brandon. But this DI hadn't asked, and Becky felt it wasn't part of her remit to talk about it.

Beth Machin drove them home, where Clare was waiting, eager for news.

Clare was surprised to see the trio approach the back door, and felt a sickening thud inside her; something was seriously out of kilter.

She flung open the door. 'What's wrong? You've found her?'

Beth held up her warrant card. 'DS Machin. We'd like to come in.'

Clare stepped aside, feeling foolish because she was blocking their entry into the kitchen. 'Sorry. I felt so worried. Becky, what's happened?'

'Can we sit down, Clare, please?' Beth's voice was gentle, and the four of them walked through to the lounge. It was a comfortable room with a large three-seater sofa and two armchairs, positioned to face a silent television. The room was warm, and Beth waited until the others were seated before sitting in an armchair.

'Clare, I'm sorry to bring you bad news, but we've found a body who we believe to be your friend, Susanna Roebuck.'

'No,' Clare whispered, then shouted, 'No!'

Katie pulled her towards her, and held her, but Clare's tears began immediately. She was inconsolable, but Katie didn't let go until her sobs were almost under control.

Becky had disappeared to make cups of tea, and Beth spoke again when Becky returned. 'I have to ask some questions and take statements from all three of you,' she said quietly, her voice calm as always. The girls responded by nodding, all three of them holding on to the mugs of tea as if their lives depended on it. Right at that moment they felt they did.

'Okay,' Beth began. 'I can see how close you are, so have any of you noticed anybody strange hanging around, perhaps targeting you four specifically, or even only one of you? Somebody lurking, or being where you are more than you would expect them to be?'

They looked at each other. 'I wouldn't say so,' Katie said. 'But with this awful weather you wouldn't know anyway. Everybody has their hoods up, or an umbrella pulled low to shield their face, and it's been like that for around three weeks now. As your boss said, the river's in full spate...' Katie paused and wiped away a tear.

'What has the river got to do with it?' Clare asked, aware she was missing something – nobody had told her how Susie had died.

Katie clutched at her friend's hand. 'They found Susie in the river.' Katie turned to Beth. 'Did DI Cheetham say the Porter?'

The DS nodded. 'Yes, the Porter runs quite near to here, in the Ecclesall Road area, but it drops down into the centre and goes underneath the roads until it reaches the railway station. That's where we found Susie.'

Clare frowned. 'But how? She was an amazing swimmer.'

'Clare, I'm so sorry,' DS Machin said. 'Susie wouldn't have had chance to swim, she was dead before she entered the water. We believe whoever killed her hoped she would be carried down the river with the water being so fast, and eventually out to the North Sea. She became trapped, and her body was wedged tightly against some large stones.'

'You're sure it's her?' Clare was heartbroken.

'Very sure, and we're expecting her parents to formally identify her tomorrow.' Beth opened her briefcase. 'Let's get these statements done, and I'll leave you to think about Susie in your own way.'

4

F rannie heard Erica enter and hang her coat in the small cloakroom. Her work was spread out on the coffee table, and she quickly gathered them up. 'I'll put these away, Erica, they can wait until tomorrow. Wine?'

'Please. I can only have one though. Just in case...'

Frannie looked up from gathering the papers into a tidy pile. 'In case what?'

'I have no idea.' Erica looked and sounded weary. 'There's something not right about this. As I said this morning, we have a dead girl who disappeared within a few seconds really, strangled and dumped in a river. The strange thing about this particular river is that it's normally quite gentle. Locals call it the Porter Brook, rather than its official title of the River Porter, but with all this bloody rain it's quite frightening. I'm meeting Susie's parents tomorrow morning for a formal identification, but they might as well have come tonight, because they're going to get no sleep.'

'Only child?'

Erica nodded.

'Shit. My heart goes out to them.'

'They want to go up and see the girls Susie lived with, after they've seen Susie. I think Olivia, her mum, needs that.'

Frannie stood. 'I'll get us that wine.'

Erica sat back and thought through everything that had happened, and the awfulness of having to go to that welcoming home and tell them of their daughter's death. Pictures of Susie were everywhere, and they had given her one so that they could begin to show it around the university campus, trying to track down what had happened between Susie exiting the theatre, and two or three minutes later being followed by Clare. In that short space of time Susie had broken all the rules. Erica looked up and smiled as Frannie returned bearing what appeared to be two buckets of wine.

'If you're only having one, make it a big one. Gin glass size.'

Erica took the glass and sipped at the Prosecco. 'Thank you. Can I bounce stuff off you, or have you got enough on your plate?' Frannie's job in child protection with social services was similar to her own in that cases lived with them twenty-four hours a day, and they tried not to bring the stuff running around inside their heads into the home.

'Of course.'

'Okay, two girls go to the university's Drama Studio. You know where it is? Between the children's hospital and the Royal Hallamshire?'

Frannie nodded. 'Been to it a couple of times. Carry on.'

'They watched *Macbeth*, which is part of the course they're both taking. They were with a group of people they knew, although they hadn't arranged to meet up with them, it happened. When the performance ended, Clare needed the loo, so asked Susie to wait outside the theatre, as they had arranged to meet up in the pub with the other two housemates from their student accommodation.'

She paused, and Frannie spoke. 'Okay, I've got the picture so far.'

'Clare came out two or three minutes after Susie, but couldn't see her. She had a good look because it was still raining heavily, and everybody had umbrellas or hoods up. She hung around for some time thinking maybe Susie had changed her mind about needing the loo, but she didn't arrive. By then Clare was feeling pissed off, and walked down to the pub on her own, where she met up with the two housemates, Becky and Katie. Susie wasn't with them.'

Frannie took another sip of wine. 'I'm going to presume this is totally out of character.'

'Absolutely. The girls wanted to contact us immediately, but Becky, who seems to be the mother hen of the group, pointed out that the police wouldn't do anything, Susie was a student and students are rather scatter-brained. She could have wandered off with some other group, and gone to a party. And she's right. We didn't know Susie, and would have said wait twenty-four hours, then come and see us. They arrived this morning, worried out of their heads. Things had taken a turn for the worse, and we had found Susie's body, although at that stage we didn't know who she was. What I want to bounce off you is that two or three minutes. Tell me a scenario.'

'For three minutes? I think the most obvious thing is she knew whoever abducted her. Possibly a car pulled up and told her to get in to shelter from the rain.'

'I thought that, but it didn't feel right. It's near the traffic lights, so whoever pulled up couldn't stay there, and there's no parking either as it turns left to go up past the children's hospital, or straight across to head towards West Street.'

'Maybe he said get in and we'll wait for your mate to come

out. If she knew him, she would do that.' Frannie hesitated, still thinking. 'Have you had the PM results back yet? Toxicology?'

'You're thinking he gave her something? An injection? Nothing's through yet. That would be the obvious thing, though, wouldn't it. Inject her with some strong drug as soon as she got in the car, and then simply drive away. We need to interview everybody who was outside that theatre immediately after the performance. I'll get Beth organising that, because I need to be available for Mr and Mrs Roebuck tomorrow.'

'You really don't enjoy working with Beth, do you?'

'Oh she's okay,' Erica muttered. 'She sometimes makes me feel inadequate.'

'She's a DS. You're a DI. Come on, you're streets in front of her, her boss.'

Erica picked up her wine glass. 'But she's clever. Bet she knew the bloody River Porter ran under Midland Station. That reminds me, I need to look it up. I need to know everything about this overgrown stream before I get to that briefing tomorrow morning.'

'That overgrown little stream was a main player in the start of the steel industry in Sheffield.' Frannie laughed. 'If ever this rain stops we'll head up to Ringinglow where it starts, and we'll follow it down to where it ends. Then you'll understand it.'

'You know it?'

'Did the walk with school many years ago. Fascinating actually.'

'Tell me what you remember. Any parts you thought might be a good place to dump a body?'

'At the age of thirteen or whatever I was, I didn't think about potential body-dumping sites. Sorry.'

'Huh,' Erica grumbled as she took another sip of wine. 'You'll never make a police officer.'

'Erica, my love, I don't ever want to be a police officer.'

. . .

Frannie smiled at the woman who had come into her life so unexpectedly a few years earlier. Erica had been part of a team investigating child trafficking, and had as a result come to her for advice. The attraction had been immediate, and two months later they had bought a house together, and followed it up with a wedding.

Frannie stood. 'Have you eaten?'

'Not had time. Let's have a takeaway. Then I'm off to bed. It's been a long day.'

'Pizza?'

Erica nodded, and laid her head back. 'This wine is nice.'

'Want some more?'

'If I use the same glass, does it count as only one glass of wine?'

Frannie smiled. 'It does.'

'Then maybe a drop.'

Frannie picked up both glasses and walked through to the kitchen. She topped them up, rang the pizza shop, and carried them back through to the lounge. Erica was on the phone, so she quietly placed her glass on the coffee table, and went to get plates for them.

Erica looked puzzled. 'That was Ivor. Wants me down at the PM suite as early as possible tomorrow to show me something. Didn't want to tell me over the phone, wants to see my reaction, and see if I sense what he's sensing, were his words. This doesn't feel good, Frannie, it doesn't feel good at all. In fact it's proper unnerved me. Do you think he didn't want me to have any sleep at all?'

Frannie laughed. 'If you can't get to sleep, I'll hit you over the head with a book or something.'

'Thanks, you're a true friend. Seriously, though, what's he found?' Erica took a long drink of the wine.

'Slow down, sounds as if you need to be sober tomorrow morning. Stop worrying about it now, let's watch some TV while we have the pizza, then go to bed. That phone call this morning woke us both, so an early night won't hurt either of us.'

The doorbell summoned Frannie, and she returned with the pizza. 'Eat,' she commanded, and Erica picked up a slice.

'Food,' she murmured, as if she hadn't seen any for weeks. 'This is so good. Will there be any left for breakfast?'

'You're a heathen, Erica Cheetham. Nobody has pizza for breakfast. Try toast instead.'

They watched half an hour of *Vera*, then switched off the television, cleared away the debris of their meal, and headed up to bed. Both were asleep within minutes.

It wasn't so in the house with only three girls in it. Clare had confessed to Becky and Katie that things had progressed with her and Susie, and Katie and Becky confirmed that they had realised that. Tears had flowed all night and the talk had centred around what could possibly have happened to their friend.

'She was there and then she wasn't,' Clare wailed. 'Why? She wouldn't hurt anybody, she'd done nothing wrong. How could somebody have taken her from me, just like that?'

'Somebody she knew?' Becky frowned. 'It had to be. She wouldn't get into a stranger's car, or even walk with a stranger. None of it makes sense. And how did she end up in the river? Where did she go in?'

'Would she walk with a female? Or get in a car with a female?' Katie spoke quietly. 'I think we're all assuming it's a man, but we don't know.'

Tears rolled down Clare's cheeks once again, and they made

the decision to go to bed, and wait until Harry and Olivia arrived to see them. Maybe they would have more details by then.

And the first day passed. No answers, only questions, intermittent sleep, and a reluctance to face a new day. Erica rolled over and disturbed Frannie, who enfolded her in her arms, wishing she could offer more comfort, knowing how bad the scene that had confronted her wife must have been, in that murky place under the station. She had nothing but admiration for the woman she loved, for dealing with the horrors that one person could inflict on another.

Becky didn't sleep. The balance of their home had been put out of kilter, and this was their second night with only three of them there. She didn't like it. It had been good to walk through the door before; now she knew the absence of one of them would be an ongoing fact for the rest of their time in the house. Forty-three Crookesvale Gardens had changed forever.

She heard a door open, then the flush of the toilet, and knew that she wasn't the only one unable to sleep, they were all feeling the loss deeply.

5

Ivor wheeled out the trolley holding Susanna Roebuck's body, and rolled the sheet covering her to one side. 'You ready?' he said and Erica nodded.

He lifted the girl's right hand and turned it so that it was palm up, indicating that Erica should move forwards.

She did, and Ivor waited for a moment before rolling Susie slightly to one side, revealing a small puncture wound in her neck.

Seconds later Erica breathed an almost silent, 'No...'

The briefing room noise subsided into silence as Erica moved to the front. She had talked the results over with Beth, and her sergeant accompanied her to the whiteboard.

'Morning, everybody. First of all, thank you for the initial work you all took on yesterday, and major acknowledgement goes to everybody who went down the culvert into that bloody river. I want two of you down there today, so make sure you've got waders, because you'll also be heading upstream. We need to know where Susanna Roebuck's body went into the water. I know it's still pissing down, but hey, nobody ever said being a copper was an easy job.' She flashed a quick smile around the room.

There was a brief round of applause at her words, and then silence fell again.

'What I'm going to tell you now I'm hoping is so far off the mark that you'll all laugh me out of the room, but unfortunately I don't think it's a laughing matter. Who was here in July twenty-fourteen?'

Four hands were raised including Beth's.

'I was a DS at the time,' Erica continued, 'newly appointed to the position and keen to make my mark. In April we had a death, a young girl called Leanne Fraser. She was twenty, worked in Marks and Spencer's, had a boyfriend who initially came under suspicion of course but had a strong alibi, and she was a regular sort of girl. Didn't take drugs, didn't even smoke, liked a drink on a Friday night unless she was down to work the weekend shift, a nice girl. She was strangled with tights that the murderer brought with him, and she was carefully posed in Boden Hostead woods. She wasn't hidden or covered in any way, he wanted her to be found. He hadn't placed her far into the woods, and it was a child on their way to school who found her. The seven-year-old boy thought it rather exciting, his mother was distraught. The post-mortem revealed one or two clues, but it was only later we realised what we had.'

Erica glanced around the room. Everybody was silent; they all seemed to be holding their collective breaths.

'There was a small puncture wound in her neck, and a drug called Propofol was found to be in her body. It's the drug that's used to sedate or knock you out prior to an operation. It depends how much you're given as to how it affects you. This was somebody who knew the dosage to give. She was then strangled with the tights, but we don't know whether it was in his car, or where she was found. It was definitely the cause of death though. After she died he slashed her right palm with a line running from the base of her palm to the bottom of her middle finger, and he removed the tip of her right little finger from the first knuckle joint.'

DC Ian Thomas held up a hand. 'Is it definitely a man?'

'We don't know. All the victims were slim, not tall, a woman could have manoeuvred them as all the bodies were placed on show not far from the roads adjacent to the murder scene. I'm using the term he loosely, you need to keep an open mind. There were three more victims before the end of July twenty-fourteen, Lucy Owen, Laurel Price and the final one, Lilith Baker-Jones. They were all left, carefully posed, in different wooded areas around the city. In every case Propofol was used, and the right hand was mutilated, but differently.'

Erica took a sip of water. 'He still removed the tips of the right little fingers, but on Lucy the slash on the palm was two parallel lines, on Laurel it was three, and by the time he'd finished with Lilith it was an IV. He was using the roman numeral system to do the body count for us. We had also realised all his victims had a Christian name beginning with L, and that he was posing every one of them. He was proud of what he was doing. All of them were naked, no evidence of rape, and we didn't find the clothing. This,' she said, as she stuck a photo on the whiteboard, 'is the hand of yesterday's victim, Susanna Roebuck. As you can see, the tip of her little finger is missing, and the palm cut is a V.' She put up a second picture. 'And this is the puncture mark on her neck.'

There was a muted chorus of shits, buggers, fuck me, from around the room. Erica sat down and Beth stepped forward.

'Questions?'

'It's almost as if it's an obsessive compulsive thing with him, isn't it? Do you think we'll have more victims? That he's missing the killing?'

'It's a strong possibility,' Beth said. 'We've certainly got to bear it in mind. It's been five years since the last killing, and now we have this. The press at the time added two and two together when they realised all the girls had L in common for their names, so called him the L-killer, but it was eventually filed as a cold case because we had nothing to go on. No CCTV, no eye-witnesses, even the victims were ordinary average everyday nice girls. The slashes on the hands were never released anywhere, so it's a good indicator that it is the same killer and not a copycat. By the end of today I want everybody here up to speed on this cold case. Nobody ever saw even a car in the wrong place, no DNA was ever left at the scene, and the killer was definitely forensic savvy. Both the boss and I were part of the investigation in twenty-fourteen and the overriding feeling was that it was a pattern he was following, and every victim had to be dealt with in the same way. Unless he is thinking of victims all with the initial letter S, we can have no clue as to where he or she will turn next, or even if it's a one-off.'

Erica stood. 'I'm leaving Beth to sort everybody out. I want this river covered every stretch of the way, we need to know where she went in. I also want everybody on this team to become familiar with the cold case that's suddenly become a hot case. I don't want one word of this leaking to the press. I have to go and meet Mr and Mrs Roebuck now, they're here to identify their daughter officially. Sort out what you're doing. If anything urgent crops up, shout straight away. Don't forget he killed four girls in three months last time he was active, we don't want a repeat of that.'

Erica left the room; immediately a crowd gathered around Beth, ready for a rain-soaked day that could involve splashing about in a river in full spate. She handed out instructions, aware that suddenly things had changed between her and Erica. They had shared an hour-long discussion before the briefing, and tossed around ideas as they relived the time in twenty-fourteen that seemed to be coming back to haunt them again. But there had been a camaraderie that had certainly not been there before, and despite the horrors of the case and the abysmal weather that was hampering them, she felt a sense of relief.

Harry and Olivia Roebuck were devastated. They clung to each other, and eventually Harry nodded. 'That's Susanna. That's our Susie.'

Erica led them to the relatives' room, and made them all a cup of tea. 'The girls are waiting for you,' she told the ashen-faced parents. 'They are aware you want to see them.'

Olivia's head dropped. 'Are they okay?' she mumbled.

'No,' Erica said. 'They're far from okay, I won't try to soften it. Be prepared for tears. They were a team, and Susie was a quarter of it. She will be missed. It's been a real shock for them almost as much as you, because they came to report her missing, and found out we had already discovered her.'

'Can I see where she died?' Harry asked. 'I'd like to spend a bit of time there if it's possible.'

'We don't know yet where she died,' Erica said. 'We have teams out today all the way up the river looking for anywhere that would give us a clue. The river is five miles long, and we are looking for obstacles that would stop anything the size of a body from traversing the full length. If we find anything like that in the higher levels, we can narrow down our search.'

'Where does the river start?' Harry was persistent.

Erica realised it would only take a quick Google search to give him the information. 'Ringinglow, on the outskirts of Sheffield. It's normally a gentle river, lots of little waterfalls on its course downwards, and was actually instrumental in starting the manufacture of steel in Sheffield. Water power from this river drove big engines, and there's a huge working water wheel still in use. At the moment, of course, it's in full spate and it's quite scary the amount of power in water. I have to ask, Harry, that you don't go there at the moment. You could potentially contaminate a crime scene and get in the way of my team. I promise, once we know the location where Susie went into the water, I will personally take you and give you all the time you need, but you can't go there yet, we don't know the location, or even where Susie died. We have so much to find out before we can tell you what we know.'

'Was she raped?' Olivia's voice was hardly above a whisper.

'We don't believe she was. All DNA was washed away because of the water, but there are no obvious signs such as bruising or cuts. I don't think rape was the intent. When you spoke to Susie, did she tell you of anything or anybody who was troubling her, or giving her any grief?'

Husband and wife shook their heads in unison.

'No,' Olivia spoke, 'she seemed incredibly happy and settled. She loved Sheffield, loved sharing the house with the girls, was enjoying the course – I don't think she complained once about anything. Student life really suited her.'

They finished their drinks and Harry and Olivia followed Erica out to the car park. 'Take care,' the DI said, as she watched them fasten their seat belts, 'and I promise to keep you fully informed.'

6

The rain was almost relentless. There had been a brief spell of dry weather during the afternoon, but the pitter patter of more of the promised downpour began in earnest after only an hour of respite. Erica replaced the receiver after speaking to Olivia Roebuck, confirming that she and Harry had spent a couple of hours with the girls before returning home.

'I spoke for some time with Clare,' Olivia had said. 'She told me of her relationship with Susie, so we don't need to avoid the subject.' Her voice had sounded strained, and when Erica disconnected, she breathed a sigh of relief. She was pleased it had come out now in case it became accidental knowledge further along the line. She made a note to tell Beth Machin, expected in at any moment after an emergency dental appointment for a tooth she had managed to chip on a piece of bonfire toffee, and Erica walked across to stare out of her tiny office window at the car park, almost a floodplain in its own right.

She scribbled a note telling Beth she was going to the search areas on the river, put on her dried out coat and ran to the car park. She skipped across, jumping over puddles until she reached her car, standing entirely surrounded by water. She waded through it, and almost fell into the driving seat.

'For fuck's sake,' she grumbled. Her coat was wet once more, and her boots were squelching. She took out her mobile phone and rang Ian Thomas to see where his team was, then reversed out of her parking place. It briefly occurred to her that sails might be a better idea than an engine.

Ian had said that he was nearing the stretch of river running by the Porter Brook Pocket Park, so she headed there, aware of how little traffic was on the roads. The rain was certainly keeping people indoors.

Getting the image of Susie Roebuck out of her mind was proving difficult. Had she been a random target, or did her killer know exactly where she was going? And had Clare Vincent had a lucky escape? Although they hadn't found anybody to confirm the theory, it was felt that for some reason Susie had got into a car, maybe to shelter from the blessed downpour that had met her on exiting the theatre. That meant she would have known the driver; surely she wouldn't have got into a stranger's car? The more Erica turned over things in her mind, the more her headache increased.

She parked the car as close as she could to Ian's targeted area and changed into her waders before walking across to the pocket park to find him. He was actually in the river, struggling to keep his balance, and staring up towards the little park.

He held his hand up in her direction and climbed out.

'What is it?' he asked, waving his arm around. 'Why is it here?'

She laughed. 'My feelings exactly. I'd no idea it was here. According to Google, the council had to remove a culvert, so decided to smarten up the area where the culvert had been and built this. It's called the Porter Brook Pocket Park, and they made it like a little amphitheatre as it's built on the slope into the river.

People bring their sandwiches on the lunch break, and eat them here by the side of the water. It's also part of the new flood defences. As you can see, when the water rises, it overflows into this park. Won an award a couple of years ago, did this little beauty.'

'Huh,' Ian said. 'Nobody will have been eating their sarnies here for a couple of weeks.'

'Exactly. Deserted in the rain. Perfect place to throw in a body, isn't it?'

'That's why I was standing staring up at it. Is there CCTV on it?'

'If this killer is who we think it possibly is, it won't help other than to confirm this was the spot Susie was thrown in. Definitely a smart arse, this chap.'

'You think it's a man?'

'I have no idea but I get so cheesed off saying him or her. Help me down, and I'll stand and stare at it as well.'

It was difficult to balance standing in the turbulent waters, and they stared up to the top of the pretty little park holding on to each other.

'You know, we've no proof, but if I was going to throw a body into the Porter, I'd choose this place. There has to be CCTV somewhere around, surely.' She looked up towards the right, to the high building about a hundred yards from the park. 'I'll get Beth to go there, see what they have.'

They battled their way up river, doling out words of encouragement to the team as they reached them; nobody had anything positive to report.

·   ·   ·

Back at the pocket park, Erica sat with Ian on one of the seats, wet through and cold. Both of them looked miserable, hair flattened to their scalps and feeling quite desperate for a cup of tea. They turned around in unison as they heard the engine note signifying the arrival of the refreshment van, followed by a small truck bearing a single toilet unit. Ian immediately used his transmitter to tell everybody to come and get drinks and food.

The men and women of Erica's team began arriving from upriver and downriver, using the pocket park to sit down, knowing they couldn't get any wetter anyway.

'Thank you, everybody,' she called. 'I know it's a lousy job, but a necessary one. We'll carry on until four, then it'll be too dark to see anything much. Back again tomorrow at eight, but we'll be higher up. I want four to start at the source, up at Ringinglow, and the rest to start where we finish off today. I'll leave Ian to sort out the logistics of who is where, and we'll have the refreshment van in the lower reaches, so the ones up at the top, bring a couple of flasks.'

Several thumbs were held up, and she responded in kind. A quick phone call to check on Beth's tooth issues resulted in Beth saying she would find out what the building was, and head down there straight away, before finding Erica to tell her.

The team drifted back towards the areas they had left for their break, leaving Erica to sit deep in thought, nursing her second cup of tea. Tonight would be a night for reading through the cold case of twenty-fourteen; a night for trying to get into a killer's mind and for pondering the whereabouts of the killer for the last five years. If Frannie was going to be in, she would talk it over with her; two brains are better than one any time, and she trusted Frannie's level-headed judgement completely. She smiled as she thought of the difference Frannie had made to her life; she had brought a calmness with her, a sense of order, and an ability to listen and let Erica work through the issues and frustrations her job created. Erica took out her phone.

Will you be in tonight? xxx

She waited for a couple of minutes, and received the response she needed.

I'll be home around eight. Lasagne? xxx

Erica smiled and typed her response. **It'll be waiting. Love you xxx**

She slipped her phone back in her pocket and turned as she heard Beth's voice. Beth was standing at the refreshment van, miming drinking. Erica held up her paper cup to show she had one, and a minute later Beth joined her on the saturated seat.

'This is wet,' she announced, wriggling around.

'You should try standing in that lot.' Erica nodded towards the turbulent waters of the Porter only feet away from them.

'You been in?'

'Yes, with Ian. We walked upstream a bit, to see what, if anything, was happening. We both feel this is a good spot to chuck in a body, but there's nothing that we've found that would indicate that was right. You been to that building?'

Beth nodded. 'I have. Yes, they have CCTV. No, it doesn't work. Hasn't worked for six months, but they've not rushed to sort it because they've never needed it.'

Erica sighed and leaned back. 'We'll catch him this time. I don't care about obstacles, he or she laughed at us back in twenty-fourteen but I'm in charge now, and they don't call me the terrier for nothing.'

'Do they?'

'Do they what?'

'Call you the terrier.'

'No, but they should.'

Beth laughed and sipped at her drink. 'So, have you had any thoughts? You looked lost in them when I walked to the van.'

43

'Not really. Our first job is to find out if anybody's come out of prison in the last month or so, after a five-year stretch. Those figures are variable. And we need to factor some things in like where the hell does he get Propofol from? I'm pretty damn sure you can't buy that from a chemist's.'

Beth took out her phone. Seconds later she showed Erica the results of her search. 'You may not get it in a chemist's, but it's certainly available online. Or what about somebody who works in a hospital? Nurse? Orderly? Doctor? Does that water come much higher than that? It's almost at our feet.'

'It does. This is part of the new flood defence system Sheffield had to install. It works like an overflow from a sink, so I understand...' Erica's voice trailed away. 'That's what's happened.'

She sat upright, and Beth looked at her.

'What's bothered me about this is if it is the same killer, and I'm ninety-nine per cent sure it is, he posed his victims. It wasn't about having them sexually, it was about saying look what I've done and isn't she pretty. That's why it didn't occur to me it was the same thing, even though Susie was naked. She wasn't posed, and we've assumed she was dumped in the river. What if she wasn't?'

Beth was listening closely. 'You mean he posed her down there?'

'No. I mean he posed her somewhere else, and the flood waters took her. What if he posed her on one of these seats? The water rose because it was spectacularly torrential that night, and took his carefully prepared body.' Erica pulled out her phone, spoke to somebody from the Forensic team, who promised to be there within the hour.

'Smart thinking, boss. I can't see them getting anything, with all this water, but for what it's worth, I think you're right. Now let's clear our rubbish up before we get arrested.'

7

The rain had stopped, but the skies threatened a heavy downpour at any moment. Erica and her team had assembled early for instructions, and Beth had been busy dividing the officers into groups of four, with details of where their search was to take place, pending forensic results from the intensive coverage of the pocket park. While the two senior officers felt that was the place where he had posed his victim, there still was no absolute proof, and work had to continue to look for any results from any other part of the water course.

The two women had met at six, clutching large takeaway coffees, to plan out the next steps. They knew every part of the five mile river had to be covered; the killer would kill again, of that they had no doubt, and he needed to be stopped before another young girl died. They had acquired a detailed map of the Porter, and its descent into the city centre. They began by drawing lines across and allocating members of their team, which had grown considerably given the new urgency that had been added to the investigation, once it was confirmed it was the same MO as their cold case killer.

Coffees finished, they headed into the briefing room. Every

officer had checked in early; even the ones who hadn't seen the body in situ had seen the photographs. This was a young girl near the start of her life, had done nothing to merit such an awful death. The whole team was waiting, ready for their instructions.

Beth took charge, handing out copies of the map to the allocated leader of each team of four. They had three teams and Erica watched with a degree of pride as everybody accepted the role handed to them, and immediately began preparations to move out.

She stood. 'Before you disappear, do not go into that water without waders, and take care. None of it is easy to walk in, and the water levels have risen overnight, so we've been told. I don't want any accidents. Your team leaders have transmitters, and I suggest you have your phones on your person in case anything happens. If you find anything at all, your team leader is your first person to tell, and they will contact either Beth or myself. Any questions?'

There were none. Every officer was keen to get on with the search, and looking forward to getting this day over with. Almost everybody in the contingent had already been out to the river, and knew what they were facing; the sooner they were done, the better.

Becky scrolled through the contacts on her phone while trying to manipulate the bagel that was dripping butter onto her left hand. Finally she found what she was looking for, and rang Zoe Wilton's number. She hoped it was the right Zoe.

Clare's sudden decision to have an hour in the gym the previous evening had caused some trepidation in both Becky and Katie, but they had extracted a promise that she would take a taxi there and back. They had offered to go with her, but she had clearly wanted time on her own, and so they pretended they weren't worried in any way.

Becky had felt a degree of relief when they had received a text from Clare saying she was okay, and staying the night with Zoe, as she had brought her car, and they were going to work on *Macbeth*. She had finished with a see you tomorrow and a kiss.

'Zoe, it's Becky, Clare's housemate.'

'Clare?'

'Clare Vincent...'

'Oh, that Clare. Hi, Becky. What can I do for you? I was so sorry to hear about Susie. We all are, but I'm sure you know that.'

'Isn't Clare with you?' Becky felt sick. She didn't really want Zoe to answer.

'No, I usually see her at the gym, but I haven't been for a few days.'

'O...kay,' Becky said slowly. 'I must have misunderstood what she said. Sorry to have bothered you.' She disconnected and turned to Katie.

'What is it?' There was fear in Katie's voice.

'She's not there. Zoe hasn't been to the gym for a few days.' She clicked on Messenger and showed the message to Katie. 'This definitely says she's staying at Zoe's. We have to ring DI Cheetham.'

The cold hit all of them as they began the searches at their designated points. Ian Thomas was glad he'd been given Flick Ardern, Mike Nestor and Sam King as his team – all reliable, and would simply get on with the job with no messing. It was there to be done, and they would do it.

'Flick, you stay this side with me,' Ian said, then laughed as he saw her struggling to put on her waders. 'Hang on a minute, I'll help.' Flick's grey eyes that turned towards him were the same colour as the rain. Her brown hair was starting to come out of her ponytail, and she appeared to be too tiny to be wearing waders. They would engulf her. He could feel her infuriation with herself vibrating out of her.

'Some people wear these through choice, to go fishing,' Mike grumbled. He seemed to be struggling as much as Flick.

Eventually all four were suitably clothed, and edged their way to the opposite banks of the river. The noise of the water was thundery as it pulsated down towards the lower reaches, and Flick wondered how much was still up in the hills driving its way down towards the visible source above the little village of Ringinglow.

The rain fell with some force once again but it seemed a secondary issue in comparison with the amount of water running by their sides, and in Ian's case, under his feet. He had dropped into the river to look at the banks from a different angle – he wanted to miss nothing. He trod carefully, moving further into the middle, then turned around to switch his view to the opposite bank. Nothing looked out of order, so he made his way to the bank that Flick was searching.

She looked up as he joined her. 'You didn't drown then.'

'No, but I've never known anything like this. There's some power in that water. I don't want you to go in, leave the river itself to us lads. It'll sweep a little 'un like you off your feet. And don't go all feminist on me, it's not about men and women, it's about weight. I wouldn't let Kev Ward go in either, he's not got much flesh on him.'

Flick held up a hand. 'Hey, I'm not arguing. I know you're right. So far I've found an empty Coke can, and that's it. I'll carry on heading lower.'

'Thanks, Flick.' He touched her shoulder, and moved a few yards further down river. The ground was treacherously unstable, and he trod carefully. Although he didn't mind going in the river, he wanted it to be under his own terms, and not propelled there in an uncontrolled kind of way.

The rain was coming down faster, and Ian tightened the drawstring around his hood. It gave an illusion of warmth, even if he was starting to feel chilled all the way through. He figured he'd give them another hour of searching, and he'd get them back to the car with the engine running, to get some warmth. Everybody had brought a flask and food so they didn't have to go seeking sustenance. A half-hour break and they could return to the job, feeling better. He peered into the water, trying to estimate its depth, but couldn't. He knew from having been in this spot in better weather that it was normally clear and sweet, but not today.

He took a tentative step, clinging on to a small gorse bush to help his descent, and felt his feet go. He scrabbled around in the most inelegant fashion, finally landing on his knees, water powering into his face. He gasped as he climbed up, and was aware of Mike Nestor by his side, helping him.

'You okay?' Mike shouted.

Ian merely nodded, feeling winded.

He leaned against the bankside and gathered his thoughts, spitting out river water. He could see Flick asking if he was okay but hadn't the strength to answer, so simply waved a hand.

Mike held up a thumb towards Flick and slowly worked his way back across to where he had been when he saw Ian go in. He had known it wouldn't be an easy day, and when he had told his wife what he would be spending the day doing, she had laughed. His fear of water and swimming was well known within his family, but there was no way he would ever admit it at work.

He was up to his waist in torrential flood waters, on an uneven and rocky river bed, and he doubted he would ever be afraid of water again. This day's work wiped out every bit of aquaphobia he had ever had.

He raised a hand to Sam to indicate that Ian was okay, but Sam was looking further down the river, on the opposite bank, binoculars glued to his face. Mike eased himself out and knelt for a moment in the mud, before clambering up to go to his partner.

'What is it?'

Sam handed him the glasses. 'That big rock about a hundred yards down. There's something...'

Mike wiped the water from his eyes, then raised the binoculars. He was silent for a moment. 'Shit,' he said finally, 'isn't that...?'

Sam took the binoculars back and looked again. 'It's a leg, isn't it.'

Mike took out his mobile phone and rang Ian. 'Think you might need to work your way down your side. There's a big rock. Tread carefully, there's something on the other side of it. Ian – we think it's another body. Looks like we can see a leg.'

8

Everything seemed to happen at once. Erica and Beth had snapped seat belts into place, and Erica had started the engine. Her phone rang out, and she answered it, registering it was Ivor Simmonite's name on her screen.

'Clever girl,' were his opening words.

'I am?'

'You are. Our blonde lady was definitely in the pocket park. We found two strands of long blonde hair. They were on the iron hand rail support, so it looks as though he wedged her on the steps, probably with her back to the upright. It's quite possible that the water reached her and took her into the river, but her hair was already caught on the upright. It's a match to her.'

'So he did pose her...' Erica breathed out quietly, feeling sick that this, in her mind, confirmed it was the same killer, surfacing once more after five years of inactivity.

'He did, it seems.'

'Thank you, Ivor. I'll pop down to see you when I get back. I've another call coming in, I'll see you later.'

She disconnected and took the next call without checking her screen, so was surprised when Becky said her name.

'Hi, Becky. Is something wrong?'

She listened to Becky's rather incoherent, garbled answer, and disconnected with the words, 'We'll be there in ten minutes.'

'Problem?' Beth asked.

'Problem. Clare Vincent didn't come home last night.'

Erica put the car into drive, and they headed for the student house, both of them hoping Clare Vincent would have turned up by the time they got there. It was only as they reached Crookesvale Gardens that Erica's phone rang again.

This time the caller was Ian Thomas.

Erica left Beth to deal with developments around Becky and Katie and headed for the source of the river at Ringinglow. Her instructions to Beth had been to remain at the house, and to organise at least one other officer to join her there. The girls were to stay put until they could sort out a safe refuge for them and she had every confidence that Beth could pull it all off without letting them know that there was a strong possibility that the newly-discovered body by the side of the river was Clare Vincent.

Beth was struggling. She wasn't dealing with irresponsible teenagers who gullibly believed everything she said, she was handling mature, intelligent women who guessed she knew more than she was saying. She felt a sense of relief when her colleague Will Bramwell arrived, and Becky quickly made drinks for everyone, before handing details of Clare's parents' address in Doncaster over to Beth.

'We didn't know whether to ring her mum, but decided not to worry her yet.'

Beth smiled at Becky. 'Thank you. We'll see to it. She doesn't have a father?'

'No, he died two years ago. Her mum isn't well, either. I hope she turns up soon so she doesn't have to know Clare is being a tad irresponsible.'

Will kept them entertained, tried to keep their minds away from the horrors they were both clearly feeling, and waited patiently with the girls while Beth left to speak to Erica, telling her the situation at the house. They agreed it was time to tell Becky and Katie the terrible news.

Clare Vincent's short curly hair was plastered to her head, and her body glistened with rainwater. This time the pose favoured by the killer had remained in place, and her hands were crossed over her stomach. Her breasts and pubic area were on display for all to see, until Forensics arrived to set up their tent. Erica confirmed it was Clare Vincent, and arranged for the teams further downriver to join them at the source. The refreshment van and Portaloo were called in, and it looked like being a long day.

Erica checked with Ian that he was okay – he had been first on scene to see the body, but she got the impression he was angry rather than upset. She knew how that felt; she felt the same. A second twenty-year-old to lose her life in two days, both girls filled with such promise and leaving distraught parents and families.

Ian was placed in charge of organising the search – this body hadn't arrived by boat, or over a bike's handlebars. It had to have been transported in a car, and in the dreadful muddy conditions surely it would be apparent where a vehicle had been.

Erica ducked inside the tent and saw Ivor with his hands moving Clare's hair. For a second she felt sick. Ivor looked up as he heard her.

'I was going to send somebody to find you,' he said. 'Look at this.' He moved Clare's head slightly to one side, and Erica leaned over him. There was a small mark on her neck, almost invisible.

'Injection?' she asked, and Ivor nodded. 'It is. I bet we find Propofol when we do the tox screen. She, like our earlier victim, has been strangled with tights and that's probably the cause of death, and I would say she's been dead around ten hours.'

'She went missing sometime last night,' Erica confirmed. 'Told her friends she was going to the gym but we haven't checked yet whether she actually arrived there. I'll find which gym it is, and go there later. I'm needed here for a bit longer, everybody's wet through and I reckon they need to see me around at the moment. Ian Thomas is squelching wherever he walks.'

'It can't rain for ever,' Ivor said.

'You sure? Can I have that in writing?' She touched his shoulder, and ducked out of the tent. Ian was standing on the bank, staring across the river. 'The levels aren't dropping at all, are they?' he said, as she came up behind him.

'Not in any way. We've had confirmation that Susanna Roebuck was positioned in the pocket park, but I think at some point during the night, when the river was running really high, it spilled over into the park, and took her body. That's what the park is there for, to act as a flood defence, so it did its job. It's why she ended up under the station, and not posed. Thank God she was caught by those big stones, or we would probably never have found her.'

'So we can call off the search of the lower levels and concentrate up here?' Ian asked.

'I'm calling it that way. I don't have a vast team to bring in, so we have to find out how he got Clare here.'

'You've ruled out it being a woman?'

'I haven't ruled anything out until we get some sort of a clue. Logistically, and because men are stronger, it looks as though it's a man because the bodies aren't simply chucked out of a vehicle, they're actually carried and manipulated. Conversely, it's not about sex. It wasn't about sex five years ago, and it's the same now.'

'You think it's definitely the same person?'

'I do. And I also think our other two girls are in danger, so I'm having them moved to a place of safety, along with two officers in attendance all the time. Five years ago he or she stuck rigidly to girls with the letter L for a Christian name, this time he's picked girls living in the same house. It's definitely an obsession, the bodies in his mind have to be linked in some way. We have to make sure he has no access to Becky and Katie. As soon as they hear this is Clare, they're going to make the connection and they're going to be scared. Until this is over and we've got the killer locked up, they have to be out of circulation.'

'Clare's dead as well?' Katie's face registered her shock, and she turned to Becky. They clutched each other's hands, and looked towards Beth.

'What've we done to cause all this?' Becky sobbed.

'Nothing, you've done nothing wrong,' Beth said. 'We want to move the two of you to a safe house, so please pack everything you're going to need. We'll be staying here with you until DI Cheetham makes the arrangements, and then Will and I can get you transported there. We'll make sure your parents are notified. Nobody can know where you are until this is over.'

'So Clare didn't go to the gym?'

'We don't know anything yet. We have to sort out the different stages of an investigation, and I imagine the main part of tracking how Clare came to end up at Ringinglow will begin tomorrow. I can start with you two while we're waiting for confirmation of where you'll be going, and I'll be contacting the university to let them know the situation. What time did Clare go out last night?'

'She set off to grab a taxi around half past six because she wanted some thinking time, said she was only going for a couple of hours and she would have a taxi back. Then we got a text to say she was staying over at Zoe's. We didn't worry because we knew she was safe. The text came from her phone.'

'Can I see it?'

Becky handed her phone to Beth, and the DS took a screen shot before sending it to her own phone.

'So you didn't actually speak to her after she left here?'

'No, we didn't.'

'You rang Zoe this morning?' Beth flipped over to a new page in her notebook.

'I did,' Becky said. 'I knew Clare had an appointment at the uni for ten, and her stuff she needed was here. Zoe knew nothing about it, she said she hadn't been to the gym for several days. That's when I knew we had to tell DI Cheetham.'

The rain pounded on the windows, and Beth heaved a huge sigh. She thought of her colleagues out on the riverside, searching for clues of any sort, and knew this was the worst possible weather for finding anything.

Katie lifted her head. Her cheeks were wet with tears. 'This can't be happening. Is it the same person who's killed Clare?'

'We don't know.' Beth's voice was gentle. 'However, the circumstances are much the same, so it looks as though it is. DI Cheetham will be going to Doncaster this afternoon to speak to Clare's mum, but we won't encourage them to see you two, not at this moment anyway. You will be in your safe house shortly, so can I ask you to go and pack what you need, please?'

Becky and Katie stood and headed off to their rooms, leaving Will and Beth downstairs.

'They're scared,' he said. 'We're not even letting them have the comfort of their families.'

'We can't. We daren't let this address be compromised. I don't know if you've had time to read the case files from five years ago, but this is a clever killer. We found nothing then, and we've found nothing now he's resurfaced.'

'You're saying "he" again.'

'It's not a woman's way of killing. It feels like a male crime. And I felt it was a he, five years ago. I think there was no sexual activity because that would have left a trace of him. He couldn't risk that, and he got his kicks from the death, not from the sex. His planning was meticulous. He picked four pretty girls with nice figures, all with names beginning with L. We never discovered the significance of the letter, in fact we discovered bugger all. Then it stopped, and despite numerous meetings where we threw around ideas, the case slipped into the cold case category.'

'It's certainly climbed back out now,' Will said. 'I was reading through it when I was called to come here. Why do you think he stopped for five years?'

'Something happened. Maybe a marriage, or simply falling in love. His mindset changed, he had achieved what he planned, and he settled down. But something is changing in his life again, and the need to kill is there. I suspect this rain has assisted him, given him a way of operating, helped by the fact that people are staying indoors. The only thing I want to stress is don't underestimate him. We missed him once, and he'll not let us get to him easily.'

9

Telling Diana Vincent that her daughter was dead ranked with one of the worst things Erica had ever had to do, and she held the fragile lady close and let her cry until she could cry no more. Taking Flick Ardern with her had been inspired; the young DC was calm, unobtrusive, and damn good at making a cup of tea without being instructed to do so.

While Flick rang Diana's sister Hazel to ask that she come over to stay with her, Erica talked to Clare's mum, gently, questioning without making it obvious she was doing so.

'When did you last speak to Clare?'

'Yesterday afternoon.' Diana's sob was almost a hiccup. 'She told me about Susie. I asked her to come home, to be safe here, but she seemed to think she was fine. She didn't want to leave Becky and Katie.'

Inwardly, Erica cursed the fact that she hadn't explained the full circumstances to the girls – the obsessive nature of the person they believed had killed Susie, and that while they had nothing concrete to go on telling them he would attack the other three girls, they should have considered it a possibility and briefed everybody remaining in that student house. Because the killer had targeted girls with the same initial letter didn't mean he would go around seeking out girls with the letter S for the start of their Christian name.

Flick brought in the pot of tea with three mugs and looked at Diana. 'Hazel will be here in ten minutes. She's packing for a few days.'

A smile flashed across Diana's face; it didn't quite reach her eyes.

'Good,' Erica said. 'You don't want to be alone at this time.'

'She came before my husband died and stayed with me. It was a hard time because he died from cancer, but this is so much harder. You've told her...?'

Flick gave a brief nod. 'I have. We'll wait with you until she arrives. Drink your tea. It can't take anything away, but it always helps.'

Erica listened to Flick talk, all too aware that this was the first time the young DC had ever notified a death and yet she was handling the situation in such a mature way. Ms Felicity Ardern was destined for a worthwhile career in the Major Crimes Unit, Erica felt.

On the drive to Crookesvale Gardens, Erica and Flick were quiet, lost in their thoughts. The arrival of Diana's sister, a slightly overweight woman with a massive personality, had allowed them to leave, and when Erica had mentioned a formal identification of Clare, Hazel had reassured them that she would accompany her sister. Erica and Flick had left with a promise to ring with details of when the sisters would be needed, and as Erica softly closed the front door, they heard both women crying.

Beth met Erica and Flick at the door, and held out a slip of paper. 'We have a safe house. This is the address. The girls are packed, but scared. They've both said they'll go home to parents, but I've carefully explained the situation with this killer and his planned obsessiveness, and now they don't want to go to their parents, they want our protection. We should get them there as soon as we can, and Will and Flick can accompany them and stay with them until we get a team organised.'

'Thanks, Beth.' They all went through to the lounge where two large suitcases stood behind the sofa, ready for the two girls leaving. Becky and Katie looked up as Erica joined them.

'I'm so sorry to disrupt your education like this, girls, but your safety is our priority,' she explained. Neither of them looked convinced, but both gave a slight nod of acceptance of Erica's words.

'Can you find him quick?' Becky asked. 'We've lost two friends in two days, plus the lives we'd planned on living for this year.'

'We'll find him or her much more efficiently if we can devote our resources to tracking him or her down, without having to worry if the killer has got to you two.' Erica hated making her voice so firm; these girls were full of grief, something that until two days earlier they had probably never experienced, and their co-operation was of vital importance.

Erica headed back to the upper reaches of the Porter. Clare's body had been removed and then a text to Erica's phone informed her that the post-mortem would start at seven the following morning. She wandered around the site, feeling relieved that the rain had ceased, albeit temporarily.

She tried to speak to everyone, to encourage them. The entire team was a sorry sight. Hair hung limply, and clothes were extremely wet. There were three people in the river, several on the riverbank and hot drinks were being freely dished out at the refreshment van.

There was an air of despondency, and Erica made arrangements for a search stop at half past four; it would be too dark by then to see much, so they could set someone on to watch the site overnight, preserving the scene, and begin again at eight the following day.

She would be at the autopsy and she knew that despite the awful weather, the cold, and the gloominess of the scene, not one of them would want to change jobs with her. Nobody liked attending the post-mortems.

Erica didn't leave her desk until eight; organising the crews who were to take care of Becky and Katie had been difficult, and she had been forced to request additional personnel. She waited until Beth returned from seeing the first two who had pulled the overnight shift, and they caught up on the day's events.

Beth looked tired. Erica reached into her drawer and took out a bottle of gin, along with two clear plastic beakers.

'You certainly live the high life,' Beth commented with a smile, and held up the pretend gin glass.

'Certainly do. I think we need this, it's been a shitty day.'

'I know, and it makes you feel so bloody helpless when you see their faces, those two girls. They don't know how to handle what's happening to them, or how to grieve for their friends. And they're scared. Even with our officers there, they're scared. They've both taken their laptops to continue their studies, but I don't think it will happen. Their concentration will be shot to bits.'

'What if he decides to play the long game?'

'What? What's that got to do with their studies?'

'Sorry my mind is all over the place. I'd sort of thought to the future a bit, after we're forced to let the girls go back to being students. If we haven't caught him by then, he's going to carry on from where he left off. That seems to be what he's done after a five-year break, so us taking Becky and Katie out of the picture will mean nothing to him. He'll simply wait. He's picked his victims and that's it. I remember the waiting game we played after we found Lilith Baker-Jones' body, and there was nothing. He played with us, until we gave up and had to wait for him to give us his next victim. Five fucking years we've waited, Beth.'

'Look, we've not had much chance to breathe, or take stock, but tomorrow morning I'll make a start on tracking down anyone who was sent down soon after Lilith's body was found. It would have to be a serious crime to get a long sentence like eight to ten years, because that's what it would take to get out in four to five. It's no good looking at people who specialise in burglary, GBH, stuff like that. This is the big boys league, so I'll pull up some names for us to look at in the morning.'

Erica grinned. 'Oh, didn't I tell you? You and me, we've an appointment at seven with Ivor, he's doing the PM.'

Beth groaned and dropped her head. 'Thanks, boss. Is it too late for me to apply for a transfer to traffic?'

Frannie took Erica into her arms and kissed her. 'Does that make your day a little better?'

'It does. I need a hot shower, whatever you want to feed me with, and an exceptionally large glass of wine. Any colour, any flavour, and a high alcoholic content.'

'It's been that good then.'

'It has. And it's been a search day. Tomorrow I've to begin with the PM on today's victim, then I'm taking Flick with me and we're going out questioning people. Beth made a start with Becky and Katie, our two remaining girls, and got some information from them, but we've got them away to a place of safety now, so I feel a lot happier about that.'

'Good. Go and get your shower and I'll make us something quick. You look dreadful, so I'm not spending all night cooking. We both need to relax. I've had a day with the Salter family, and their increasingly mucky kids. It's getting close to our taking them away, I've never seen them look so bad as they looked today. I've called a case meeting for tomorrow, but it may be an evening meeting because two of the people I want there can't make it till after work. We're so bloody overworked, it's getting ridiculous. That new one who started last week, moved here from Luton, she's got three meetings tomorrow. She'll be moving back to Luton soon, she'll not be able to cope with this northern lifestyle.'

'We'll be like ships that pass in the night,' Erica joked, as she climbed the stairs. 'God knows what hour I'll be home for the foreseeable. In the meantime, don't forget me.'

'As if,' Frannie responded, and blew her a kiss.

'Nice wine,' Erica murmured, and laid her head on Frannie's shoulder. 'You do know, by the way, that the only reason I fell for you was because my head fit so neatly into your shoulder.'

'Of course I know that,' Frannie said. 'But did you love me a little as well? Or am I really only the pillow that's the right fit? Or maybe it was my exotic job in social services...'

'Yes.'

'Yes what?'

'Yes to all of it. Now shut up and kiss me. And I could manage a refill if there's any going.'

10

Beth looked around her lounge and knew Evan had been in. The key he had dropped through her letter box the previous week had meant nothing – he had clearly had a second one cut. She could sense him, sense his presence without him being in the room, and her anger grew.

Their separation had been acrimonious; the list he had presented her with where he outlined everything they had bought together showed how nasty he could be, and he wanted his half share of everything.

Turning around she covered each area, and realised the television had gone. A half smile formed on her lips. She had no problem with his removing that; he had insisted on a massive set because, in his words, 'you couldn't watch Sky Sports on a small screen'. She didn't care about watching Sky Sports on any size screen, so she walked upstairs to the bedroom, unplugged the thirty-two-inch, and carried it downstairs. As she set it up, she smiled at the speed with which she had cancelled Sky. Evan had only been gone a day.

Tomorrow would be a day to organise a locksmith to change the locks on front and back doors, and to attend the post-mortem of a twenty-year-old. Evan really was a mere blip in her existence so far, and it was time to admit to a feeling of relief that he had gone. Beth vowed to tell Erica about it, get it out in the open, and move on.

'And I thought he was the love of your life!' Erica looked closely at Beth. 'Clearly he wasn't.'

Beth shrugged. 'We wanted different things. He wanted other women, I didn't want other men, that sort of thing. Five years is long enough to work out I don't even like him, let alone love him. I thought I'd better tell you, before you wrote your Christmas cards.'

'I don't send Christmas cards.'

'That's okay then. We're both sorted. Thank God I didn't marry him, it's been hard enough getting rid of him without having to divorce him as well.'

'So he took your television?'

'No, he took *his* bloody television. It's big enough for him to nearly be able to play on the pitch, so I was glad to see the back of it. I've connected up the bedroom TV, and I'm quite happy with that. Don't have time to watch much anyway, with this job. No point starting to watch any serials, I'd miss most of the episodes. And I'm saving nearly £100 a month by cancelling Sky. Result.'

'Then I'm happy for you, but you know, I have to say the obligatory stuff like "if you ever need to talk" and "don't ever feel alone, I'm here", but actually I do mean it. It might feel good at the moment, but then you'll hit a memory and wonder if you really did the right thing.'

Beth laughed. 'You're going all philosophical on me, and it's only half past six. You want another coffee before we go to this PM?'

Erica looked at Beth and knew she would be okay. 'Why not? I'll give Diana Vincent a ring later, and get her organised for Clare's formal identification, but what I really want to do is go over the twenty-fourteen evidence, or lack of it, to see if there's anything we could possibly have missed. Do you have any feelings on it?'

Beth handed Erica the freshly poured coffee, and sat down facing her. 'In twenty-fourteen I didn't think for myself. I was a mere foot soldier for the likes of you. You were what I aimed to become, and there was a bit of hero worship in the mix, I think. I had started seeing Evan, and so I really was only there to take orders, not make waves and not contribute other than searching the crime scenes. Times have changed, and I spent last night listening to music and going through the old files. The press haven't picked up on it yet, that he or she has returned, so that's good. Some smart arse will before much longer. Have we got a strategy?'

Erica sipped at her coffee. 'I haven't, but you know me and the press. The words "no comment" were made for me when confronted by them. There's people higher in rank than me who can deal with that stuff, I've a killer to catch.'

Standing by the side of the autopsy table left Erica and Beth in no doubt that the same person had killed both girls. Ivor turned over the right hand, and there was VI cut into it, along with the missing tip of the little finger.

'Number six,' Beth said quietly. 'Thank God we've removed his seven and eight.'

Ivor looked at the two police officers. 'Don't underestimate him.'

'You think it's a him?' Erica's response to his comment was swift.

'I've no idea. It's just... dead bodies are heavy, and even more so when you're battling the elements. But let's not write off it being a fit woman. Anyway, I'm starting to record now.'

He took them through the main points, all of which were basically the same as the autopsy performed on Susanna Roebuck, and eventually Erica and Beth left the suite feeling queasy and concerned.

'Are we in danger of underestimating this killer?' Beth asked.

'I'm not. This is the sixth post-mortem I've attended that's a direct result of the actions of this one person. Let's go and find a café, grab some breakfast, and talk things through. Then I'll ring Diana and get things moving there.'

They walked to the outside of the building and Beth stopped. 'That's sunshine.'

'Thank God for that. We've got teams out on the riverbank again today, but I'm calling them back in tomorrow. We've interviews to do, searches and stuff, but it's important to get the crime scene cleared as soon as possible.'

'And I want to start on tracking down anyone who hasn't been around for five years.' Beth glanced at her watch. 'Half eight. I'll ring a locksmith while we're waiting for breakfast, then that's ticked off my to-do list.'

It was quiet in the office. Most of the team were at the river, and Erica and Beth had opted for computer work.

Erica angled her screen carefully to cut out the winter sun that was directly on it, and pulled up the file from twenty-fourteen. There had been no physical contact between the girls who had lost their lives to the L-killer, but the link between them, their names, had been obvious. 'What if that wasn't the link,' she mumbled, but with nobody else near her she received no answer except one inside her own head. *What if?*

Had they, he or she, been influenced by the press jumping on the bandwagon with their L-killer headlines? Could it have been something else? Erica pulled up a second file headed Leanne Fraser.

Leanne had been the first to be discovered, at the end of April in twenty-fourteen. A seven-year-old boy, Finn Draper, had run into the woods on his way to school, and found the posed, naked body. He had been interviewed, swore he hadn't touched anything because he watched *CSI* on television. His mother had cried through most of the interview. She had been distraught that her only child had seen such an awful sight, and she had been unable to prevent it. Finn had been quite blasé about the whole situation. However, they had been unable to help with anything other than finding her.

Nobody else had seen anything, the significance of the slash on her right palm wasn't obvious at that stage, and even though the Propofol was found in her system, they could find nothing to point them to the killer.

Erica read through Leanne's employment history, her family life, and nothing helped. It was very much a live investigation by the time it reached mid-May, and on the eighteenth a second posed and naked body was found in woods near to where the Pennine Trail passed through Woodhouse, on the outskirts of Sheffield.

Once more the body was placed so that it would be easily found, and still nobody suggested an idea that the two slashes on Lucy Owen's palm meant anything other than he'd slipped with whatever he had used to cut off the tip of her little finger.

It was obvious it was the same killer, and the newspapers made noises about serial killers. This was squashed by the police. Yes it was two bodies, but two bodies do not a serial killer make, was their take on the matter.

The third body had. *Serial killer strikes again* was the gist of the headlines and this time nobody denied it. Laurel Price died in July, on the ninth, but wasn't found until the afternoon of the tenth. Two boys riding bikes through Rolleston Woods found her and freaked. They had heard of the other two murders, and knew they needed help. One boy stayed nearby, too scared to be too close, and the other went to the edge of the woods to meet the police, after calling them on his mobile phone. They too watched *CSI* and knew they hadn't to touch anything at the scene.

Erica read through them carefully. She digested every word until these old cases became as clear in her head as the new ones did. Laurel was the oldest of the four victims at twenty-three, was about to marry, and this fact gave her prominence in the newspapers. Her fiancé was distraught, as were her parents, and although the fiancé hadn't had an alibi, he had for the first two murders.

She made a note of his name, Nicholas Payne, and decided to check if he had alibis for Susie and Clare's murders. Rule him out once and for all.

Lilith's murder had been the final one, and the one that had confirmed what the palm marks meant. She was number four, with an inherent promise of there being more. Except no more appeared, not then. Lilith had been found in Ecclesall Woods, in the south of the city, and gave no more clues than any of the others. She had been found on the twenty-seventh of July, a beautiful sunny day; she never saw the sunrise.

Other than the letter L, they had found no link between the girls, but Erica knew there had to be one, she felt it. Somehow the killer had known the girls, had chosen his victims because of their names, but initially he or she had known them. They had to find that connection with the help of the knowledge they were picking up from the new murders. He or she had known them.

Erica's page was filled with notes, yet nothing of outstanding interest had occurred to her other than Nicholas Payne's name, and that was a kind of straw-clutching exercise really, and she knew it.

Four girls with families that still hadn't had full closure, a killer who was seemingly proud of their work, and who was forensically well informed, leaving nothing at the scene to give them any information.

'I'll find you this time, though, you bastard,' Erica whispered, closed down the file and walked across the office to Beth's desk.

Beth looked up. 'Okay?'

'Kind of. I'm heading out to the river, see what's happening if anything, then I'm going home. If you need me, ring. One thing I have learned is that the kids of twenty-fourteen all seemed to watch *CSI*, thank God. Maybe we should have that as part of the qualifications you need to have to get into the police.'

11

Beth went home at three and met with the locksmith, who secured everything for her. Although unafraid of Evan, she felt much happier that he could no longer invade her home. After saying goodbye to the elderly man who had given her peace of mind, she spent some time moving furniture around.

No longer would everything be focused on the television, and she cleared a corner for the installation of a small desk. It had always occurred to her that a laptop wasn't actually meant for a lap, and so she would have a desk. The friendly Argos website said they could deliver the same day, and she mentally prepared herself for an evening of flat-pack assembly.

The sound of a key in the lock caused a spasm of fear to pass through her, and she knew who it was on the other side of the door. She slid over to the window, and glanced outside. Evan's car was parked across the road. She waited.

The key was inserted for the second time, and then she heard a thud as he kicked the door.

A couple of minutes or so later she heard the same key insertion sound, but this time in the back door. Then he banged loudly. 'You in there, Beth?'

She remained quiet. She had to stifle laughter as she heard a muttered 'Fucking woman. Think you can change locks and keep me out? Fucking woman.' She was tempted to move towards the kitchen window and wave at him, but she didn't really want to have to arrest him for harassment or breaching the peace, or probably even GBH. She wanted to spend her evening building a desk, not down at the station booking her ex.

He eventually gave up and she moved back into the lounge, watching as he walked down the road towards his car. He sped off with a squeal of tyres, and she finally gave in to the laughter. He hadn't known of her change of car which was parked on the kerbside; four doors away had been the nearest she could get to her home. He had obviously worked it out that she wasn't in. She briefly wondered what he had come to take this time, but dismissed it as irrelevant. From now on she would decide what he could have.

Erica walked up and down the riverbank, talking to members of her team who were fingertip searching. With the onset of the afternoon rain following the hopeful sunshine of the morning, everyone was looking wet, and shortly before four, satisfied that everything possible had been done, she called off the activities.

'Okay,' she called, and her team stopped, hoping the instruction wasn't to move to another area. 'Time to pack up and go. Please check in every evidence bag when you get back to the briefing room, and I'll see you there for a quick chat, then it's home time.'

There was a brief but heartfelt cheer, and Erica asked Ian to make sure the crime scene tape was still secure around the small area where Clare's body had been found, before heading back to her car.

For a short time she sat and let her thoughts wander. This

had been a nightmare week and she hoped she had stopped it getting any worse by hiding away the other two girls. They had to step up the search for the killer – he or she had a pattern, and she sensed their brain wouldn't allow them to deviate from that plan. Two girls from the four-girl group had gone, and she suspected he would wait until the remaining two went back into society. They couldn't keep them locked up for ever, they would have to resume their university life one day.

As Erica started the car her phone rang, and she sat with the engine running while she answered Frannie. 'I'm frozen.'

'I imagine you are. You at the river?'

'I am. We've found nothing, Fran.'

'So what will you do next?'

'I have no idea. Sit and think about it, for a start. What time are you home?'

'Should be no later than nine. I did put it in your journal. You know, Erica, I can cancel it if you need me there now...'

'No you can't. It's your job. I'll be fine. I made some notes when I went through the twenty-fourteen file, so I'll work on them, see if they clarify anything. I'll put jacket potatoes in about eight, and they'll be ready when you get home.'

'Okay. Let's have something exotic with it. How about curry?'

'That's exotic?'

'It's tasty even if it's not exotic, and it's already in the freezer. I'd better go. Wanted to check in with you, make sure you're okay.'

They said 'love you' and disconnected. Erica put the car into drive, and set off down towards the city centre, and her office. The team would all appreciate an earlier night, and hopefully return the following morning feeling refreshed and alert. They would need to be – most of them would be out doing door-to-door interviews.

She would be going back to the beginning, she decided.

What had sent this killer from random girls with L names, to a group of girls all living together? Where had the information come from? The university?

Time to stop the initial evidence-gathering, she needed to move on to the real work, and start thinking like a killer. She would get the girls to write down a list of their tutors, and as many as they could remember who had been there for Susie and Clare, then she would head for the university, already armed with a certain amount of knowledge. Technology had moved on since twenty-fourteen, and she intended making full use of it. The tutors' names would be fed into HOLMES within minutes of her getting them, and maybe something out of kilter would hit her.

Beth couldn't believe how simple it was to erect the desk. Even the two drawers had been almost easy, and she sat on the typist's chair she had ordered at the same time, and surveyed her kingdom. Queendom. Well, whatever.

It looked so cosy now she didn't have to have everything worked around watching football, and she opened up her laptop, firmly ensconced on the desk and not falling off her lap. She entered her complicated password that had taken her three days to learn, and, as usual, felt inordinately pleased that she had got it right. She opened up the files she had spent all day collating, asked Alexa, the tiny round machine she found invaluable, to play her some piano music, and settled down to work.

Six names were on her list, all men who had been given long sentences in twenty-fourteen, and were out in the community once more. There were no women, and she wondered if she hadn't looked in the right place.

. . .

By the end of the evening Beth was at the hot chocolate stage, and satisfied that she had a core list of eight – seven men and one woman who came into the particular time frame. There had been others she could discount – too infirm, too elderly, residing out of the country, and she ruled out anybody living too far north or too far south. She closed down her laptop, blew out the candles and made her way upstairs feeling satisfied with the work she had done, and more than satisfied that she had kept Evan out of her home and at the same time turned it into a warm, comfortable haven.

She checked the road as she closed the curtains, then checked again before getting into bed. There was no sign of her ex-partner, and sleep came easily for the first time in weeks.

It was almost eleven before Erica and Frannie went to bed. After eating their curry-topped jacket potatoes they talked – Frannie explaining what had happened at the meeting, how they would check on the children causing them concern for one more week, then it would be decision time as to whether they would be taken into care or left with their inadequate parents.

'How do you feel about it?' Erica had seen the quiet times when the children had been on Frannie's mind, and she knew it was a really difficult decision they would have to make as a group.

'It's a poisonous atmosphere these children live in, but it's going to devastate the mother if we remove them. The father is a horrible man, never seems to be sober, and controls everything. If we could remove him and put him in care it would solve everything. We could give the mother the support she needs to get her clean of both alcohol and drugs, which in turn would make the lives of the children so much better, but that's not how it works.'

Erica nodded. She had seen the same scenario so many times, felt the same anguish Frannie was feeling at the unfairness of a situation. 'And everyone is of the same mind?'

'Everybody is of the mind that we should kill him, painfully, and then give the help that's needed. But we've all agreed in principle that it can't go on for much longer, so we'll have a meeting in seven days, and if nothing has changed we have to get those children to a place of safety. We'll sort visitations out once they're settled. The appointments will be carefully monitored, and there'll have to be massive lifestyle improvements before these children are allowed back to the family home. So, lovely lady, how's your case progressing? Anything you can talk through with me?'

Erica laughed. 'I can talk anything through with you. I think we've been together long enough to know that trust is a major component of our relationship. If only there was something to talk through...'

'It's not progressing well?' Frannie frowned at her wife.

'It's progressing marginally because two of the girls who share that student accommodation have been killed, so we can see the pattern. We've removed the other two to the safe house so hopefully that's stopped him, even if it's only temporarily.'

'It's definitely a he, then?'

'I think it has to be. The terrain on the banks of the Porter is pretty rough in places, and to be carrying a body in that area isn't going to be easy, so I'm not convinced a woman would have the physical strength for it.'

'I'm not saying you're wrong, Erica, but if you saw some of the women who go to my gym, you'd change your mind about that. The women who work mainly with the weights are proper tough cookies, could easily carry a body. But you're right, carrying it on a slippery riverbank is different to picking up a weight and lowering it to its resting place on a block.'

Erica sighed. 'I know. This killer hasn't been off my mind for five years now. He or she might have gone quiet, and I know there's a reason for that, but they're back and I have to find who it is. We start tomorrow with interviews. We need to find out what the connection is that led this fuckwit to our girls, and let's face it, the one thing they do have in common above all else is the university.'

'Fuckwit. Love it. Professor Fuckwit of Sheffield University. It has quite a ring to it.' She clasped hold of Erica's hand. 'You'll find him, I know you will. You're not a lowly DS anymore, Cheetham, you set the rules. Go get him.'

12

Erica was getting out of bed when the telephone rang. She grabbed at it hoping to silence it before it woke Frannie who finally seemed to have dropped off to sleep. They had both had a disturbed night, and she knew Fran didn't have any early meetings scheduled. She slipped quietly out of the bedroom before speaking.

'Morning.'

'Morning, ma'am. It's PC Fisher, front desk.'

'That's fine as long as you're not ringing me to tell me we have another body.'

There was a moment of silence, and she guessed he was trying to decide whether she was joking or not.

He decided she wasn't. 'Sorry, DI Cheetham. A dog walker has reported finding a body. A female. He says she's naked, so I guess she's yours.'

'Where's the body?'

'A bit downriver from where everybody was yesterday. The man who rang it in is a bit shaken up, but he says he can see the police tape around the previous site. Who do you want me to call, ma'am?'

'Can you get hold of DS Machin? Tell her I'll meet her there ASAP. And then get in touch with the same message to Ian Thomas, Flick Ardern, Mike Nestor and Will Bramwell. And put a call in for a Forensics team to get out there.'

Disconnecting after Fisher's assurance he would follow instructions, she immediately rang the safe house, getting the officer to check that both girls were there. He swiftly reassured her they were, he could see both of them still fast asleep.

Erica grabbed some warm clothing, left a quick note to tell Fran the situation, and headed up to Ringinglow. Erica's head was spinning. She had thought they had possibly stopped him, or at least delayed his plans with the removal of the other two girls, but they hadn't caused him any heartache, he had simply chosen someone else. Or had he been out-thinking them all the time?

The girl's body was posed exactly as the others, and she was pretty, as the others had been pretty. Her shoulder-length dark hair with the flash of turquoise in the fringe was wet from the incessant rain, as was the rest of her body. The Forensics team had arrived at the same time as Erica had got there, and were busy setting up the tent they had removed from the earlier scene.

Monday Susie, Tuesday Clare, Wednesday Jane Doe, Erica's thoughts were churning. Was that his plan? A girl a day? A beautiful girl a day? They couldn't hide all the beautiful girls away, that was for sure, but they needed to get the message out not to go anywhere alone. She thought of all the students in the city from all around the world, and shivered as she realised how much the problem had escalated.

With Ivor's arrival she followed him into the tent.

. . .

'We have to stop meeting every day like this,' he said. 'We'll be talked about.'

'We certainly will. Do I need to ask if this is the same killer?'

'Let's look.' He gently lifted the girl's right hand and turned it over to reveal a VII carved into the palm. The tip of the little finger was missing. 'It is, I'm afraid.'

'Shit.'

'I take it this isn't one of the other girls?'

'No, they're tucked up in bed in a safe refuge. I checked before I even left home. We know this killer works to a pattern, there's something linking the victims, and of course it was obvious it was that student house. He's thrown us a curveball with this. Showing that's not his pattern at all, it's something else. Susie and Clare were on the same courses, maybe this girl is as well.'

Ivor confirmed death formally, and added that it was strangulation by tights, and again they had been left around the neck. He lifted her hair slightly and found the tell-tale mark of a hypodermic on her neck. 'And I expect to find Propofol when we do the tox screen. Let's get out of the way and get the photographer in. I've a flask in the car, come and have a coffee. You look like you need one.'

The riverbank was once more filled with uniforms searching for clues, but feeling demoralised before they started. Too much rain, too many consecutive days of dead bodies, everything was simply too much.

Erica had requested that if anyone reported a missing girl of around twenty, she was to be notified immediately if not sooner, but as with all the other bodies, nothing had been left at the scene other than the girl herself. No clothes, no bag, no soul.

Erica left Ian to organise the teams, pleased to see how well he responded when gravity and professionalism were called for, and walked back to her car. She felt the need to contact Fran, to hear her voice tell her to hang on in there, things would work out and they would find this killer.

The call went through to voicemail, and she left a brief message saying it was only a catch-up, and she would see her that night. No need to ring back.

She sat for a while staring out of the windscreen at the bleakness of the scene in front of her. The rain ran down the glass like mini rivers, all meeting up at the bottom and forming a large puddle. Halloween was the following day, and she guessed it would be a washout if this rain continued. Thousands of disappointed children, thousands of happy parents trying to look upset for the sake of their sons and daughters who had been planning outfits for a couple of months – and she realised they had nowhere near enough Haribos in the house to cater for the usual amounts of children who turned up on their doorstep because they went to the trouble of decorating with ghosts, witches, wizards and pumpkins. That problem would have to be rectified before Thursday evening. She couldn't assume nobody would be out in the rain, and apart from that, she and Fran loved Haribos. For the first time that Wednesday morning she allowed a smile to cross her face, and the tiny sweets had put it there.

Was it really only Wednesday? Her thoughts drifted back to Monday morning, to the phone call that had dragged her out of bed. *What the hell had prompted the killer to start again?*

By eleven they had a name. Imogen Newland. Her boyfriend had reported her as missing; he couldn't track her down. She had been out Tuesday night for a gym session followed by a meal with colleagues because he was on nights, and when he arrived home shortly after seven in the morning, she wasn't there.

Pete Vanton had gone to bed, thinking she had probably had a drink so decided to stay with a friend, but following being woken by an Amazon delivery driver at a few minutes after nine he decided to ring her at work. She hadn't arrived, and she wasn't answering her mobile phone.

He spoke to one of her friends, and she confirmed Imo had been with them, but didn't go for the meal. She had complained of a headache and decided to head home.

By ten, Pete decided enough was enough and he rang the police. He'd heard the news about the two dead students. He didn't go back to bed.

Erica was impressed by the young man. He spoke well, waited, still in his dressing gown, until she sat, and watched as Beth disappeared into the kitchen to make them all a coffee. His face showed some unease and Erica was keen to progress, to help that unease disappear. He deserved that much.

She took out her notebook and carefully asked questions. She had already seen the photograph of Pete and Imogen that was standing on the coffee table, and knew she was about to impart the worst of all information to the young man with the blonde hair and watery blue eyes.

Beth returned with the coffee mugs, and he looked at Erica. 'What aren't you saying, DI Cheetham? Has Imo been in an accident or something?'

Erica leaned across and picked up the photograph. 'Is this Imogen?'

'It is. Will you please tell me what's wrong?'

'I'm so sorry,' Erica spoke gently, 'but we believe a body found this morning is that of your Imogen.'

He seemed to crumple in front of their eyes. 'A body?'

'Yes. I'm so sorry. We will need to ask you to make a formal identification, but having looked at this picture I'm sure Imogen is our victim.'

'Victim?' He stood, agitated. 'What do you mean? She's been murdered? Or is it an accident?'

'We believe the killer to be the same person who has already killed twice this week, but I can't give you any more information than that.' Erica took hold of his hand and gave a gentle tug. 'Please sit down. We have a few questions we need to ask you. I understand you worked a night shift last night?'

He nodded, almost unaware of tears falling from his eyes, and she continued. 'Where do you work?'

'I'm... I'm a night manager at a twenty-four hour Tesco in Rotherham,' Pete said, sitting down. He took a tissue from the box on the coffee table and wiped his eyes. 'Sorry...'

'Please don't apologise. Take your time. You didn't leave your workplace at all last night?'

'Not for a minute, there are twenty members of staff who will vouch for that, but so will your colleagues. We had some bother about two this morning with some drunks who'd fallen out of a nightclub and called in to see what alcohol they could get from us. They dropped a couple of bottles of wine, so I went to deal with them, but they waved the broken glass around and I sent for the police. They were there until shortly after four. Arrested the lot of them.'

'And you were home for just after seven?'

'Yes. I finish at six, but because of the trouble it took longer than normal to do the handover. I had a form to fill out, that sort of thing, and it delayed my departure. When I saw Imo wasn't here, I assumed she'd stayed with one of her mates. They're a crowd of six or seven, all work for the same solicitors in the city centre. They go out a couple of times a month, so I didn't worry then. It was only when I woke at nine to take in an Amazon delivery that I realised she'd be at work so I rang her. Her mate said she'd gone straight home after the gym session because she had a bad headache, so I tried her mobile. Nothing. By ten I thought there must be something wrong so I rang the police. And now you're here telling me I've lost her.'

'I really am deeply sorry. Is there anybody we can call for you?'

He shook his head. 'No, I'll ring my brother. He'll come over. You're sure it's Imo?'

His eyes said everything, and Erica could have cried alongside him. 'I'm sure. You're not married?'

'No, we're engaged. Oh God... her mum and dad...'

'Would you like us to notify them?'

'No, that's my job. I'll get dressed after I ring my brother, and he'll run me over to tell them. I'll make the formal identification, DI Cheetham. I can't ask them to do that.'

Erica put down her mug, and the two police officers stood. 'We'll leave you now. This is my card... if you think of anything that could possibly have some bearing on these cases, please ring. Anything at all, Pete. Any tiny detail.'

He followed them to the door and watched as they walked towards their car. Only then did he let himself cry properly for his Imo.

13

E rica felt angry. How could she be attending her third post-mortem of the week, and it only be Wednesday afternoon? She saw Ivor's head lift and look across at her, and she waited.

'DI Cheetham? This young lady was pregnant. I would say around eight weeks.'

Erica felt the anger escalate, knowing she would have to tell Pete Vanton this news. He hadn't only lost his fiancée...

She breathed in and out slowly. 'Thank you. And everything else is the same as the others?'

'It is. We're waiting for the tox results, but I don't doubt the drug will be present.'

'Why the hell are these girls getting into this car? It has to be a vehicle, and this weather is probably helping the killer. Offering them a lift because it's raining – good call. But surely they must know him. Or think they do. Even that mark for the hypodermic leads us to think he's in the driving seat, and he simply reaches across with the damn needle and injects it into them.'

'I fear your reading of the situation is accurate. Now you have to weigh up how much to release to the general public to keep them aware, and how much to hold back. I don't envy you your job.'

'Thanks, Ivor. We have to go. I'd like to bring Imogen's fiancé in tomorrow for the formal identification. Will she be ready?'

'She will. I'll finish tonight with her. You're going to tell him she was pregnant?'

'I am. It will come out eventually, and I'd rather he knew from the beginning. Let's hope we're not meeting up tomorrow for another PM, this week surely can't get any worse.'

The university was obliging, and had allocated a small office for police use during the investigation. The Tech department had set up two computers, and Erica and Beth walked in, looking around with a degree of surprise.

'This is smart,' Erica said. 'Puts my cubbyhole to shame.'

Beth picked up a note leaning against one of the monitors. 'They've organised for the first two on our list to be available at four. They're better organised than we are.' She looked at Erica. She knew she was thinking about the issue of having to tell Peter Vanton about his baby.

'Wouldn't take much to be better organised than us,' Erica snapped. 'Since Monday morning we've had three bodies pass through our system, despite our taking people out of the way to keep them safe. Who's first on that list?'

'That girl in the wheelchair, Jenna...' Beth hesitated while double-checking her list, 'Jenna Armstrong, followed by Dom Andrews. Then there's a further list of six for tomorrow. That's all the people who went to the *Macbeth* performance and who saw Susie there.'

'Okay.' Erica checked her watch. 'Shall we have a coffee before Jenna Armstrong arrives?'

Beth moved over to the coffee machine, and spent a couple of minutes working out how to use it. Eventually it was sorted and she turned to Erica who was checking something on the computer. 'While we're drinking this I'll fill you in on what happened last night.'

She picked up the two mugs and walked across to Erica's desk. 'I had my locks changed,' she said, moving to her own desk. 'All went well, and when the locksmith had gone I set about changing stuff, moving the furniture around, that sort of thing. I ordered a desk from Argos which was delivered last night, but at one point I thought my heart was going to stop.'

Erica lifted her head. 'Why?'

'I heard a key in the lock. I knew it was Evan, and of course he couldn't get in. He kicked the front door, said a few choice words, then went round to the back door. He tried to unlock that one, but I've had everything changed, plus extra bolts on, so he's not getting in at all. It scared me, made me feel... oh, I don't know, inadequate I suppose.'

'He didn't know you were in?'

'No, I parked higher up the street, and he doesn't know I've changed cars. He would have thought I hadn't got home from work.'

'You want me to have a word?'

'Not yet. If he continues it might come to that, but I wanted you to be aware, just in case.'

'You think he would attack you?'

'Six months ago I would have laughed at the idea, but he's changed. Don't worry, if I feel he needs some heavy-handed treatment, I'll tell you. Now, how do we handle these students? Gently, I assume?'

'With care, definitely, unless we feel they're holding back on something. I should imagine the women are feeling uneasy. I know our third victim wasn't from the uni, but they don't know that. And that little fact tells us that whatever is connecting these victims in this murderer's brain isn't the university. It's something else.'

'Pretty girls? All three girls have been really attractive, all had good figures which is what he likes the world to see. I don't think it's really that, it's too simplistic. In twenty-fourteen it was all about the pretty girls and the way he displayed them, but their names did all begin with L, which was a much bigger link. I don't think it's only about them being physically attractive, it's more than that, and until we recognise that link he's going to carry on killing.'

'Let's hope the link isn't one body a night, because if it is we'll be up early again tomorrow.' Erica sipped at her coffee. She looked up in response to a knock at the door.

Beth moved around her desk and helped Jenna manoeuvre her wheelchair through the opening that was only just big enough to accommodate it.

Erica smiled at the girl with the glowing cheeks.

Jenna shrugged off the all-enveloping rain cape and ruffled her hands through her curly red hair. 'It's pissing down again,' she stated, 'and I'm fed up with being wet. I'm Jenna Armstrong, although I suppose you've guessed that.'

'Kind of.' Erica laughed. 'You need a paper towel or something to dry off? A coffee?'

'I'd love a coffee. I'm chilled through. Bloody weather,' she grumbled.

Beth stood. 'I'll get you one. Milk?' She took the cape from

Jenna and hung it on the coat stand in the corner of the room, then pushed it closer to the radiator. 'That should dry it out, but I can't control how wet it gets when you go back outside.' She couldn't help but smile at the vivacious girl in front of them.

'Milk and one sugar, please,' Jenna confirmed. 'I'm not sure if I can be of any help to you, but I do realise you'll be talking to all of us who were there that night. It wasn't only uni people though. Others who simply enjoy Shakespeare.'

Erica gave a slight nod in acknowledgement. 'We realise that, but we're making life a little easier by starting with those who knew Susanna and were there with her. I understand you sat next to her?'

Beth passed Jenna her drink, and Jenna smiled. 'Thanks. I need this. Yes, I did. I like... liked Susie and Clare. Susie was in the end seat, Clare next to her, so I parked my wheelchair in the aisle and sat with them. It's easier for me if I stay in my chair.'

'Did you have any concerns about anything? Did anybody speak to them who you didn't know?'

'No, Dom and Danny were behind us, as were Maria and Anya, the twins, and during the interval we chatted with them. Dom went for some cans of Coke for us, but other than that we didn't move, didn't chat to anybody else.'

'That would be Dom Andrews? Do you know the other lad's surname?'

'We all call him Brummy Danny, but that's because his Birmingham accent is so strong. His actual name is Daniel Irving.'

Beth glanced down the list they had been given, and put a star by his name. She had noticed a twinkle in Jenna's eyes when she had spoken of Brummy Danny, and guessed their flame-haired interviewee was interested in the lad who had sat with them in the theatre.

'Jenna, can I ask how you came to be in a wheelchair?' Erica spoke carefully.

Erica had decided to get the elephant out of the way so they could ask more probing questions. Jenna Armstrong was an extremely pretty girl with what appeared to be a slim, attractive figure and as such needed to heed the warning that she never accept a lift from anyone... conversely, if she was able to walk, a wheelchair would enable the transport of bodies to be undertaken very easily, with hardly a passing glance from members of the public.

'Of course. I was knocked off my bike when I was twelve. It caused spinal damage, and I'm fine from the waist up, but from the waist down I feel nothing. I don't let it stop me doing anything, and this university has been so accommodating of my needs, it's unbelievable. I have a specially adapted car, although I rarely use it during term time, I get about on this little workhorse.' She tapped the arm of the wheelchair.

'Thank you for that. So, you came out of the theatre. Did you stay in the foyer, or go straight outside?'

'I stayed in the foyer for a couple of minutes while we were deciding what to do, then Clare said she needed a wee. It was rather crowded because most people were waiting inside for their lifts to arrive. It was raining pretty heavily. Susie and I decided to wait outside, thinking Clare would only be a minute, but when we got outside Danny and Dom were waiting for us. I drove up to them, on this, not the car of course, and Susie said she would wait for Clare to come out, and see us down at the pub. I've no idea what happened after that. I eventually saw Clare in the pub, but not Susie. I went down to the pub with

Dom and Danny. Clare was in the corner with Becky Charlesworth and Katie Davids. I must admit I didn't think anything of it, simply assumed Susie had decided to go home.'

'Let's go back to when you came out of the theatre,' Erica said. 'Close your eyes and picture the scene.'

Jenna complied, and the two officers waited.

'Okay. It was raining heavily, as it had been for what seems weeks, and there were quite a few people hanging around, or getting in cars that pulled up to take them home. Lots of umbrellas. Lots of faces hidden by umbrellas. Dom and Danny were standing higher up that little road at the side of the theatre, and I saw Dom wave. Susie told me to go to them and head off to the pub, to get out of the rain as quickly as possible. I left her...'

There was a catch in Jenna's voice as she narrated the events of the evening when her friend had disappeared.

'And I haven't seen her since,' Jenna finished quietly. She picked up her drink and sipped at it, looking at the two officers. 'In fact, to carry things on a day, I haven't seen either of them since, because Clare has been killed as well. What's going on? Is it someone with a grudge against Clare and Susie, or are Becky and Katie likely to disappear also?'

'Becky and Katie have been moved to a safe place,' Beth said. 'You don't need to worry about them. We won't bring them back here until we've caught the person doing this to your friends.'

'Are we *all* in danger? Is he targeting girls from here?'

'Jenna, there is a third victim. We found her this morning. She has no connection to the university as far as we're aware. But we will be putting out an announcement tonight on *Look North*, recommending that nobody gets into any car other than a car they're expecting to get into.' Erica hesitated. She felt somehow she was breaking rules. 'I believe, and this is only me, that somebody the girls knew well enough to trust, offered them a lift home or something, to get out of this blessed rain.'

Jenna stared. 'Should I be worried? I'm rather vulnerable.'

'Yes. Every pretty woman in this city should be worried. But I do believe a vehicle of some sort is part of the MO, so only ever get into your own car, and don't give anybody else a lift, no matter how well you know them. Because you don't know them.'

14

_____

Dom Andrews was waiting to enter the office as Beth opened the door to allow Jenna to leave.

He smiled as he saw her, and bent to kiss her cheek. 'If you wait till they've finished with me, I'll walk you home.'

Jenna hesitated, then nodded. 'I'll sit out here and read.'

Dom sat down, and then Erica asked him to stand. 'I'm sorry about this, Dominic, but can you empty your pockets, please.'

He looked puzzled, but complied. He took out his wallet, and Erica glanced through it. There was only a ten-pound note in the paper money compartment, and in the card pockets there was a debit card, a credit card, a gym membership card for the Starlite Gym, and a driving licence. She half pulled out the ten-pound note, and he shrugged.

'Hey, I'm a starving student.'

Erica smiled at him, and checked through all the other items he had placed on the table. She pushed them across the desk to him, and he refilled his pockets.

'Now your backpack, please.'

By the time he had emptied it, there was quite a pile on the desk. Paperwork from whatever tutorial he had attended, a journal, several pens, a book on criminology, a bag of Skittles, a pencil case... Erica frowned. The pens were lying around loose in a bag when he had a pencil case. She carefully unzipped it, but it contained nothing more sinister than rulers, coloured pencil crayons and a rubber. She looked through everything while Beth searched the bag itself.

Eventually they handed everything back to him. He said thank you.

They waited, but he didn't ask why they had checked him out, so Erica spoke.

'You're not curious why we've checked everything you have on your person?'

'No, you didn't find the dagger down my sock.' His face was deadpan.

'Our killer doesn't use a dagger.' Erica's face was equally straight.

Beth laughed. 'Stop it, you two. We've looked at everything for a quite simple reason, Dom. We've heard you ask Jenna to wait for you, and you'll see her home safely. That's the sort of line our killer seems to be using, so we're making sure you don't have the killer's trademark tools on you before we let you take Jenna anywhere.'

'As if,' he countered. 'As if I'd hurt a hair on that lass's head. So you're happy I'm not going to bump her off on the way home? Do I need permission to take her for half of lager?'

'No permission needed,' Erica responded, 'but you might need more than that tenner in your wallet. Now, can we take you back to Sunday evening. *Macbeth*.'

'Excellent performance,' Dom said. 'A really good night. Heavy rain of course, but we dry, eventually, don't we.'

'You were outside before Clare and Susie?'

'Yes, I saw Susie with Jenna, so we waved to them to let them see where we were standing. Jenna drove up to us, and left Susie by the roadside. Jenna said Susie was waiting for Clare to come from the ladies and they'd see us in the pub. We left straight away, and walked down.'

'Okay,' Erica said. 'I need you to go back to that scene. The rain is tipping down, there are cars collecting theatregoers to transport them home, what else can you see?'

He hesitated, and Erica knew he was taking himself back to Sunday night.

'Umbrellas. Lots of umbrellas. A couple of people struggling with theirs because it was windy as well as raining heavily. People huddling together. Groups. No individuals on their own except Susie. Waving.'

'To you?'

'No, she was looking up the main road. Her back was to me.'

'You're sure it was Susie?'

'Yes. She had on a bright red coat with a hood with fur round it. Quite distinctive.'

Erica and Beth exchanged a glance. Could this be the first clue as to what had happened on that dreadful night? 'After she waved, what happened?'

'I don't know, I'm sorry. Jenna reached us, and we set off to walk to the pub straight away. We were soaked by this time, we didn't have an umbrella.' He smiled. 'We got to the pub pretty quick, I'm telling you. It got really busy, and I didn't think any more about Susie and Clare, because I'd spotted Becky Charlesworth at the bar, so assumed the four of them were all together. They always seemed to be together, didn't really do anything separately. I can't imagine how Becky and Katie are feeling. They okay? They've not been here today.'

'We've moved them away for their safety. We'll get them back as soon as we can.'

'Shit. You think this bloke's after all four of them?'

'We don't know. No doubt Jenna will tell you, but there has been a third victim today, there'll be something about it on the news tonight. As far as we know the latest victim has no connection with uni, she worked at a solicitors. But obviously we're taking no risks, so Becky and Katie will be held safely until we catch who is doing this.'

Erica stood and held out her hand. 'Thank you for coming in, Dom, and I apologise for checking everything you have on you, but now is not the time to take chances. Enjoy your lager, and make sure she arrives home safely.'

Dom grinned. 'Not my job. Danny will take over when we get to the pub. I've never known him have a dagger in his sock, but there's a first time for everything... he's got a bit of a thing for Jenna, and she's got a bit of a thing for him, so I reckon he'll see her safely inside, not merely to the door.'

Erica and Beth sat for a moment, discussing the two interviews. 'It seems to me,' Erica said thoughtfully, 'if Jenna hadn't zoomed on that nifty little chair up to Dom and Danny, Susie might still be alive. Jenna going left Susie on her own, and whoever planned this took the opportunity to get her in the car. She waved at him, for fuck's sake! She knew him well enough to recognise him, or her, through a rain-covered windscreen. Or did she simply recognise the car? I want every house and every business on that stretch of main road, both sides, visiting. I want CCTV checking. Let's see if we can find this red coat with an arm raised, waving at somebody, and let's see who the bloody hell she's waving at.'

'You're swearing,' said Beth.

'Too damn right I am. We're clutching at tiny straws like Dom saw her wave at somebody. We have no idea who that could possibly be, or even if we can find any evidence of that action on any CCTV. We know it's not on the theatre's, that's been checked. And I do swear. Occasionally.'

'It wasn't a complaint. It was an observation of different behaviour in my ranking officer.'

'You've changed.' Erica stared at Beth. 'What's with this frivolity?'

'Evan's gone. It's given me a new life. Should have happened years ago, but now it has, this is the new me, so get used to it.'

'Crikey,' Erica muttered, closing down the computer and switching the phone to her mobile number. 'This is becoming scary. The worm has turned. Thank God for that.'

Erica followed Beth home at a discreet distance. She saw Beth's indicator light go on, and she pulled in about fifty yards from her home. She walked down the road and let herself in the front door.

Erica waited five minutes then rang her DS.

'Beth?'

'Yes. What's wrong? Don't say we've another one already.'

'No, I'm checking everything's okay with you. No intruders or anything.'

Beth laughed. 'No, it's all quiet. Let's hope he's got the message. You at home?'

'I am,' Erica lied. 'Ring if you need me. Night, Beth.'

Frannie was already home when Erica arrived, and they prepared their evening meal together, enjoying a glass of wine while they chopped vegetables and cooked.

'We had one of the neighbours ring today.'

'One of our neighbours?'

'No,' Frannie said with a laugh. 'Sorry, my head was in front of my mouth, I think. One of the neighbours of my problem family. She said there was an ambulance outside the house. I rang the ambulance service to find out why, and it seemed the mum had fallen down the stairs. Again. Anyway, I went to the hospital, checked her out. It might be genuine. She said she fell over a toy. She could as easily have been pushed. I was there for about two hours. They patched her up and discharged her, so I drove her home, checked out the kids were okay, and gave him the gipsy's warning about any further injuries to either his wife or any of the kids, and he'd have injuries of his own to contend with.'

'You supposed to say that?'

'Nope. Not at all. You going to arrest me?'

'Nope. I'll help you with the injuries though. Beth's going through a similar thing at the moment. She's split from Evan, and he's become threatening. I followed her home tonight, before I came here. I wanted to make sure she got in okay, and he wasn't lurking in the bushes or anything. I rang her after a few minutes, pretended I was home, and she said she was good. She seems a lot happier, lighter with her comments, that sort of thing. Best thing she could do, get rid of him.'

Frannie sprinkled cheese on the top, and put the pasta dish in the oven to finish off. 'Twenty minutes. Eating in front of the telly, or at the table in here?'

'Is *Vera* on?'

'Eight o'clock.'

'In front of the telly then. I feel like being swept away by somebody else's crime tonight. I can't do anything with my own till tomorrow morning now.'

'I saw *Look North*,' Frannie said. 'Nice chap. Said it like it is, told everybody about the third one, then stressed not to get into anybody's car, always be with somebody else, that sort of thing. You any further on with it?'

Erica shook her head. 'Not so you'd notice. The whole team are feeling frustrated by it. We've another six students to see at the uni tomorrow, although I may send Beth to lead that, let her take Flick Ardern. I want to do some door knocking and sabre rattling. People will think more seriously if it's a DI asking the questions, I reckon, and tomorrow I want an answer to one particular question.'

'Go you! Now you sound scary. Don't forget I'm here if you want to talk about it.'

'What I really want is for this bloody rain to stop, give us a chance to search properly instead of destroying everything with our own sliding footprints. It's a killer on these banksides, and it's so damn tiring battling against the wind and rain all the time. They get into the shelter of that refreshment truck and they collapse. Dear God,' she said emphatically, 'give us some sunshine.'

15

The sunshine came out around ten that morning; Erica felt an uplift of her spirits, which had been dropping lower and lower as she had requested CCTV to no avail. The sunshine and the CCTV appeared almost in the same second.

The elderly lady had greeted Erica and Sam with a smile once Erica had flashed her ID. 'I do indeed have CCTV. I'm not sure if it will cover all the area in front of the theatre though. It's not been the slightest bit of use for the five years I've had it, but my son insisted I get it. You're welcome to look at it. Do you know how to use it?'

Erica smiled. 'We'll work it out. Can I have a quick word while I summon one of our experts to come and take a look?'

'You certainly can. Would you both like a cup of tea?'

Erica and Sam said yes, and within minutes were sitting in a lounge that was spectacularly old-fashioned, and utterly comfortable.

Sam sank back into the armchair and heaved a huge sigh. 'I really shouldn't like this room, I'm too young to appreciate doilies and stuff, but it's brilliant. It's like my nan's, you want to nod off as soon as you sit down. And look at that bookcase! It's groaning with books. You think she's looking for a grandson to adopt?'

'Doubt it. Go and see if she needs help to carry in the drinks.'

Erica tried hard not to let her excitement show. The technician had found the relevant time that coincided with the theatregoers coming out of the theatre, and had taken it slowly when the girl in the red hooded coat came into view. The scene was in black and white, but Susie's coat was recognisable as being of a shade. They watched as she held up her arm in a wave, and saw a small black Fiesta pull in to the kerb.

'Okay, freeze it,' Erica said. 'Can we get that number plate enlarged?'

The numbers and letters became clear quickly, and Erica rang the main office back at the station. She wanted an address and she wanted it yesterday.

Erica was angry. She felt cheated. The number plate belonged to a red Peugeot that had been sent for scrap, and was originally from Leicester. They were no nearer finding the driver of that car than they had been back at the beginning.

Parking as close as she could, Erica climbed out and headed across the flattened and muddy grassed area towards the source of the River Porter. It was still torrential, despite the temporary cessation of the rain, and she knew it would be fast-flowing for some time as the rain-soaked hills that formed the backdrop to her home city gave up the water they had accumulated over the prolonged period of heavy rainfall.

Her first thought was that it was actually quite beautiful, if a little frightening. They believed the girls had been dead before they'd arrived at the river, and Erica hoped that was the case; if they were still alive, they would have been so terrified. The noise of the water was scary enough, without knowing you were going to die either by the side of it, or in it.

Being there alone was something she felt she had to do, to get a feel for the place when it wasn't overrun by teams of searchers. She looked all around, before taking a tentative step towards the river itself. Frannie had described it as a gentle brook, bubbling out from its source and gathering momentum as it dropped down for two miles towards the city centre, before it widened to go under culverts and ultimately to the confluence with the Sheaf, under railway platform five.

Erica stood quietly, listening to the roar, and taking in the surroundings. She didn't feel overawed by it, but she did feel something. Was she feeling a connection with the three girls who had died there? She thought not; she had seen many bodies during her career, and the binding she had felt with them was purely to seek their killer. In most cases it had been finding the proof to convict the person she felt had done it, but this bastard had eluded her for too long. It was time to lock him up, time to stop feeling her thoughts drifting back to twenty-fourteen at odd times when she was working on a different case. The one that got away. Clichéd, and true.

The CCTV had shown that they were on the right track with a car being used to entice the girls, but they hadn't been able to see if it was a man, woman, or a two-year-old child driving it, although, she thought with a grin, she reckoned they could rule out the child. However, they had a picture of the car and it would be on *Look North* that evening, asking for the public's help, but also warning them to be aware of it.

The on-screen picture would block out the registration

plates as it was quite possible the killer had several sets, and swapped them around with each attack – they didn't want the public confused by thinking the car they could see across the road couldn't be it because it had different number plates.

Erica pulled her jacket as low under her bum as she could get it, and sat on a rock. Thinking time.

Could he have hung on to the car from twenty-fourteen? It certainly hadn't looked to Erica's untrained eyes as though it was a newer model – she took out her phone and asked Will Bramwell, who she knew lived and breathed cars.

'Twenty-o-two to eight,' he said immediately. He didn't need thinking time.

'Thanks, Will. So he could have been using it the first time around.'

'Definitely. You in the river, boss? The water sounds loud.'

'If I fall off this rock I will be. I'm not in it yet. I've come up to Ringinglow for some thinking time, hence my question about the car.'

'I have a question that's running around my head about it, but I'm not sure my answer lies here.'

'Oh?'

'I'm probably thinking this because I'm only twenty-four and in my prime...'

Erica laughed. 'Love it, and you wish. What's your thought?'

'If it's a man, why isn't he screwing them?'

Erica remained silent for a few seconds.

'Boss? Sorry if that sounded blunt, but it's what I'm thinking.'

'It's what I've thought from the beginning. It's why I struggle to commit to it being a man. These girls, and the girls back in twenty-fourteen, have all been stunning. There's a certain sexual aspect to it in that they are posed in a way that offers their bodies to the finders, but unless he gets sexual gratification from playing with them, touching their bodies, it doesn't make a lot of sense.'

'But if it's a woman, she'd have to be fit.'

'I know. Look, Will, I want you to bring these thoughts up at the briefing, let's get everybody coming up with theories, because if I know my team, they'll all be like you and trying to make sense of everything. Call them in for a briefing at four, will you? Then they can get off early, I am aware it's Halloween.'

She sat for a further ten minutes then walked down to where she could see the crime scene tape that surrounded where they had found Imogen Newland. Imo, Pete had called her. Imo, the woman he clearly loved.

The officer left there to guard the scene jumped up. He too had utilised a rock as a seat, but he had had the foresight to bring a small blanket and a flask with him.

'Ma'am? Can I help?'

She flashed her warrant card at him and he blushed.

'I'm sorry, ma'am, I'm new. I didn't recognise you.'

'You had any sightseeing visitors?'

'A man and woman with a dog walked over, but that's all. I took their names just in case...'

Erica was impressed. 'Good. Hand them in when you return to the station. I'm heading lower down, so I'll see you on my way back.'

He smiled. 'I'll remember you next time.'

The waterfalls that would have been not much more than trickles in the summertime cascaded over, and she took out her phone to snap some pictures, purely for her own pleasure. This really was a lovely river, and she understood now how it came to be a major player in the manufacture of Sheffield's famous steel. The force of the water was enough to turn any waterwheel, and she knew one day, in the summer, she would come with Frannie and they would make better memories of this stretch of the river, and visit the still-working wheel.

She sat on another rock for some time, looking, letting her thoughts gather apace; the forefront of her brain held the image of that car. She knew within seconds of Susanna getting into the vehicle, a syringe would have been stabbed into her neck, and she wouldn't have been awake longer than a few seconds.

Susie Roebuck was the only one of the victims they could actually pinpoint the time and place of abduction. She obviously was the one on which to concentrate; and yet Erica still felt they knew nothing. Back in twenty-fourteen they had also known nothing – no abduction area because they hadn't had information on the last sightings of any of the four girls. They didn't know where either Clare or Imogen had climbed into that car, and yet every single victim had probably known the driver. Nobody gets into a car with a stranger. This mantra was constant in Erica's mind.

Nobody gets into a car with a stranger.

It was a day to be alone, to think. Erica stopped at McDonald's for a late lunch shortly after two, completed some thoughts in her notebook, and enjoyed her cheeseburger Happy Meal. The minion toy joined all the other McDonald's toys in her glovebox.

Her couple of hours by the river had made her restless, and it was with a feeling of unsettlement that she entered the briefing room. She had a car boot seemingly half-filled with Haribo sweets, and a glovebox filled with McDonald's toys. Was she old enough to be doing this job?

She stared around at the roomful of people, took a deep breath, and approached the whiteboard.

'Okay, everybody. I know you've all been beavering away on various follow-up jobs this morning, and thank God we didn't have another call-out, but this isn't so much a briefing as a thought-gathering exercise. When we've finished, get off home and wait for the witches and wizards to come visiting.'

She heard a few groans and smiled. She loved Halloween. 'Mardy arses. Now, this car. I spoke with Will earlier, because we both feel this car is possibly the same one used in twenty-fourteen. I don't think it's on the roads other than to abduct the victims and transport them to wherever he wants them to be posed. Will?'

'That's right, boss. I reckon it's kept in a lock-up, and I think that needs to be mentioned when they do the broadcast and show pictures of the vehicle tonight. If we can get everybody watching lock-ups or out-of-the-way garages...'

'The car was made in the early to late-noughties, we can't be sure of the exact year, and has almost certainly been used to offer lifts to all three of our current victims because of the bad weather. They would accept gratefully, especially if they knew the driver well. I think they did.'

'Are they going to push the serial killer aspect tonight? Make people more aware?' Flick's voice came from the back of the room.

'He isn't a serial killer,' Erica said, letting her voice carry. 'If there are three victims or more in any thirty-day period, the killer becomes a spree killer. We need to stop this spree before it becomes a rout.'

16

E rica continued with her captive audience, keen to get them on their way home. Most had children, and she recognised the need to be with them at special times in the year.

'So,' she began, capturing their attention with the one word. 'I've done a lot of thinking today. I've spent quite some time up at the river, and I had occasion to ring Will to ask him about the car, what year it was probably made, that sort of thing, and he countered with something he'd clearly been mulling over, sex.'

There was some laughter, some ribald comments, but she saw a grin on Will's face and knew he could take it. She held up a hand and silence descended once more. 'It started because I said "he", in reference to our killer. Will quite hesitantly queried that statement, because he felt if it was a man why wasn't he screwing the girls. His words, not mine, I might add. You can see from the photographs on here,' she pointed behind her, 'that all of these girls, women, are extremely pretty, have stunning figures, and yet there's no evidence of sexual activity. In view of Will's words, I have asked Ivor Simmonite to double-check if there could be any evidence of even gentle sex. I'll let you know what comes from that. He did confirm there was no evidence of semen anywhere on the bodies.'

There was silence. Then Flick spoke, still somewhere at the back of the room.

'It could be a woman? I know we've always said we'd keep our minds open on this, but is it more than keeping them open now? Is it a strong possibility that it is a woman?'

Erica took a deep breath. 'Right from the start it's been on my mind that a woman should never get into a car with a stranger. This killer is not a stranger to them, and they would feel reassured that it was a woman. I can't say this with any definition, as you know, but I think it should be something we're looking at closely, instead of *it's a man* being always at the forefront of our minds, because deep down we don't want to believe a woman could do this.'

'I couldn't do it,' Flick said. 'I'm simply not strong enough. These bodies up the top end of the river had to be carried some way, and I know I'd give up after a few steps. Could a woman do it?'

Erica laughed. 'I'm married to a woman who takes two wheelie bins out at the same time, ours and our neighbours. Some women are strong, maybe you need to go to the gym.'

There was some laughter and everything settled. 'There is one other thing. I feel the rain has a lot of bearing on these deaths. I suspect because the rain has been so bad, these three women willingly got into the car, even if it was purely for shelter. Last night the rain eased, and this morning we weren't all tipped out of our beds to attend another death. The rain's coming back sometime Sunday afternoon, and it's going to be as bad as we've had it for all these weeks. Let's hope we're not called out early Monday morning. There's no pattern to the victims. Imogen didn't know Susie and Clare. We can't warn anybody. I'm not bringing Becky and Katie back, in case I'm wrong, but the link to these girls is different to the L Christian name back in twenty-fourteen. I think the link this time is more random, I think it's the River Porter.'

Beth smiled. This was so good, and this was how a boss should be. Erica had her team in the palm of her hand, and the DS concurred with everything Erica had said.

Beth allowed her thoughts to wander, trying to think how they could possibly have over five miles of river under constant surveillance, and knew they'd need an army platoon to do that. It simply wasn't going to happen. And if Erica's theory about the rain was right, how the hell could they cover Sunday night?

'There's one other thing,' Erica said, 'something I need checking. Flick, I'll leave this in your capable hands as you don't have enough muscles for heavy lifting. This is computer stuff. I want you to go back to twenty-fourteen and look at the following dates for the weather. I'm giving you dates for the day before the bodies were found, because the murders all seem to happen in the evening, and be found the next day. The dates in question are...' she glanced up to check Flick was ready. 'Twenty-seventh of April, seventeenth of May, ninth of July, and twenty-sixth of July. Take your time, make sure the information is accurate for Sheffield, and come and see me as soon as you have the report. It will do tomorrow morning. Thanks, Flick. Okay, that's all my thoughts from my riverbank walk and my McDonald's lunch, does anyone have anything they want to add?'

'Did you have a Big Mac?'

She couldn't see who had spoken, so glanced over in the general direction of the voice. 'No, I like the toys so I had a cheeseburger Happy Meal. With banana milkshake. Now go home, enjoy your trick or treating, and let's have you in early tomorrow morning, please.'

Beth got them both coffees then followed Erica into her office.

'A thinking day, then?' she said, as she handed her boss the hot drink.

'I needed it. I met a nice young officer who didn't know me, and I walked a fair way downstream. I imagine in the summer it's a beautiful spot, but the water is still really powerful, quite scary. Court go okay?'

Beth had spent three hours at Crown Court giving evidence in a drug case, and she hadn't appreciated having to leave a current investigation of such magnitude to go and make sure somebody who was clearly guilty was sent down.

'It went well. They couldn't argue with our evidence, we'd got him bang to rights, it was something I could have done with not doing at the moment.'

'Everything okay at home?'

'Fine. No phone calls, no knocking on the door, and I made a start on sorting out the DVDs and CDs. He's only having what's his, not the whole lot. I went to bed around ten, and slept through till the alarm woke me. It's like... finding peace. Let's hope it lasts.'

'Nine nine nine is the number if you ever need it. And don't hesitate if you do. Sort him once and for all.'

'I know. But to get back to your thoughts today, we've got definite proof she got into that car?'

'We have, but that's all we've got. She must have recognised the driver, because I don't see how she could have known the car. I don't think the killer would bring it out on the roads other than when he needs to abduct. It doesn't have genuine number plates, and that's soon picked up these days.'

'You're still saying he,' Beth said. 'This is bloody annoying not knowing what we're dealing with.'

'Easier to say he. You bought some sweets for tonight?'

'Had an Asda delivery at the weekend, more sweets in it than vegetables, I can tell you. I emptied the bags, looked at the stuff on my sides in the kitchen and thought, that's a healthy shop, Beth. I remembered the sweets but forgot the milk.'

Erica laughed. 'I can't wait to see Frannie's face tonight when I carry in the load that's currently sitting in the car boot. I don't understand these miserable sods who say they don't like it, I love to see the kids all dressed up.'

'Do you dress up?'

'I do. Frannie hides behind the door. I've got a Professor McGonagall outfit, so I wear that. We put some lights and stuff in the windows last night so the kids will know we're not grumpy old tarts, and for a couple of hours tonight I'll have a fab time and try to stop thinking about this case.'

'Good luck with that. I was sitting in that courtroom today, and all I could think about was what was happening back at work. Does everything feel frustrating to you? Who the hell is doing this? And why? Even the clues about the car are proving to be non-clues. Seven people dead and we know nothing.'

'Whoever it is has possibly a connection with a hospital, might even work in one, because not everybody can lay their hands on Propofol. The only alternative is to buy it from some dodgy website in the States, like the one you showed me. They're forensic savvy because they leave nothing of themselves. This is why, despite Will saying why isn't sex involved, I'm still inclined to think it's probably a man, because he could take photographs of what he's done and get his pleasure later from looking at the picture. That way he's not leaving semen at the scene, pubic hairs anywhere, nothing of him.'

Beth nodded her agreement. 'And none of that supposition

helps. It's all well and good having feelings about things, but none of it is factual, and we're actually no further forward than we were in twenty-fourteen.'

'True.' Erica drained her cup. 'Let's go home. Let's have our night with the witches and wizards, and come back tomorrow refreshed and full of Haribos.'

They walked slowly down to the car park, and Erica looked at her car covered in mud and grass. 'Look at that. It's a mess.'

'You went to the river in your own car? Why didn't you check out a squad car?'

'Didn't think. Got the idea and went. I'll maybe call at the car wash on the way home. See you in the morning, Beth, and enjoy your evening.'

Frannie was already home when Erica arrived with her sparklingly clean car. She handed Erica a drink as she walked through the front door, kissed her, and said welcome home.

'Something smells nice.' Erica wandered through to the kitchen with her glass of wine in her hand.

'Boeuf Bourguignon. Be ready in about half an hour. That okay?'

'It is. We haven't had any witches or skeletons yet?'

'No, thank goodness. If we ever have any children, Erica, you can do Halloween with them.'

Erica laughed and dumped her briefcase and cardboard box full of sweets on the kitchen side. 'I'm knackered. As soon as the door knocks are done with, I'm off to bed. I've been at the river for ages today, cold, wet and a miserable place to be. Beautiful spot though.' She emptied the sweets into the big plastic orange bowl.

'You went on your own?'

'Kind of. I did know we had an officer on duty, so I wasn't entirely on my own. I needed some thinking time, needed to work things through in my head. Will Bramwell wanted to know why there was no sex. Why did the killer go to the trouble of removing all their clothes, choosing really pretty women, and yet not having sex with them at any point, either pre or post mortem? I didn't have an answer. The only thing I could offer as something to discuss was that maybe it was a woman.'

'You think?'

'It's one answer. I think one or two people don't agree with it, because it would take strength to carry a dead body, so I told them you could manage two wheelie bins at once. They were impressed.'

Frannie's laughter echoed around the kitchen. 'God, I love you, Erica Cheetham. You make me laugh all the time. You want some more wine?'

The knock at the door was loud, and Erica put her glass down. 'Maybe fill it up, I have some witches to attend to.' She grabbed the orange bowl and headed for the door.

17

Beth looked in the mirror and laughed. Calling in to pick up some milk from the local store had tempted her into buying a witch hat with an attached wig – bright orange hair that floated across her face every time she moved – and it totally changed her. She took a quick selfie and sent it to Erica with the message *I'm ready*, then headed for the lounge.

She carefully emptied all the sweets into a large fruit bowl, then opened a can of soup. She wasn't hungry, knew she would be dipping in and out of the sweets all night, and she'd also accidentally picked up a delicious crusty loaf, so tomato and basil soup with grated cheese on it was exactly the ticket, she reckoned.

Carefully pouring the hot soup into the dish, her hand reached for the grated cheese. She heard the knock at the door, and grabbed the sweets.

Two witches and a skeleton stood outside, a woman dressed as a ghost waiting at the end of the path.

'Trick or treat?' the children yelled in unison, and Beth laughed.

'We'll go for treat.' She held out the bowl. All three children thanked her, and the woman at the end of the path held up a thumb to also say thanks. Beth held up the Haribos, silently asking the mum if she wanted a treat, but the woman laughed and shouted no thanks, she would help the children with their sweets later.

Beth watched as the children walked down the path to rejoin the woman, then she quietly closed the door.

She had washed her dishes before the second knock came, and this time it was two larger skeletons and a fairy. The fairy clung grimly on to one of the skeletons; she was hardly big enough to walk on her own, but clearly determined to join in with whatever her big brothers were doing.

Beth looked around. 'You're not with your mum?'

'Yeah,' was a skeleton's response. 'She's down the road waiting for us.'

Beth held out the dish and grumbled inwardly that her visitors were taking most of the Swizzels lollies. She smiled and waved as they disappeared out of the front gate, running down to meet their mother.

Beth carried the bowl to the console table. 'Best take one before they all go, Beth.' She removed a Swizzels lolly and placed it in the drawer.

The evening passed with multiple visitors, and at eight o'clock Beth decided it was probably all over. The knock made her jump, and she picked up the dish for what she guessed would be the last set of visitors for the night. The previous two or three groups had been ten- to twelve-year-olds, the little ones from earlier probably tucked up in bed.

She straightened her hat and wig, opened the door with a

smile and felt the punch to her jaw. She staggered backwards, and the intruder followed her in, hitting her again.

This time she went down, the hat and wig skittering across the floor. His foot connected with her ribs and she screamed.

'Shut up, silly cow,' Evan snarled. 'Thought you could get away with changing the locks, did you? Payback time, darlin'. I'm here for what's mine.'

This time his foot connected with her head and she knew nothing more.

Erica was reading through her notes, occasionally dipping her hand into the sweet bowl that still held quite a few of every variety known to man.

'Good night, wasn't it?' she said, lifting her head as Frannie brought hot drinks in for them.

'If you say so,' Frannie answered, half laughing. 'Thank God it's only once a year.'

'You'll be telling me next you don't like Christmas.'

'Love Christmas, as you know. I simply think Halloween is a bit...' she searched for the right word, 'paganish.'

'That a word?'

'No idea, but you know what I mean. You and the devil in cahoots, what could be scarier. What are you doing, anyway?'

'I'm looking through some reports – I missed a lot of input by being out and about today. I've got Beth's list of people who've been released, and she's redlined three out of the eight but the fourth one has a row of question marks against it. Harvey Orgreave. He was sentenced in January twenty-fifteen, released about two months ago. It's the right time frame. I'll give her a ring, I think, and ask her about the question marks.'

She picked up her phone, selected 'Favourites' and hit the call button. There was nothing other than a connecting ring.

She waited patiently and then it disconnected. She waited a couple of minutes, then tried again, but still received no answer.

She searched for Beth's landline number and called that, and once again there was silence. Erica felt uneasy, but returned to reading the notes.

There was still no response half an hour later and she immediately put in a call to the station.

'Steve, DI Cheetham. We got any squad cars around DS Machin's home address? She's having some bother with her ex, and I can't raise her. I'm a tad concerned.'

'Lives in Crookes, doesn't she? Hang on, ma'am, I'll put a shout out.'

She could hear his voice in the background relaying Beth's full address, and then he returned to her.

'They're one minute away, ma'am. Want to hang on?'

'I do. Her ex is a bully. She's recently changed all her locks to keep him out, so...'

'So you're worried. Hang on, you'll know soon enough.'

She waited, her patience at an end. She needed to know Beth was okay. She hoped she was in the bath, or had already gone to bed, but somehow she knew that wasn't the case. Detective sergeants always had their phone switched on.

There was the sudden clattering of the phone being picked up, and Steve spoke. 'Ma'am? They've found her – the door was open and she was lying in the hall. They've sent for an ambulance. There's a lot of blood...'

'I'm going there now. ETA ten minutes. If you hear anything else, ring me.' Erica felt her head spin as panic overwhelmed her. She should have followed her gut reaction after the first phone call had elicited no response.

She put down the phone and grabbed her coat. 'Don't wait

up,' she said to a startled Frannie. 'It seems Beth is injured. Lot of blood they've said.'

Frannie gave a brief nod in acknowledgement, then hugged her. 'Go. Let me know how she is. Calm down, you'll be no good to her in this state.'

Erica drove, her foot hard to the floor. She reached Beth's house to see an ambulance and three squad cars outside – when one of their own was injured, forces gathered.

She climbed out of her car and ran, waving her warrant card needlessly at the young constable who was preventing anyone getting through the crime scene tape who shouldn't be there. He knew who she was. He lifted the tape as she approached.

'Paramedics with her now, ma'am,' he said, and she thanked him.

Beth was lying on the hall floor, unconscious.

Erica stood, feeling utterly helpless. She watched as the paramedics attached connectors to Beth, then shocked her with the defibrillator. To her police eye there seemed to be no response, and she wanted to scream at them, to tell them to bring her friend back, to make her breathe.

The ambulance travelled with blue lights flashing and a siren to warn all recalcitrant witches and wizards to get out of their way. Erica followed in its wake, never leaving the back doors more than about eight feet in front of her.

She spoke briefly to Frannie to fill her in on what had happened, and Frannie had been warmly supportive with the usual platitudes of she was sure Beth would be fine, strong woman, keep your chin up, but Erica had seen the faces of the paramedics as they had battled to bring her back to life.

'Love you,' Frannie had concluded. 'Stay as long as you're needed.'

'I will,' Erica said. 'Love you too. We're at the Northern General now, so I'll see you later.'

She pulled into the car park nearest to the ambulance station and ran back up the hill to join Beth. A doctor had been waiting, it seemed, and she had to hover to hear what was to happen next. A nurse pressed a cup of tea into her hand, saying she looked as though she needed it, and Erica smiled her thanks before sipping gratefully at it.

It seemed an age before she saw the doctor; Beth was heading for surgery, and did Erica know her next of kin.

'I've already contacted her parents,' she said. 'They're on their way. I've told them to go to A and E, I'll meet them there.'

'No. A and E will direct them to the relatives' room. Wait in there, DI Cheetham. It will be comfier for you, and will save you having to arrest the drunken skeletons and witches we always get on Halloween.'

'Thank you. You'll let us know...'

'Of course. You're close colleagues?'

'Very close. Beth is my sergeant. Currently working a case that's making us see each other differently, and as a result we seem much closer. She's in here right now because I felt uneasy, not because of good policing or anything. If we hadn't been close she wouldn't have been found until tomorrow, probably.'

'And that,' he said, 'would have been much too late.'

He escorted Erica to the relatives' room, and left her with a promise that he would keep her fully informed.

Erica finished her second bottle of water, and nipped out to find a ladies toilet before risking a coffee. She was washing her hands when her mobile rang, and she saw it was the number for the station.

'Steve?'

'Yes, ma'am. We've got him.'

'Evan Yeardley? You've got Evan Yeardley?' She had passed his name on within a minute of seeing Beth lying on the floor of her home, with little hope of anything happening quickly.

'Drunk as a fart if you'll pardon the expression, ma'am, and covered in blood. Big carrier bag of CDs and DVDs. He was sitting on the floor of a bus stop singing a Bob Dylan song when the squad car stopped to investigate. He'd taken the sleeve out of the case to read the words, blind drunk.'

'Has he said anything?'

'Nothing much beyond he feels sick.'

'Steve, for God's sake don't let him choke on his vomit. I need that fucker in front of me answering questions, and let's pray it's not a murder charge he's facing.'

Steve's tone softened and she knew he didn't want whoever was there to hear him. 'Erica,' he said, 'you look after that lass. And don't worry about this plank here, it'll be dinnertime tomorrow before he's fit to be questioned. You've heard nothing yet?'

'She's in surgery. I'm expecting her mum and dad to arrive anytime now, and the doctor said he would keep us informed as soon as there was anything to say. I'm staying here until I know she's stable, then I'm going home for a couple of hours' sleep before I tackle that cretin you've got in the cells.'

'No worries. You take care, you hear, and I'll check in tomorrow to see how things are going.'

She gave a half smile. 'You're a good 'un, Steve. Oh, and Steve, leave that light on in his cell all night, at its brightest. Let's have him waking up to the mother of all hangovers tomorrow, and no paracetamol available.'

'Yes, ma'am,' he said, and she heard his chuckle as they disconnected.

18

Hiding from the Halloween trick or treaters by going to the gym hadn't helped Tanya Lacey at all. There were several others who had staggered in over the three hours she had spent there, all laughing in an embarrassed sort of way as they admitted to not liking the annual event. Four of them had left their homes in desperation after continually answering the door, and had figured half an hour getting fit was preferable to walking up and down a hallway, false smiles stuck on their faces.

Tanya had enjoyed the planned evening but now felt tired, she was ready to go home and not looking forward to the walk. The offer of a lift, as she and another escapee stepped outside to feel rain on their faces, was gratefully accepted, and she sank into the passenger seat of the small black car.

'Nice to see you again, and thanks for this. I live quite close...' She said no more as she felt the soft touch of a hand on her right breast, followed by the sharp prick of a needle as it sank into the flesh of her neck.

. . .

Erica arrived home shortly before four, grateful for the lack of traffic at that time in the morning. The Machins had opted to stay by their daughter's side in HDU, saying they would find a local bed and breakfast place later. Beth's mum had looked relieved when Erica told her they had Evan Yeardley in custody; her father looked angry, and Erica suspected he had hoped he would get to Evan before the police did.

Frannie had been asleep, but stirred as she felt Erica slide in beside her.

'Everything okay?'

'No. She's out of surgery, but everybody's being non-committal. Wait and see seems to be the general consensus. Her parents are with her in HDU, and they're going to ring if there's any change. I spoke to the doctor on the way out, and he more or less shook his head. He actually said keep every finger crossed if you don't believe in prayer. Hold me, Frannie, it's been a shit night.'

'Has he said anything?'

'Evan? He's too drunk to be coherent, according to Steve.'

Frannie pulled her close, and stroked her hair. 'Go to sleep, sweetheart, try for a couple of hours at least. What time do you need to get up?'

'If I forfeit a shower and breakfast, I can sleep till eight.'

'Then do that.'

Steve rang her at seven. 'Some of the shelf-stacking staff at Waitrose can see a body propped up where the culvert starts. I'm sending a car for you, ma'am,' he said. 'I imagine you've had little sleep. I've sent a team already, they'll be waiting for you when you get there. Any news on DS Machin?'

'She's out of surgery,' Erica said, struggling to get herself out from under the duvet. Her feet seemed to be tied together. 'I'll be ready in ten minutes, Steve. I take it it's a girl's body.'

'Yes, ma'am. Exactly like the others.'

Forensics were installing a tent when she arrived. She thanked her driver and said she would grab a lift to the station later, but he was adamant he had to wait for her.

'I'm here to help, ma'am, and make sure you're ferried about today. We're all really sorry to hear about DS Machin, and you've apparently been with her most of the night. Best accept today is about making you safe, and I'm your designated driver until I drop you off at home.'

She wanted to cry. Instead, she thanked him, and clambered down towards the river.

Ivor was in the tent and she popped her head inside.

'Morning.'

He looked up. 'Morning, Erica. And so we have another one. The River Porter seems to be the gift that keeps on giving, doesn't it?'

'Everything's the same?' She felt a rage building inside her.

'It is.' He gently lifted the girl's breast, turning her arm slightly at the same time. 'This is the needle mark at the base of the neck and we'll do a full tox screen but I think we both know it will show Propofol. No clothing anywhere. As you can see, she's posed so that her genitalia and breasts are on show, and once again she's pretty with a good figure. Wants approbation, doesn't he?'

'Or she does.'

'You think?'

Tiredly, Erica swept a hand across her brow, pushing back her hair. 'God knows, Ivor. We're getting nothing. This bloody rain keeps potential witnesses indoors, and washes away any forensics, as you know. The river seems to be the common theme but it's about six miles long and I simply don't have enough personnel to have them standing here on the banks twenty-four hours a day for the foreseeable future. And yet again we've no idea who she is, why she knew the person who gave her a lift – and that bit's guesswork at the moment but it's been a common theme with the others – and we're probably going to have to wait until somebody rings in with a missing person query. I'm tired, I think we're losing Beth, and I've got to go and face the bastard who hit her.'

Erica burst out crying, and Ivor quickly stood. 'Hey, come on.' He wrapped his arms around her and held her close.

She took in some deep breaths as she battled to control her emotions. The cameraman slipped out of the tent to give them privacy, and Ivor held her until she brought herself back to a kind of normality.

Ivor quickly changed his coverall and shoe protectors, then headed back into the tent. He'd never seen Erica anything less than the cool professional lady that she was, and he felt... startled... by the revelation. So she was human after all, he mused, and bent over the body. The ice lady had melted quite spectacularly.

Erica sent Flick and Sam around the Waitrose staff, interviewing them all, and concentrating on the three who had initially spotted the body. None of them had anything at all to add to the investigation. They were going off shift when it had been spotted, yes they had been on duty all night, and no, they had seen nothing untoward on the banks of the now-infamous river. Contact information was taken and they were finally allowed to finish their shift.

Erica was driven back to the station and much as she tried to dismiss her driver he was certain he was going nowhere, he told her. Steve said he was hers for the day, and he couldn't disobey Steve.

She actually shook her head in wonderment. He could disobey the order of a DI when she said he could stand down, but he couldn't disobey the order of Sergeant Steve. In the end she gave in, and sent him off to get them a sandwich lunch that had to include two of the biggest and best coffees Starbucks could provide.

Waiting for her was the report from Flick that she had requested concerning the weather back in twenty-fourteen. She wasn't sure why it was relevant, but felt it was some knowledge she could acquire. On every single night the four girls had died, it had been heavy rain.

She sat back in her chair and let that fact run around inside her head, and knew it was yet further confirmation it was the same killer. Rain kept people indoors. Heavy rain even kept dog walkers confined to their back doors at night, with the poor dogs merely let out into the garden for their ablutions. Drivers hesitated before venturing forth in heavy rain, and children were made to stay indoors by parents who didn't want to have to deal with sodden offspring and their clothes.

The killer needed time to set up the display, time for the rain to do its cleansing work in case there had been a transfer of bodily fluid, skin cells and suchlike, and most of all the effect of the body when it was discovered had to be perfect. He or she must have been incredibly fed up when Susie had been dislodged from her position in the pocket park and forced downriver to where she had been found.

Erica headed towards Flick's desk, wrote a little note that said *thank you for the weather report*, smiled at the wording and headed back to her own office after a brief glance at the murder board. It would be extremely full once the new case was added.

Back in her own office, resplendent in the middle of her desk, was a large chicken and stuffing sandwich, an iced doughnut the size of one of the rings of Jupiter, and the biggest cup of coffee she had ever had. Her driver had scribbled a little note telling her to ring him when she needed to go anywhere.

Once again she felt close to tears. People really shouldn't be nice to her, she wasn't good at accepting niceness. Or was it simply that she was so goddamn tired and so worried about Beth that coping was a step too far.

And she still had that toerag Evan Yeardley to deal with. Word from the custody suite was that he was definitely under the weather so probably the optimum time to interview him was around one. He would still be feeling the effects of the alcohol, but sober enough to answer questions.

Evan Yeardley looked up from his thumb-twiddling hands as the interview room door was pushed open. Erica and Flick walked in, and took the two seats opposite him. They started the recording and introduced the three of them plus the duty solicitor, Jeffrey Galloway, who looked with some disgust towards his client. He was obviously getting the bulk of the waves of alcohol that were emanating from Yeardley's body.

Flick opened the proceedings. 'You do not have to say

anything, but it may harm your defence if you do not mention when questioned, something which you later rely on in court. Anything you do say may be given in evidence, Mr Yeardley. Do you understand the caution?'

He looked down to his hands and mumbled.

'For the recorder, please, sir.'

'Yes. Fucking yes.'

Erica slammed her papers down on the table, and he jumped.

'Okay, Evan, let's begin with what's going to happen at the end of the interview, shall we?'

His solicitor looked across at her with a degree of surprise.

'At the end you will be charged, probably with an initial one of attempted murder, but that of course may change.'

Yeardley tried to lever himself upright, but the officer standing quietly in the corner moved across the room towards him, and he sat down.

'What's that silly cow said?' Evan demanded.

'That silly cow can't say anything following emergency surgery through the night, and little hope of a recovery.'

There was a brief moment of silence, then he looked wildly around. 'But I didn't...'

'Unfortunately, you did. I hope you think that a few CDs and DVDs were worth the sentence you're going to get. Time to start limiting your alcohol intake, I think, Evan. It's going to be a long time before you get another drop.'

He turned to his solicitor, who merely pointed forward and said, 'Answer the questions, Evan, answer the questions.'

Yeardley slumped in his chair, then ran his hand through his hair. 'I've got a fucking headache. I can't deal with this.'

'Medication will be provided after the interview if it is still required. We don't treat headaches. Now, Evan, tell me what happened last night from... oh, let's say five o'clock, shall we? I want to know everywhere you went, everything you did, and eventually we'll end up in the charge office – but that's some time away yet.'

19

With a confession to what had happened, or the tiny amount Evan Yeardley could remember after a night of beer, vodka, and wine, he was formally charged with attempted murder and placed in custody, prior to a magistrates hearing scheduled for the following day.

Erica rang her driver and he appeared immediately, as if waiting outside her office door.

'Ma'am?'

'Can you take me to the hospital, please? Then you can stand down, I don't know how long I'll be so–'

'I'll wait,' he interrupted. 'I can park anywhere and sit and read until you ring me. Sorry, DI Cheetham, I have my instructions, as you know.'

Erica stifled a laugh. He was so formal. And clearly enjoying his day in the limelight with the serious crimes squad.

'Okay, thanks. What's your name?'

'PC Lee Jesmond, ma'am.'

'Okay, Lee. Let's go. And try not to get a parking ticket.'

. . .

Beth's head was swathed in bandages, and apart from the gentle rise and fall caused by her assisted breathing, she looked... dead. The nurse explained Beth's parents had gone to find a hotel for a few days, but she had her instructions to ring them immediately should there be any change.

'The young man who was on guard duty outside the door has also gone,' she said.

Erica pulled the blue plastic chair a little closer to the bed and sat. 'Yes, we've been able to call him off. We've arrested someone, and he's been charged. I don't believe there's any danger now, Beth simply needs to get better.'

The nurse looked at her for a few seconds. 'It's a very serious head injury, you know. They're monitoring her closely, and there's every chance they may need to operate again. You may not get back the Beth you once knew, although I haven't said any of this to her parents.'

Erica gave a brief nod. 'I understand. And you're going to tell me this is one of those cases where there's no time limit. She'll come round when she comes round.'

'That's true, although we will lessen the sedation if she begins to show any signs of emerging. That's not going to happen yet, though, she needs rest to recover from the attack and from the surgery.'

Erica took hold of Beth's hand, and stroked her fingers. She felt helpless. 'Hi, Beth, it's me. I don't know whether you can hear or not, but I'm going to talk anyway. It seems it did rain every evening in the twenty-fourteen lot, so this bugger is simply carrying on. We need to find a psychopath who loves the rain.'

The nurse turned slowly. 'You two are working on the three young girls who've been killed?'

'We are, or at least I am, now.'

'The last one, Imogen Newland, I knew her. She goes to my gym. I wasn't there on the night she was taken, I was on duty here, but we'd chatted a few times. Lovely girl, and incredibly happy.'

Erica's phone vibrated, and she pulled it out. It was a text telling her there had been a positive ID on the girl from the morning. She stood. 'I have to go but I'll try to get back later. This isn't public knowledge yet, but will be by tomorrow. We had another body this morning, and she's now been identified. If you're on next time I come, I'll maybe have a couple of questions for you, although I do realise you weren't there that night. But you did know Imogen, so keep thinking. Anything could lead us to this killer.'

Erica sent a swift text to Lee, placed a gentle kiss on the back of Beth's hand, and walked down to the hospital entrance. Lee was waiting, and drove her back to headquarters.

Ivor was waiting for Erica. 'Her name is Tanya Lacey. Twenty-four, and her prints are on record. Minor drug offence five years ago, non-custodial sentence but obviously prints taken. Nothing since that. I'm running a tox screen as we speak to see if she still imbibes.'

Erica sat down at his desk, facing him. 'Thanks, Ivor. I've come from seeing Beth – traumatic. She looks lifeless. There's a machine breathing for her, and she's bandaged around her head.'

'Give it two or three days,' he said gently, recognising the stress showing on her face. 'There'll be a noticeable difference.'

He passed across the report that indicated the name of the new arrival in his autopsy suite and remarked she was another beautiful girl.

'And there was no sexual activity?'

He shook his head. 'No, little fingertip missing, and VIII carved into her palm. You considering a profiler?'

'I am. Or at least I'm considering asking if we can have one. This has escalated so fast. Four bodies in a week. It was over five months back in twenty-fourteen, and Beth had been doing some work on prisoners who've been locked up and released since the last of those four murders, but from what I can see of her report, it's leading nowhere. So what else could have given us a five-year hiatus? A change in lifestyle? He or she fell in love? Possibly got married but is currently going through a rough time? An illness? Something serious that stopped the killing but is now much improved and the urges have risen again?'

He shrugged. 'I'm no profiler, Erica, but it strikes me that if this was an ex-con doing this, something would already have been highlighted. HOLMES throws all sorts of oddities at you, and you would have picked up on it. This is somebody who stopped for a reason back in twenty-fourteen. Did he fall in love with someone? Was he unhappy then happy? Minds are strange things, as you know, and I suspect his mind is stranger than most. Something happened to trigger the first one and he gained a lot of satisfaction from it, so he didn't stop until the fourth. Where did he come across the fifth? Was she special to him?'

'Go on.'

'I can't, but I started to think, as you can tell. All these beautiful girls I'm doing post-mortems for, it's so wrong, Erica. So wrong. But of one thing I am sure – he venerates them. He wants people to see how beautiful they are unclothed.'

'You've studied psychology?'

'I have a degree in psychology, but my real love was forensics, so I acquired a second degree.'

She stood. 'I have to go. Now that we have a name for this latest victim, I have parents to inform before something is leaked to the press. Please keep thinking, Ivor. You've opened up my mind, even though I've no idea how to track down this one person. But we will do it. I don't want them falling in love with the next victim and stopping all over again. This time we get him and lock him away for ever.'

Tanya Lacey had two younger sisters and a mother and stepfather living in Peterborough who adored her. She had rung them from her small flat in Sheffield to say she was going to the gym to escape the constant knocks of the ghosts and fairies, and she'd see them at the weekend. They had no idea she was missing, believing her to be at work in an office in Sheffield, where she was training to be an accountant.

Officers from the Peterborough force had notified the family, and explained they would take them to Sheffield to formally identify the body of their daughter.

Tanya's whole family was devastated. They had heard of the ongoing spate of murders in the steel city, but as with everything in life, had assumed it could never happen to them. Yet it had.

Erica sat at her desk and woke up her computer. She pulled up all witness reports, friends' statements, anything she could find – there was a niggle in the back of her mind.

The piece of A4 paper looked too pristine, so she turned it around to landscape it and drew four lines top to bottom. Then she headed each column with the names Susie, Clare, Imogen, and Tanya. There had to be a link and she was going to find it, or find a suggestion of it.

She scrolled carefully through everything they had on Susie, but almost from the beginning saw slight differences. Susie was the practice model. Susanna Roebuck hadn't remained in situ, she had been swept downriver by the torrent that was the Porter in its current state. The killer had become more careful in his, or her, positioning after that.

Susie had been picked up and that pick-up had an almost accidental feel to it, an opportunistic move on the part of the killer.

The other three shared a noticeable link once everything was written down on the paper. A gym.

Was it the same gym? Clare Vincent had tried to escape the horror of her girl-friend's murder by going to the gym for a couple of hours, but according to Starlite Gym had never arrived. That information had been treated as a dead end in view of the fact that she had never arrived.

Imogen Newland had gone to the gym – the same one – for a girly night out, confirmed by Starlite, and Tanya Lacey had rung her family to say she was going to the gym to escape the Halloween visits. The same gym? Could the Starlite Gym be the link between the last three victims?

One other factor linking all four was that none of them had used a car, and in fact only Tanya had owned one, although hadn't used it, on the night of her abduction.

Did the killer know this? Did this mean that Tanya Lacey was a second opportunistic abduction? He wouldn't have been able to lure anyone into his car to escape the rain if they already had a car of their own.

Erica's mind was buzzing. It felt to her that this was almost the first time she had been able to sit down and view the facts, make some sense of them. The murders had happened seemingly one after the other, and they had only started on investigating each individual one, then another happened. Now she could see the four as a whole, and knew she had seen something new to chase. Starlite Gym. She needed to know whether Tanya had been a member there.

. . .

Erica showed her warrant card, as did her colleague Flick Ardern. The receptionist initially said she couldn't give them the details they wanted, but soon backed down when they talked of closing the gym to facilitate their investigation. Flick knew it wouldn't happen; the receptionist didn't.

It appeared that all four girls were registered with the gym, all four living fairly locally to it. She also confirmed that Susie hadn't attended on the night of her death and hadn't been for about two weeks prior to that. Clare had last visited on the same night as Susie. She hadn't shown up on the night of her death. Both Imogen and Tanya had been there on the night they were abducted.

'There you go.' Erica smiled. 'That wasn't too hard, was it?' She handed her card to the grumpy-looking receptionist. 'My email is on that card. I would like the complete membership list, please. Names, addresses and telephone numbers.'

'But...'

Erica held up a hand. 'Don't even begin to say you can't do it. You can, and I want it by the end of today. I don't need to remind you this is a quadruple murder investigation. Quadruple so far, that is. And I need to know attendances over the last three months of every member.'

Flick sank into the back seat, alongside Erica. Lee put the car into gear and pulled smoothly away. 'Phew, that's why you're the boss and I'm a lowly DC. Think she'll do it?'

Erica laughed. 'Oh, she'll do it all right. And you're not a lowly DC, I'm moving you to acting DS until we get Beth back again. That okay with you? It'll look good on your form when you take your sergeant's exams.'

20

Erica's headache was worsening, so she went home early. Flick was only too happy to write up the notes from their trip to Starlite Gym, and everybody said an inward little prayer that there would be no more early-morning call-outs to bodies found near to the River Porter.

Lee dropped Erica off, and seemed quite unhappy at it being the last time he would be needed, but she was adamant.

'Honestly, Lee, thank you for your chauffeuring skills, but tomorrow I'll have had a good night's rest, I hope, and I'll take my own car.'

She watched him drive away, a smile on her face. Maybe she could ask for him to be put on temporary assignment to her team. Lord knows, they needed all the bodies they could grab with four murders to sort out.

Frannie's car wasn't on the drive, so Erica guessed she would be on her own. Take a couple of painkillers to divert the headache from thinking it was migraine material, and close her eyes for an hour. Bliss.

. . .

Frannie didn't wake her. She'd spotted the paracetamol packet on the coffee table, alongside the glass of water, and knew Erica was hurting, so quietly closed the lounge door and headed for the kitchen.

Frannie opened her laptop after making a coffee, and entered the notes from the house she had recently visited before heading home. Things seemed to be on the up for the family since the permanently drunk boyfriend had found some other poor woman to take him in. Frannie was close to adding them to her six-monthly visiting list, and made a note to that effect. She would visit in a month's time, and if the level of cleanliness in the home and with the children continued to improve she would make the list transfer.

She closed her laptop and sat back with a sigh. Her thoughts spiralled as she sipped at her coffee, and she let them travel where they would. Meeting Erica had saved her, of that she had no doubt. She had been going through a deeply black period a few years earlier when the woman with the beautiful smile that could light up a room had lit up her life. Frannie had tried to hide her sexuality, but with Erica's arrival it had been a natural progression.

Moving in together, marrying, the blackness had lifted and her life had changed for ever.

Frannie looked up as the kitchen door handle clicked, and she smiled as Erica appeared.

'Feeling better?'

Erica walked across and stood behind Frannie, wrapping her arms around her, and kissing the top of her head. 'Much better, thank you. Headache only an ache now, and I've caught up a bit on sleep. This case is bloody harrowing, Fran. Can we have something light tonight?'

'Eggs on toast?'

'Perfect.'

'You need to work?'

'It depends on whether that receptionist at the gym has pulled out all the stops and done what I asked of her. If she hasn't, I might watch TV.'

Frannie laughed. 'Let's watch TV. Have some time for us. What could be better than poached eggs on a tray in front of the telly, and the two of us.'

'You're right. I'll put up with the guilt tomorrow.'

Frannie felt better as she climbed into bed, and she knew it was all down to Erica lifting her spirits. They had watched *QI* and laughed for the entire show, opened a bottle of wine, although only having one glass each, and talked. Generally a good night all round. Maybe she could get through this without having to seek help for the stress related melancholy she was beginning to recognise, maybe Erica was all the medication she needed.

Erica remained downstairs reading. Her nap earlier in the evening had helped with the tiredness, and she suspected it would be a restless night. It was better if Fran dropped off to sleep before she joined her, then hopefully one of them would get a good sleep.

She opened her Kindle, then closed it again and rang the hospital. No change, the nurse told her. Erica thanked her and said she would be at the hospital the following day.

She dragged a fleece blanket over her and settled into the furry cushions. She read a few pages and within ten minutes was asleep.

. . .

Erica was at the hospital by eight o'clock and sat silently by her friend's side, holding her hand.

'There's no change yet,' the nurse said gently, 'but don't give up on her. She's young, I don't doubt she'll fight to live. It was a brutal attack, but we have the best surgeons...'

'There's been nothing?'

The nurse shook her head. 'No, and her parents have been here most of the time, talking to her, but no response at all. It's early days, give it time.'

Erica leaned towards the silent Beth. 'Wake up. I need you.' She kissed the back of Beth's hand. 'We got him, Beth. He's going down for a long time. Come back to us soon.'

She looked up at the nurse. 'I have to go, it may be Saturday but I need to go in to work.'

The nurse smiled. 'You and me both.'

'If there's any change...'

'I'll ring.'

The briefing room seemed full. Apparently there wasn't only her who felt the need to work. There was a chorus of 'Morning, boss' from around the room, and she acknowledged them with a wave.

Entering her own office she started her computer and pulled up her emails. There was one from the Starlite Gym.

The receptionist had sent two documents: the membership list and one headed 'atendances over the last three months'. Erica smiled at the misspelling.

She opened up the attendance document first, deciding to print it off so she could write notes and thoughts that might occur to her. She wandered into the main office to pick up her printout, and banged on a desk.

Everybody stopped what they were doing and turned to look

at her. She gave them a brief update on Beth's condition, and
heard one or two groans as they digested how serious her
injuries were.

'Why are you all in?'

'Following up on stuff,' Ian Thomas said. 'And it's not
raining. Thought a couple of us might go down to the river...'

'Don't forget your waders,' she said with a smile. 'And don't
drown. Has this overtime been agreed?'

'Erm... we didn't ask.'

She gave a slight nod. 'Leave it with me. Thank you,
everybody. Ian, can I speak with you for a minute?'

Ian followed Erica into her office. 'Boss?'

'You think we've missed something?'

He shrugged. 'I don't know. Something's nagging at me, but
I'm damned if I know what it is. I mentioned it to a couple of the
others last night, and they said they'd come in this morning and
we could go down en masse, so to speak. Honest, boss, I don't
know what it is, but I do know it's four beautiful young lasses
who've lost their lives, and it's not the river that's to blame, it's
the bastard who strangled them. Maybe the river can tell us
more, maybe it can't, but we won't know unless we look.'

'There's another link. I mean apart from the Porter. I'll be
filling everybody in on Monday morning, but it seems all four
girls had a membership at the Starlite Gym. Susie wasn't there
on the night she was taken. Clare was on the way to the gym
when she disappeared, and Imogen and Tanya were leaving the
gym when they were abducted.' She waved her printout. 'These
are attendees, dates, times, etc., for the last three months, and I
have a full membership list to work through, so can you make
sure we have a seven o'clock start time on Monday, full briefing
then.'

'I can, boss. Flick's in if you need her to help with the lists.'

'No, I want to take my time, make sure we don't miss

anything. It'll be hectic next week, we'll have a lot of these names to interview.'

Ian went to leave but turned back. 'You're doing a cracking job, boss, and we're all gutted about Beth. You'll tell her when she comes round?'

Erica nodded. 'But it's if, Ian, not when.'

Erica stuck to drinking water. Memories of the previous evening's headache were in the forefront of her mind, and she guessed it had been caused by a surfeit of caffeine. Today would be a day for a clear head and gallons of water, she reckoned.

She had sheets spread around her desk with different headings, and arrows pointing to links that were obvious. Things were further split into male and female, and she quickly realised the scale of the task.

'Do all gyms have this amount of members?' she grumbled.

Five of them went down to the river, gathering initially in the pocket park. Ian took his list out of his pocket.

'Sam and Kev, take your car and go up to the source. Waders on, and if it's safe get into the water and look, initially. Make a note of anything you see, even if it's not relevant. It might be. Easiest to use the voice recorder on your phones. Then get up onto the banksides, basically look everywhere. A couple of hours should do it, but if you see anything that's likely to help, ring me and we'll all get up there to meet you. Mike and Will, we'll start here and work upwards towards the source. Any questions?'

They all said no, and Sam and Kev headed back to the car park to drive up to Ringinglow.

. . .

The crime scene tape was still around the pocket park, and a man and woman walked up to it. As the three officers struggled into their waders, the woman called down to ask if they wanted a hand.

'No thanks, love,' Ian called back to her. 'You're frightening us.'

She laughed. 'Can you tell us when we can use this place again?'

Ian walked towards them. 'You use this place a lot?'

'We do. Most lunchtimes to get away from the office when we have a sandwich, and sometimes when we're in town in the evening we come here. It's lovely during the summer. We came here... you know... that night when the girl died.'

Ian stopped securing his waders and looked at them. 'Did you see anything?'

She shrugged. 'The river was too bad. We couldn't sit down anywhere, it was way over the top of that bottom stretch. We only stayed a couple of minutes and then went home. It was pissing it down and we were soaked.'

Ian felt disappointment. 'Can I have your name and address? My boss might want to talk to you. I know you didn't see anything, but we like to build a picture.'

'Yeah, sure,' she said, and the man wrote on, then held out, a card.

'That's where we live,' he said, 'but we both work here.' He indicated the building behind him.

Ian nodded his thanks. 'And there was nothing to see? What time was this?'

'Tennish,' the man said. 'We didn't see anything here, but there was a car in the car park.'

'What sort?' Ian held his breath.

'A small black one, oldish, maybe a Fiesta,' the man said. 'I only took notice of it because the driver took her top off over her head. She must have been wet through.'

'Woman? You're sure?'

'You don't get boobs like that, and in a black lacy bra, on a man, believe me.'

21

E rica listened to the excited intonation in Ian's voice, and swiftly wrote down the name and address he passed on to her.

'Are they still with you?'

'No, boss. But they'll be available whenever you want to speak to them.'

'Okay. I'll give them a ring, maybe get them in, although that could be a waste of time at this point. When we get a suspect, they'll be brought in then to see if it's the same woman.'

'You're not surprised, are you?'

'That it's a woman? No, I'm not. Don't take this the wrong way, Ian, but when it's a man there's always evidence of either a condom or semen. We've seen nothing of that, in eight murders. This is the first glimmer of a breakthrough in all that time. Well done for talking to them.'

He laughed. 'They spoke to us. The woman offered to help us put on our waders. Right, I'm going in the water now, and I'll leave our couple to you.'

. . .

It was cold as Ian dropped down into the fast-flowing river, and he stumbled. This wasn't going to be a load of laughs, he realised, unless one of the others fell flat on their face.

Mike and Will had already moved ahead, and had claimed bankside positions. He tried to keep a central line, his head swivelling, looking, seeking anything that looked out of place. They moved inexorably forward and an hour and half later saw Kev and Sam in the distance.

They clambered out when they eventually met up, and neither team had anything at all to report.

'Dead loss really, wasn't it,' Sam said, a look of disappointment written on his face.

'No. I've something to tell all of you, but let's find somewhere to have a cup of tea, and I'll fill you in. And it's been confirmation there's nothing here to find, so we can discount the river and concentrate elsewhere. It needed doing, and we've done it. Well done, lads.'

The café was warm and welcoming, despite their attire. Ian had shown his warrant card, and the café owner had set them up on a corner table, giving them some privacy. It was next to a radiator, and slowly they thawed.

Ian waited until they had bacon sandwiches and two pots of tea in front of them before telling them about the young couple he had encountered purely by accident at the pocket park.

'A woman?' Sam looked shocked. 'A woman?'

Ian nodded. 'Seems so. Unless this woman had been for a quick dip in the river fully clothed and she's nothing to do with the murders, then it's a woman. The car fits. They had no registration for it, but it seems the one she uses doesn't belong to the car anyway, and that probably means she has several sets of plates. But it was definitely a black car and the man said probably a Fiesta. I've passed the info on to the boss, she's going to do the follow-up. She wasn't surprised. She'd always felt it wasn't a man, despite us all saying he.'

They digested what Ian was saying, along with their bacon sandwiches, and remained quiet while the café owner removed their empty teapots and replaced them with fresh ones.

'So are we finished with the river?' Sam asked.

'We are unless there's more young lasses taken and killed,' Ian said. 'But no, we won't be back here, I think we've covered every bit of it now. She's a canny one, whoever she is. She's leaving nothing that could take us to her, and it's only chance that brought that young couple to us this morning. I wonder if she, the killer, knew they'd seen her. Bet she didn't, 'cos I reckon they'd both be dead now. Thanks, everybody, for coming here with me this morning.' He raised his cup of tea in salute to them.

'No problem,' Kev said. 'I think it's knocked us all for six, this last week. Four cracking young women all dead. And we've still no idea why. Is being a psychopath enough reason to start a career as a serial killer? You think it's a case of she simply can't help it?'

Will joined in. 'I'm sure she can't help it. There's not even a real link between them other than this blessed river, is there.'

'There is,' Ian said. 'I'm not sure of any details yet, and there's a briefing at seven on Monday morning to go into this in more depth, but it seems they all have a link to one of the gyms. Star something. Stardust? Stargazing? Something like that. The boss told me as we were leaving, but that's as much as I know.'

'Starlite?' Sam said.

'That's it! You know it?'

'My ex used to go there, probably does still for all I know. I've picked her up a couple of times after she'd finished a session. Big gym, large membership so I understand.'

Ian looked around at his colleagues. 'Keep it to yourselves

until after the boss has had chance to investigate more into the gym, and told everybody what she's found. Thought I'd give you a heads-up. We nearly ready? We've a fair trek back to the cars. I'll get these.'

He walked to the counter and waited while the bill was printed, then placed his card over the card machine. He heard the familiar beep and put his card away before picking up the receipt.

They headed for the door and waved at the owner, who clapped.

'Think she guessed where we've been and why?' Sam said before the two groups separated to collect their cars.

Ian pulled at his waders and laughed. 'I think she probably had a pretty good idea. Nice lady.'

They arrived back at the police station within five minutes of each other, and removed their wet outer garments before heading up to the office. Ian could see that Erica was still in her room, so popped his head around the door.

She smiled as she saw his face. 'Ian, come in. Good morning's work from all of you. I've agreed the overtime, so tell the others, will you? Did you find anything at all?'

'Nothing, boss. This is the card that chap gave me.' He handed over the visiting card. 'And I'll ask Flick to email everybody and get them in for seven on Monday.'

She thanked him and placed the card in her in tray. 'You have any expenses from this morning?'

'No, I treated them to tea and bacon sandwiches after we'd done, but that's okay.'

'Give me the receipt,' she said. 'You did get a receipt?'

'I did,' he said, and went into his wallet. He handed it to Erica.

She looked at it, and frowned. 'You paid a penny for four pots of tea and five bacon sandwiches?'

He took it back and read it for the first time.

'Blimey,' he said. 'She clapped us as we left, so we guessed she'd realised who we were and what we were doing in our waders. I didn't even look at the price, simply waved my card over the machine.'

Erica laughed. 'Then screw it up, I'm definitely not claiming 1p on expenses.'

Erica smiled as the door closed. She liked Ian. Older than most of her team, he had taken on the role of leader almost by default, and she knew he would have no trouble being promoted to sergeant when he felt the time was right. He merely needed a little persuasion to take that next step, and she would make it her mission once this damned case was out of the way.

She returned to the lists she had in front of her, and continued with the cross-referencing task she had set herself. Nothing so far had rung alarm bells, but it did briefly occur to her that if ever all their membership turned up at one time for a session, the building would explode. Even the people who had turned up on individual nights must have made the place seem really busy. So far as she could tell, there were no quiet nights, simply busy nights and busier nights.

She'd never felt the inclination to join a gym, despite Frannie's enthusiasm for enjoying a workout. It all sounded like hard work to her, and life was much too short to waste it on exercise.

Erica was deep in concentration when Flick brought in a coffee.

'You're not drinking enough,' Flick said.

Erica grinned. 'You're right, didn't want to get up and interrupt the flow of my thoughts. You must have read my mind.'

'It's not good to sit here all day. I'm heading off home now. Do you need anything before I go?'

'No, I'm leaving the membership lists until Monday, and taking tomorrow off. I'll finish off the work I'm doing on the attendance lists, then go home. It's been a good day – we now know it's a woman, so it means we can cut the lists by half.'

'You're sure it's a woman?'

'I am. It's the first slip-up she's made, but I'm sure it's the killer. The car fits, the time fits, and she was taking off clothes which were probably wet. And she thought she was unobserved. In my mind it's a massive breakthrough.'

'So, motive?'

'No idea, but one day I'll bloody ask her.'

Flick paused for a moment, then nodded, and left Erica to her thoughts and lists.

Frannie was mashing potatoes when Erica walked in. 'I'm in the kitchen,' Frannie called, and tipped a small pile of chopped spring onions into the mash. 'You hungry?'

'Starving,' she called back, as she hung up her coat.

She walked along the hallway and into the kitchen, picking up the glass of wine Frannie had poured while waiting for her. 'Bloody long day. Is it chicken?'

'Is it Saturday?' Frannie countered. 'You want a shower before I serve?'

'Give me ten minutes. I need my PJs. I need to not be DI Cheetham.'

She ran upstairs still clutching her glass of wine and Frannie shook her head in amusement. Not to be DI Cheetham? That was a good one. She was always DI Cheetham.

Taking the pâté out of the fridge, she made them a small starter and placed the plates on the table ready for Erica returning, then lifted the chicken onto the side. She enjoyed cooking, and during the years they had been together she had developed into the one who sorted the meals, sometimes with a degree of reluctance when she felt too tired – it was simpler that way with the irregular hours that came with Erica's job.

Frannie heard the bathroom door close, and a minute later Erica joined her.

The evening was uneventful; Erica wouldn't have had it any other way. She felt she needed time out, time to stop thinking, to make her journal entries that were more relevant to home life than work life, to enjoy her book. Together they finished the bottle of wine, and Erica felt almost normal by the time they went to bed. A lie-in was on the cards, and a full day of doing little, before Monday and the interviews and follow-ups.

The river flowed, the rain fell, and Beth remained in a coma. Evan Yeardley didn't sleep much – the pain from the beating of two hours earlier was overpowering, and he was hoping to God that the bitch would die, then it might make all this worth it.

22

Frannie woke Erica with tea and toast for both of them, then sank back into bed. 'The way I see it, we can stay in bed for the day, or we can get up, put on our boots and go for a walk in the rain.'

Erica looked at her, horror etched into her face. 'You don't think I've been wet enough this week? You ever seen underneath the Midland Station?'

Frannie thought for a moment. 'No, but I'd like to. We need permission?'

'I understand we don't, and I definitely don't with my magic wand of a warrant card, but as it's still cordoned off with crime scene tape that might be a warning not to go there. However, crime scene tape notwithstanding, my lovely wife, anybody can go. You walk through the culverts, which on a bright summer day would be something to explore, but it's early November, it's been flood conditions for over a week, and it's simply not advisable. Now eat your toast and let's think of something else to do.'

. . .

The something else proved to be a shared shower followed by a drive to the local supermarket to stock up on everything in one go, instead of the haphazard corner store shopping they'd been doing all week. Frannie had pointed out they were running out of Haribos, and might need more normal food.

The rain fell all day and eventually the two women gave in, returned home after a short half-hour walk, dried off and settled down for the evening. A Chinese takeaway was the general consensus, and duly ordered, and by the time the two of them retired for the night it was agreed the day had been exactly what they both needed.

Monday the third of November began shortly after six for Erica. She left a still-sleepy Frannie in bed, and was on her way into work by half past six. The weather forecaster on the radio told her it was likely to be a dry Bonfire Night and she sighed. Bonfire Night. Every fifth of November was a nightmare for all the emergency services, and yet the British people loved it.

Her first job on reaching her office was to ring the hospital for an update on Beth; her team would want to know how she was doing. The news was neither good nor bad. Beth was still heavily sedated, with no visible changes, but tests would be performed later in the week. Erica thanked the nurse and said she hoped to be able to call round later.

She put down the phone and rubbed her arms. Tests being performed had sounded ominous to her, and she decided not to mention that. It was enough to say there was no change and she was still under sedation. But the mention of tests being performed worried her. Brain stem?

Erica gathered her papers together and walked into a full briefing room. 'Is everybody here?' she quietly asked Flick.

Flick nodded. 'Yes, boss. You're good to go.'

Erica tapped on a desk, and the room became quiet. 'Okay, this is a briefing session, but I want all bums on a chair or a desk, we're not here for two minutes and then out. I want to hear thoughts, I'm going to give you new information, and by the end of this week I'm hoping we'll be moving on to the next case.'

She waited through the clatter of chairs being moved, and once everybody was settled she moved across to the whiteboard. She pointed to the pictures. 'We let these four girls down. In twenty-fourteen we didn't catch the killer who has ultimately moved on to killing these four beautiful young women. As you already know, it's definitely the same person. The roman numerals carved into the palms was never revealed, neither was the removal of the little fingertip and yet it has carried on with this new set of murders. Even without the presence of DNA it is unquestionably the same person. There are too many similarities to even doubt that.

'However, things are moving on apace. We received a valuable clue on Saturday which is a kind of confirmation that the black car used to pick up Susanna Roebuck was driven by the killer. That same car, an older-type Fiesta, was seen around ten o'clock in the car park adjoining the pocket park on the banks of the Porter where we have DNA evidence of Susie being left there by the killer. When Ian went to the park on Saturday he was offered help with putting on his waders by a young woman.' She waited while the laughter and claps for Ian died down before continuing, and trying to hide the grin on her own face.

'Ian being Ian, he declined the offer, but talked to the young woman and her partner, who, it appears, have been in a cottage in the New Forest for a few days. They've only caught up with the news since Friday night when they returned home, so went down to the pocket park on Saturday to see if there was any police presence still there. And there was our Ian.

They told him on that Sunday night, when we know Susie was positioned in the park, they had a walk to the park to look at the river.

'They decided not to go down to it as it was dangerously high, so remained at the top and then set off back for home. They saw the car in the car park, and watched because the driver was sitting in it removing clothes. The driver had breasts in a black lacy bra apparently. They stopped, figuring the person needed privacy, but it was only with hindsight, after they returned home from their break, that they realised the significance of what they had seen. She was most likely removing wet clothes, because she pulled on a red jumper after taking off the black one.

'She drove off immediately after putting on the red jumper. They're not convinced they could identify her because it was dark, but the man said he could identify her breasts. I think he was joking. What this means, of course, is I think we can start saying her instead of him/her, and it also confirms Will's query of why no evidence of semen or condom use on any of the eight bodies. I'm aware one or two of us thought it was more likely that it was a woman. Any comments?'

'They're reliable, this couple?' Will asked.

'Yes, I spoke with them over the phone on Saturday. They're both chartered accountants, work for the same company, and although both of them have a sense of humour they were quite serious about what they saw. They've written everything down, and they're coming in on Wednesday to give a statement. Nice people. They were telling me that during the summer they use the pocket park most days, at lunchtime, and they litter-pick it before returning to their offices. The red jumper may not be totally accurate, but it was the impression both of them got. It was definitely a different, lighter colour than the black top she took off.'

Will nodded his thanks. 'So you think when they saw her she had already placed Susanna on those steps?'

'I do, but I think Susie had already been washed away, and that's possibly why our killer was so wet. It also explains why our couple saw no trace of a body when they first went to look at the river before deciding it was too dangerous to go down to it. Our killer was out of practice with the first killing for five years, wasn't she? The next three were all positioned away from the pocket park, and on banksides.'

There was a brief moment of silence while everybody digested the information, and Erica turned back to the whiteboard. By Susie's picture she wrote 'member of gym', then 'on way to gym' by Clare's photo, and on Imogen and Tanya's pictures 'at gym on night of abduction'. She tapped the board and turned to face her team.

'We have a second link apart from the river. All four girls have a membership with the same gym, the Starlite. I've made some notes,' she said, waving sheets of paper in the air. 'Please take one when we've finished. I've listed all attendees on the nights the girls were killed, the times they were there and the times they signed out, although most of them apparently forget to sign out. Everybody has to sign in, however, or they don't get anywhere near the equipment. All of these people have to be interviewed, and I want them all seeing today. I've allocated them by area to all of you, and that list is on the back of the sheet. You'll be interviewing in pairs. Nobody goes anywhere without accompaniment from a colleague. This woman has killed eight times, give that fact the respect it merits and be constantly aware. Thoughts?'

Flick held up a hand.

'Flick?'

'Were the first four girls members of gyms? Or were we led by the nose because they all had Christian names beginning with L? This woman is strong, we know that, she carries dead bodies considerable distances. Is she strong because she trains constantly? Did we miss this link in twenty-fourteen?'

'My answer to that is I don't know. So here's my gift to you, smart arse, I'll leave you to find out all about that.'

Everyone laughed, and Flick held up a finger in the general direction of her boss.

'Insubordination,' Erica called out, over the laughter. 'Okay, on doorsteps by nine o'clock, so I've requested early availability of breakfasts in the canteen if anyone wants one, my treat. You have to say my name to whoever's on duty.' She watched in amazement; the room emptied as if a switch had been used.

Flick laughed. 'I'll stick to my breakfast bar and a coffee, boss. Want one?'

'Thanks, I will. Come into my office when you've got the coffees, will you.'

'Good briefing, boss,' Flick said as she placed the coffee and a granola bar in front of Erica. 'I'll get straight on to checking the L girls out when I've had this.'

'Thanks, Flick. Back in twenty-fourteen there was never a hint of gym involvement, but quite honestly, there was never any hint of anything. It was almost as if we were waiting for the next body in the hope something, anything, would be revealed as a new clue. That's a bad place to be in. But forget the case for a minute.'

Flick took a sip of her coffee. 'Okay.'

'I rang the hospital before the briefing in the hope that I could tell the team there was some improvement with Beth. I thought it would send them off on a high. However, there was no change, she was still in a deep coma, and they would be doing tests later in the week.'

'Shit.' Flick said the word quietly.

'I couldn't tell them that, but if anyone asks you, you can give them the truth. I will. As it stands at the moment, we're the only two that know that, but I'm hoping to go to the hospital and see her parents later.'

'You want me to go with you?'

Erica shook her head. 'No, I'll leave you here to co-ordinate what's happening with the interviews in case anybody needs help. You can cope?'

'I can.'

'And at tomorrow afternoon's briefing I'm going to tell them that in view of your upcoming sergeant's exams, I'm making you acting sergeant until Beth returns. Maybe that will make Ian pull out his finger and put in for his promotion.'

23

Flick pulled her keyboard towards her, and with a couple of keystrokes began the job of rereading statements, and in particular looking for the word 'gym' in any document pertaining to the twenty-fourteen investigation.

There was nothing. She then tried looking at the timeline as far as they knew it for the day of death for each individual girl, to see if anything at all was common to them beyond the L name. All four had been at work, although none of them had any connection with any other of the victims, and Flick realised how frustrating this must have been to the investigation team. They all worked in different industries, again with no obvious connection.

The weather, she knew from her earlier work, was the only other connecting link. Every victim had been killed during a rainstorm. Either the killer was a meteorologist, or one who didn't plan too far in advance. She took advantage of promised rainfall, offered the girl a lift home because of the weather, and had a handy prepared syringe in the car, ready and waiting. But still there was a degree of obsessive compulsive disorder about her. She had to have known the girls, she knew their names. She had to have been familiar with their working routine, and she had to have known where to take them to pose them for the unfortunate walker who found them. They weren't random girls; once she had set them into her mind, they were as good as dead. And then she had stopped.

For five years, nothing. What had retriggered the psychopathic tendencies? What had changed in her life that would make her seek the satisfaction that murder gave her? The death of someone close to her? A marriage breakdown? Had she suddenly become happy five years earlier, but the happiness was evaporating? Maybe routine and boredom had set in?

Flick sighed and opened up the files for the current case. She began with Susanna Roebuck, checking what the other three housemates had said in their statements about Susie's activities prior to her visit to the theatre.

It had seemingly been an ordinary day. She had got up around eleven after watching a film on Netflix with Clare. They had made cheeseburgers for lunch for all four housemates, taking Becky's lunch to her room because she was working on an essay to be handed in before the evening was over.

In the afternoon Clare and Susie had snuggled on the sofa under a quilt, both reading *Macbeth* and making notes, waiting until the play started at half past five.

Flick sat back for a moment, thinking about the two girls. Within forty-eight hours they would both be dead, along with whatever relationship had been growing between them. It was an horrific thought, and Flick shivered. She wondered if their removal of Becky and Katie had thrown a firework of immense proportions into the plans of the killer, or if she had merely shrugged off the inconvenience and chosen somebody else – Imogen Newland.

How had she known Becky and Katie were out of her reach? Maybe she had guessed what would happen after the death of the second housemate, maybe she was one hell of a smart cookie who was one step in front all the time. But Flick would bet everything that the killer didn't know about having been seen in the pocket park area on the night Susie was killed. Was this the only fact they had but she didn't? If so, how could they use this to their advantage? Announce it to the world?

Flick rubbed her forehead. An irritating little headache was starting, and she knew it was because her mind was rioting. Was the way forward to push her, to tell her that she had been seen and identification was close? Which way would she go? Back down or try for a ninth victim...

Erica walked onto the ward and immediately saw Beth's parents, huddled together and holding each other tightly, crying. Her immediate reaction was to turn and run in the opposite direction; she didn't want to know why they were in tears.

She walked slowly towards them.

'Erica, she moved!' Mr and Mrs Machin spoke in unison, and Erica immediately understood the reason for the tears.

'Thank God.' She looked through the tiny window in the door of Beth's room. The staff were pulling her up the bed slightly and her ventilator had been removed.

Erica's smile was huge as she turned back to the elderly couple. 'Has anybody said anything?'

'Not yet, they sort of threw us out. She moved her head and tried to take the tube out of her throat and the nurse hit the alarm button, then asked us to leave while the doctors attended to her. We cried.' Norma Machin turned to her husband and clutched at his hand.

'I feel like crying too,' Erica confessed. 'I thought...'

'So did I,' Owen said, 'but Norma here never gave up hope.'

The door opened and a doctor came out, moving towards

them with long, easy strides. 'You can go in to see her, but be gentle. She's still fragile, and she may not be awake for long, but now we have hope.'

Beth had little colour, but she did have the tiniest of smiles. Her voice sounded raw, as if she had smoked twenty cigarettes before speaking, but she managed to say, 'Mum.'

Norma promptly burst into tears again, and Beth turned her eyes to Erica.

'Erica.'

'I'm here, Beth. Don't talk, gather your strength first. You're safe now, and we're all batting for you.'

Norma reached forward and grasped her daughter's hand. 'We're here for you, sweetheart. Sleep when you want, we'll still be here when you wake. I don't think Erica will be, she's a killer to catch now you're slacking.' Norma smiled.

Beth gave the smallest of nods, and closed her eyes.

There was jubilation that afternoon in the briefing room when Erica gave them the news. It appeared that everybody had avoided asking after Beth, because they didn't want to know if it was a bad prognosis.

Erica let them talk amongst themselves for a few minutes – it was rare to have something good to pass around in the briefing room, but she eventually tapped on the desk and there was silence.

'Reports from interviews yesterday. Ian, can you collate them all and have them on my desk by noon, please. In the meantime, was there anything significant from anyone?'

Ian waved a bundle of papers. 'Already done, boss. Only Sam had anything significant. Sam?'

'Yes, boss. It's in my report. One of the men I interviewed said he'd seen the car before, recognised it because it was the same model as his son's, and he'd seen it outside the gym. He'd actually made a move to go towards it, thinking it was his son stopping by to pick him up, but then realised it was a different number plate. But that's as much as he could tell me. He'd no idea who was driving, or even what the number plate was. Other than that I got nothing. Sorry, boss.'

'Thanks, Sam. And thank you, everybody. Sterling effort completing that list. Not given us much to go on, but it had to be done. It's ticked off now, and I'm going into my office and starting work on the membership list. And we have temporary congratulations for Flick because I've made her acting DS until Beth is well enough to return to us. This may be for some time, Flick, but thank you for agreeing. Flick, as you all know, is soon to take her sergeant's exam anyway. Maybe others amongst you, Ian,' Erica said pointedly, 'might like to consider this brave move.'

Ian laughed. 'Good on you, Flick! Not for me, though, boss. Not yet, anyway.'

'We'll see,' Erica said, half joking and half serious. 'Okay, I need two of you to go out to visit our hidden girls, Becky and Katie, show them that car, see if they know it. Decide who's doing that, and I'll need the report first thing tomorrow. Check up on their general welfare, and tell them we're close to finding the killer. That will keep their spirits up.'

'Are we?' Ian asked. 'Close to finding her?'

Erica looked around the room, then spoke slowly. 'I think we are. I think one tiny piece of evidence is all we need. God knows what that is, but I promise all of you, this will not be a repeat of twenty-fourteen, and she'll pay for all eight of these girls.'

. . .

Flick waited until Ian had organised Sam and Kev to go and see the girls, then popped her head around Erica's door. 'You okay, boss?'

'Feeling a bit overwhelmed,' she said with a smile. 'My worry for Beth has been immense, and to see her and hear her has made my day. They seemed to take it well, your temp posting.'

'They did, but they all knew I was going for sergeant anyway, and I'm just waiting for the exam date. They're a good bunch, don't think there's anybody I don't get on with. Kev can be quiet but he takes everything in. I know this is changing the subject, but it's Bonfire Night tomorrow.'

'I know. I'm starting to become slightly paranoid about it. You don't like it either?'

'No, not at all, but even more so this year. Everybody knows our emergency services are all on full alert on that night more than any other time in the year, and we've got a serial killer wandering the streets of Sheffield possibly looking for victim number nine. If I was that serial killer, I'd take full advantage of that situation.'

'My thoughts exactly. The worst part of it is that I've no idea what to do about it. So... let's assume you're the killer. What would you do?'

'Go to one of the civic bonfires, and pick somebody up there. You could easily latch on to somebody who's on their own, suggest going to the pub, and she only needs to get them into her car. She's proved that.'

Erica gave a slight nod. 'Okay, so how can we negate this a little?'

Flick thought for a moment, then smiled. 'I see where you're heading. We need to get it out there that the killer is a woman, probably comes across as really nice and helpful, and we need to tell them on this evening's news programmes. There may even be bonfires tonight that she could visit.'

Erica stood. 'Come on, we need to speak to somebody higher up who will deal with this. Count this as part of your training, acting DS Ardern.'

A look of concern flashed across Flick's face, and Erica laughed. 'Don't worry, not all supers are like they are in fictional stories. Ours is okay, usually amenable, although a bit touchy on this one. He'll think of this as a positive step forward. We'll get the information about the car and that we believe it to be a woman we are looking for out in the general arena, and see where we go from there. Let's hope lots of people watch the news.'

Quarter of an hour later they were in the canteen enjoying a coffee.

'Told you he'd be okay,' Erica said.

'Okay, I'm a fan. You have to report everything to him?'

'I make a point of doing so. I send an email every day, keeping him informed of what we're doing, and of any progress we've made. We had a different Super in twenty-fourteen, so all that side of it has been fairly new to this one. To be fair, he's read up on the cold case, knows as much as we do about it.'

'And he's good in front of a camera. A presence. Let's hope it has some effect, we can't have another body, boss. We simply can't.'

24

November the fifth arrived without rain. It wasn't exactly sunny, but it was bright and when Erica woke at seven it was to a feeling of relief that it was her alarm that had pealed out its tune, and not a call on her mobile phone.

Frannie got up at the same time, and they shared breakfast and news of their intended day.

Erica was all too aware of the hard day in front of Frannie. Social Services were removing three children from the dubious care of their parents, albeit temporarily, but it had to be done. The parents needed help and possibly counselling; they needed to be taught how to look after their own children, and a short sharp shock was usually a good place to start.

They talked it over, and then moved on to Erica's day, where she confessed to a feeling of relief that no early-morning call had woken her.

'Flick and I had a conversation yesterday about the possibility of a further killing because it's bonfire time, so at the moment no dog walker has found anything untoward.'

'Maybe it's helped putting out that warning on the news.'

'I hope so. It's also helped the killer though. She's now aware we know it's a woman.'

'Lucky for you that couple saw the car in the car park.'

'More than lucky. We'd still be at the he/she stage without them. Good day yesterday though. The team interviewed everybody who attended the gym on the nights all four girls were killed. Big job, but they saw everybody except one, and Kev went off last night to speak with the final one. I can't imagine he got anything from it or he would have rung me. But it's cleared up that line of enquiry.'

'You still think the gym is the answer?' Frannie leaned forward, her marmalade knife in her hand and a quizzical, thoughtful look on her face.

'God knows, but that's police work, isn't it. I can't barge in and accuse all and sundry, we have to eliminate. The gym was definitely a link between the four girls, but the gym is almost next door to the university so does that give us another possibility?'

'A student? Maybe a mature student in view of the fact that this case is linked with your twenty-fourteen one? Shall I shut up?'

Erica laughed. 'Don't be daft. Any input is welcome, and you know almost as much about this case as I do, as all I seem to do is rabbit on about it. It's become personal, as you probably realise. Eight beautiful young women, never going to reach their potential in life, and you've been designated chief sounding board.'

Frannie reached across the kitchen table and squeezed Erica's hand. 'Always here for you, talk all you want, you know it goes no further. Expect me when you see me tonight, I have no idea how today is going to play, but I'll be thinking of you.'

'And you take care. Bit of a thug, isn't he, the dad?'

'He is, but we take police protection. I'll be careful, don't worry. And I can handle myself, anyway, I'm the one who can move two wheelie bins at the same time, remember?'

Flick placed a coffee in front of Erica, and sat down.

'You here to talk?' Erica asked.

'Yes, is this the way a DS would do it, or is it insubordination again? I'm good at getting things wrong.'

Erica closed her computer and waited.

'I'm not sleeping,' Flick stated, 'and I'm not sleeping because of this case. I've realised that this second case has thrown up things that should have been done in the first case, and I also think this bloody rain may be a link between the two but it's not a planned link, it's a link that she uses when it occurs. Get me?'

'Go on.'

'Okay, the link in the cold case is the letter L, but how did she do that? Where did she get girls with the initial L? Surely she didn't know them all? I couldn't name four female acquaintances all with the letter L – or at least I could, but they'd all be Lisa, and that's not what she wanted – but if she, killerwoman, belonged to some sort of group that was for women, it would probably give her the choices she needed. And let's not forget there was a time lapse between each L killing, so the last couple may have been new members.'

Erica frowned. 'What sort of group? You've ruled out a gym, so what would a group of twenty-plus-age women attend?'

'I had no idea on that one when I fell asleep at five. What I'm really getting at is I think L isn't the real link. That was a little foible. I think we've no idea what the link is yet, but I think we need to go and talk to boyfriends and parents of the L girls, dig deeper into their lives instead of thinking there's no DNA, or nobody has spotted anything, or this killer's too freakin' careful.

At the most we'll have eight interviews or so, and who knows where that might lead us?'

Erica sipped at her drink. 'I completely agree. I've been trying to work with both cases concurrently, but all the time it's showing the only link between the two is the same killer. We need more than that. Well done, Flick. Now we need a starting point. We need a list of parents, husbands, boyfriends, even their dogs and cats if they're relevant. When you've done the list, let me have it and I'll set up appointments for tomorrow. We can't drop in on them, I want it to be more formal than that so that they realise we've never let this case go. I think most of them assumed we had. Okay, making guesses time. At what sort of gatherings could this bitch have met them?'

Flick shrugged. 'Pilates? Art classes? IT classes? There's all sorts run at any moment in time, so I guess we need to be asking that sort of question tomorrow. The WEA – Workers' Educational Association – have been running classes for years, so maybe we could ask them for membership lists for that particular period when the girls were killed, if all else fails.'

'If she's a student or a tutor her name will be on the list, and possibly also on the membership list of the gym. I've had to ask for a new list from the gym, much to the receptionist's disgust. I've asked her for two separate lists, male and female, because I was coming across too many names that could be either. I didn't want to miss an Ashley because I assumed it was a man, but there was a Hilary, a Lindsey – so I took the best way and asked for it to be broken down.'

'So the gym membership list hasn't been checked yet?'

'No, only the attendance one, and we could have halved that job if we'd known she was a woman earlier. Although in all fairness, only one man was visited, the rest were women. It appears men prefer not to visit the gym in the rain.'

'Okay.' Flick stood. 'I'm on it now. I feel as if we're finally making headway, but I'll be glad when tonight's over with the bloody bonfires. You going to one, boss?'

'No, I want to be at home when Frannie gets there. She's got a big case today and is likely to be home late, exhausted and emotional. That comes before any bonfire.'

Flick gave a brief nod and left Erica to her thoughts and her sleeping computer.

Erica looked up the number of the WEA and spoke to a secretary, who went into meltdown at the mere request of a student list, so she asked to be put through to someone who could organise it without the need for a court order, but one could be arranged if it was necessary.

Within five minutes it had been sorted, and although he couldn't promise a speedy response he said he would prioritise it. The issue, he said, was it was five-year-old information she was requesting, but he would start from a month either side of her dates and get the information she needed.

She thanked him, said she would cancel the court order, and put down the phone. She put a tick against the action on her to-do list. Result.

Beth stared around the room, and her father smiled at her.

'Hi,' he said. 'Your mum's gone to get us a coffee and a sandwich. She'll only be a couple of minutes.'

'What...?'

'You're in hospital, sweetheart. Welcome back to the world. You've been asleep for five days, but you're on the mend now.'

'Evan?' Beth croaked.

'He's where he belongs, Beth. Erica saw to that. She was the one who alerted everybody to you needing help. She couldn't raise you on the phone, so asked your colleagues to drive past and check on you. You're safe now, love.'

He stood as Norma entered the room, bum first, trying to carry two coffees and two sandwiches, with two packets of crisps dangling from her mouth and her purse tucked underneath her arm.

'She's awake,' he said, and Norma dropped the crisps.

And so bonfire afternoon melded into Bonfire Night. The council had organised four different fires around the city, but many households had taken advantage of the rain being non-existent and had built one of their own. It was a good way of getting rid of unwanted furniture, chopped-down trees, and anything else grateful neighbours handed over to be added to the pyre.

Erica was home by five, knowing that once all the lists started arriving in her inbox the next day, she would be working until she could work no further. The broadcast from the previous evening was repeated on *Look North*, and Erica watched it over the rim of a glass of fruit juice. She'd decided no alcohol was her best course of action, so scrambled egg on toast and orange juice had been her evening meal.

She walked to the window and stood mesmerised by fireworks lighting up the night sky, many colours, flashes and bangs that sounded like bombs. She might hate the whole concept, but the show was spectacular.

She couldn't settle. She tried reading, decided to put in a load of laundry, changed the bedding, wiped down the interior of the fridge, placed a couple of pieces in the jigsaw they'd been doing for six months at least, but still her mind wouldn't rest.

. . .

Frannie arrived home shortly after ten, kissed her and held her tightly. 'Shitty day,' she murmured into Erica's hair, 'very shitty day.'

'The children are safe?' Erica remained still, enjoying the feel of arms around her. 'You stink of cigarette smoke.'

'The whole bloody family smokes. I could have snatched one from them at one point, I was so stressed. It's frickin' hard being an ex-smoker. I'll jump in the shower in a minute, I promise. I just need to hold you at the moment. Anyway, the children are safe, and with no trouble from the dad. The mum, however, flew into a screaming rage. Maybe she simply didn't believe we would do it, perhaps she thought we were all talk, but she knows different now. I've spent a long time with her explaining what she has to do to get the children back, the work she has to put in to give them a good home environment and not the crap they have been living in, so let's hope she took everything on board. I've made arrangements to return next week, and see how she's doing, and organise her seeing the children, but supervised. Sometimes, Erica, I wish I had your job instead of mine. I'm sure chasing killers up hill and down dale isn't as stressful as the stuff I've experienced today. I got your text about Beth, and I'm so chuffed. Come on, let's sit down and collapse. We don't need our jobs right at this minute, we need each other.'

25

There was a pall of smoke hanging over Sheffield. Three people had been taken overnight to Accident and Emergency with burns, two from firework explosions and one from falling on the bonfire severely inebriated.

There was a mist of rain, not heavy drops that would add to the River Porter flow, but a wet damp haze, nevertheless. Winston Leonards stared at his dark brown face in the mirror and grinned. The dark brown knitted hat he'd pulled on merged his visage into one dark brown blob with a slash of shiny white teeth breaking up the ebony effect.

'Max!' he called to the little black and white Jack Russell he'd adopted when his friend had gone back home to Jamaica to live. 'Pee time.'

The dog gave a small woof of pleasure, and waited patiently for Winston to attach the lead. It was only half past five, but as always Winston had an early start at work; Max had to be sorted before he could open up the shop. Running a newsagent's was interesting and he met lots of nice people, but early mornings were imperative.

Winston slipped on a warm jacket, zipped his mobile phone

into the inside pocket and opened his front door, conveniently situated at the side of the shop he had managed for the last four years. A brisk half-hour walk, and he and Max would open the shutters and start work for the day.

They reached the kerb and Max obediently sat, waiting for the gentle tug on the lead that indicated they could cross the road safely. Next stop would be the fields and the freedom of being off the lead for twenty minutes, before their return to the shop.

Winston was wet within the first five minutes; the mist was all-encompassing, and combined with the somewhat acrid smell of still smouldering fires it wasn't quite the pleasant walk he was used to, even during the past couple of weeks of more torrential rain. He bent and slipped the lead for the first time in over a week, watching Max race off in the direction of the Porter. Winston knew he would return on command. During the investigations by the police, he had kept Max on the lead, but the area seemed to be a police-free zone so Max could enjoy his freedom.

And then the little dog was gone. Winston called his name. Since the river had been in full flood, Max had seemed to recognise the danger and had stayed back on the bank, but now he wasn't even in sight.

Winston gave a piercing whistle, and heard a small bark. 'Max! Here boy,' he called and heard a more prolonged two or three barks. He swerved and followed the sound, while glancing at his watch. 'Don't prat about, Max,' he said under his breath, 'we open up in quarter of an hour.'

The longer grass, away from the well-worn path, soaked Winston's boots, but Max barked again and Winston could tell master and dog were pretty close. The bark wasn't a bark of 'let's play', it was more a bark of help requested.

He dropped down towards the water and saw the little dog, facing a naked woman, barking at her as if he could wake her. Winston knew that wasn't going to happen. 'Here, Max,' he said softly, and tapped on his knee.

Max looked at the woman, and hesitated. Training took over and he left her, walking back to his owner. He waited until his lead was attached, then tried to pull Winston back towards the woman.

'I know, Max, but this isn't for us.' He took out his mobile phone and dialled three nines. He knew of the four other bodies that had been found next to the river, but all crime scene tape had gone now, and this stretch of the river hadn't really been affected anyway, other than the search he had noticed at the weekend. His shop wasn't going to be open yet, he acknowledged, when the nice lady on the other end of the nine nine nine call asked him to wait until police arrived.

Erica answered her phone shortly before six. She asked that her team be informed, and she wanted the refreshments truck on site all day.

Flick handed her a coffee, then sipped at her own. 'Do we know anything?'

'Not yet, other than that chap with the little dog found her.'

'The one walking away from us over the field?'

'Yes, he owns the local newsagent's, and needs to open up. I've asked him to say nothing, and we'll go and chat to him later. He's a bit shaken, but fine. The dog found her.'

'Ivor here?'

'In the tent. There's an IX carved into the hand, and her fingertip is missing. I don't expect anything to be any different to the others.' Erica sounded tired. 'It's one step forward and two steps back all the time, isn't it?'

'It is. You okay?'

'Tired. It took ages to get to sleep. Frannie had the day from hell, and she tossed and turned all night, and I was worried this would happen today. It was a perfect night for it. But we knew, didn't we? Admit it, we both expected to be called out.'

Flick gave a brief nod. 'We did. Could we have prevented it? Should we have had patrols up and down the riverbank?'

'We couldn't have prevented her death. This river is merely the display cabinet. They're dead before they get here. At the best, we would have driven her to find a different place to pose her. I feel so angry about it. Once again nobody's seen anything. The chap who found her actually lives on the main road, but because it's a main road the odd car parked on it won't be noticeable. That's what roads are for, cars.' She sipped at her coffee. 'When we eventually catch this cockwomble of a woman, I'd love half an hour in a room on my own with her. And we will catch her, never doubt that.'

'I don't. Cockwomble?'

'My grandmother was Scottish. It was a major part of her vocabulary. Come on, let's go see if Ivor has anything to tell us.'

The text from Frannie asking if she was okay lifted Erica's spirits. She said she was and that she would ring later, then took a deep breath before entering the autopsy suite. Ivor had promised a speedy one as they needed to identify the woman as soon as possible.

Ivor gave a small wave of his hand as Erica took her position on the viewing platform. She was alone. Flick had gone to write the report of their morning's activities and it briefly crossed Erica's mind that she had been pretty quick to volunteer for that task. Although, when the alternative was an autopsy...

She listened as Ivor began his preliminary findings, and he started with the right hand, confirming it was IX on the palm, and the tip of the right little finger had been removed post mortem. He gave an approximate time of death as between eight and ten the previous night, she was between twenty and twenty-five years of age, and there had been no sexual activity although she had recently given birth.

Erica felt a shiver run through her and she leaned forwards to speak into the microphone. 'How recently, Ivor?'

He looked up. 'Three, maybe four weeks.'

'Ivor, see that I get the full report, will you? I need to start the search on this one right now.'

He held up a thumb in acknowledgement, and she slipped quietly out of the viewing area.

There were six people in the briefing room and she gathered them in front of the whiteboard.

'We have a potential major problem with this one.' She tapped the question mark on the board that would eventually be removed and replaced with a victim photograph. 'We don't know who she is, her fingerprints aren't on our database for anything, but we do know she gave birth three or four weeks ago. We need to know where this baby is, who has him or her, but most of all we need to know the baby is safe and well. Thoughts?'

'Hospitals,' Flick said. 'First port of call, I reckon. We know she's white so we can rule out any other races. Let's start with Jessops, that's the main maternity one. We'll move on to the

Northern General if we have no luck there. Let's hope to God she's a Sheffielder, and not from out of town.'

'Okay, immediate start on this one, Flick. I feel sick at the thought that this poor little one is on its own. Let's hope it's with grandparents or a partner, but if it is they may not realise our victim is missing.'

In the end baby Noah Urland came to them, tucked warmly into a smart navy-blue pushchair, without a care in the world.

His grandparents, Victor and Pamela Urland, were out of their minds with worry. They had looked after their four-week-old grandson to give their daughter a break, but they had been unable to contact her all day. Victoria had promised to collect Noah by eleven, and simply hadn't appeared. She hadn't rung, and they had repeatedly rung her mobile, to no avail. They had given in at midday and driven to the police station, as scared as they had ever felt in their lives.

The quivery, scared voice of Pam Urland explained Victoria had been going to meet friends at one of the council bonfires the previous night, but had texted at seven to say change of plan, going to a local one. She had asked if Noah had settled, and when they reassured her he had, that was the last they had heard from her.

Erica, newly arrived back from watching CCTV of the crime scene, took them into the room reserved for when they needed quiet, and broke the news to them that a body had been found. Pamela produced a photograph, and as soon as she saw Erica's face she knew. Her husband took her in his arms and simply held her. He clearly didn't know what else to do.

The baby slept on, unaware that his life had changed for ever.

26

The turbulent tumbling waters of the Porter had calmed; they were a million miles away from being at summertime flow, but the officers seeking clues on its banks were all aware it was less frightening, less worrying.

Ian had been left in charge, a role he stepped into without giving it any thought, and he split up the team, sending couples into different areas. He left them to it while he went across to talk to the newsagent owner, to get his morning actions down on paper.

The shop was empty, and Winston Leonards was sitting on a stool behind his counter, reading a paper and eating a sandwich. Max was on his dog bed, chewing happily on something that resembled an elephant tusk, but proved to be a reindeer antler.

'Mr Leonards? DC Ian Thomas.' He showed his warrant card, then took out his notebook. 'I have a few questions, then I'll leave you to the rest of your day. We will need you to come in and give a statement at some point though.'

Winston nodded. 'No problem. Tomorrow's my day off, I can do it then.'

'What time did you leave the shop?'

'Around half past five, give or take a couple of minutes. I open up at six – obviously I was a bit late this morning.'

'And neither you nor your dog went near the body?'

'Not at all. It was obvious she was dead. Max was about a metre away from her, barking at her so I put him on his lead first, then rang it in. Max barked, quite a lot, but I think it was fear. I'm pretty sure he didn't go anywhere near her, he was too scared.'

'You didn't know her?'

'Not at all, and obviously I know lots of people around here, it's the nature of my business. Is it the same sort of death as the others?'

Ian paused for a moment, unsure how to answer. He sighed. 'Yes, it is. Don't broadcast it, but I suppose it will be in the newspapers you sell tomorrow morning.'

'Poor lass. And so pretty as well. At least whoever is doing this isn't mutilating them.'

Ian didn't respond verbally to this, simply put away his notebook and handed Winston his card. 'If you think of anything that could be relevant, give me a call, will you? And don't forget to pop in and give a formal statement. Thanks for your help, and I'm sorry you two had your morning walk ruined. I wouldn't advise going that route tomorrow, it will have crime scene tape everywhere.' They shook hands, and Ian walked out of the shop. He stood for a couple of minutes staring across the road to the grassed area that ultimately led to the river, his mind churning things over.

He returned to the shop seconds later. 'Mr Leonards – from this shop to where you found the body – which would be the most direct route of getting there from here? The route you took with Max or some other?'

Winston laughed. 'Definitely a straight line almost, from here. It was a miserable morning, I wanted to get out there, let Max do his business, and get back to the warmth of the shop.'

'You have CCTV?'

'I do. It's rather cranky, definitely old, but you're welcome to check if anything's on it.'

Ian walked back inside the shop, dropped the latch on the door and turned the sign around to say Closed. 'We'll only be a few minutes,' he said, 'and you can open again.'

'Come through into the back room, the monitor is in there.'

Ian followed Winston through, and watched as the man's fingers clicked on keys to bring up the picture.

'What time do you want to see it from?'

Ian thought for a moment. 'Let's say eight o'clock last night.'

'It'll be grainy, but here goes.'

The picture flickered and filled the screen.

At nine thirty-two a dark-coloured Fiesta pulled up across the road from the shop, rendering the number plate invisible; the angle was wrong and the camera too basic. But it was clearly an older-model Fiesta, and of a dark colour. Nothing happened for five minutes and then the driver's door opened slightly. It remained like that for two minutes, then opened fully and a figure got out of the car. The gender was unclear, and dressed in black.

The figure leaned against the car, back towards the camera, but the action was clearly that of a smoker. The cigarette was finished and tossed casually away towards where the grassy beginnings of the field met the tarmac pavement.

'Shit...' Ian breathed. 'Can you pause it while I go and search for that cigarette?'

'Want me to come with you? I'll take you to the exact spot.'

Against all the odds, mainly the rain, they found it. Ian carefully picked it up and dropped it into an evidence bag before shaking Winston's hand. 'Thanks, mate. Let's go and see what happens next.'

Winston restarted the recording, and the figure opened the back door. A large suitcase was dragged out and dropped heavily onto the pavement. It was hoisted upright and the handle elevated. The figure glanced all around and grabbed at the handle before wheeling the suitcase onto the grassy bank. It took a little effort to get it up the initial small slope and onto the more-level field, but that was as far as the camera's view went.

Ian turned to Winston. 'I'm so sorry but you're going to have to keep the closed sign up. I have to bring Forensics in to download this, and I need to speak to my boss.'

Winston laughed. 'Don't worry about it. At this time of day it's mostly kids who come in for sweets, and they pinch more than they pay for. I'll write today off, I think.'

'Good idea.' Ian took out his phone. 'Boss? Can you get somebody from Tech or Forensics to come out to Winston Leonards' shop? Remarkably interesting CCTV footage. It's not crystal, but clear enough for me to have picked up a cigarette end the killer threw away after she'd smoked it. And before you ask, no it's not obvious it's a woman, not from this camera. And guess what? She's not superhuman. She doesn't carry the bodies, she wheels 'em.'

Ian and Winston were enjoying a cup of tea and a bag of crisps when Erica arrived, and she gratefully accepted Winston's offer to make a cup for her. 'The Tech boys are following me so I'll hang on till they get here before looking at it.'

She listened to them describe what they had seen, and Ian showed her the remains of the cigarette. 'It was the only one we found in that little area, so I'd be prepared to swear it's the one she threw away. I'll hand it in when I get back,' he said, and popped the bag into his pocket. 'I took photos of the exact spot before I picked it up.'

'And neither of you could come up with a description?'

Winston and Ian looked at each other. Winston shrugged. 'She's tall, I would say. But I can't say for definite it's a woman. The figure leaned on the car roof at one point, before turning away from the camera. You'll see what I mean. I felt tallness.'

Ian agreed with him. 'And using a large suitcase to transport the body does explain the puzzle of how could she carry a body over the distances. And nobody would query anybody pulling a suitcase behind them, would they? Blood hasn't been an issue...' and Ian stopped speaking, aware that Winston wasn't actually part of the investigation.

Fortunately, the two Tech people arrived at that moment, and they all went through to the back room where Erica saw the recording for the first time. They were silent while watching it, then Erica and Ian followed Winston back through to the shop, leaving the Tech men to do their job.

'Thank you so much, Winston,' Erica said. 'Hopefully this takes us a step nearer to finding out who this evil... person is.'

'No problem. Happy to help, and my day's been nowhere near as boring as it usually is.'

Ivor had completed the post-mortem and proved to be amenable to the parents asking to see their daughter.

Flick took charge of the baby, and Erica, her head still full of having watched the killer ferrying their daughter to the banks of the river, accompanied Pamela and Victor down to the autopsy suite. They confirmed it was Victoria, and suddenly Erica and Pamela found themselves supporting Victor, a panic attack threatening to overwhelm him. They sat him on a chair, and Erica spoke slowly and quietly, coaching him in his breathing. Eventually he regained some colour, and the two women sat on a chair either side of him.

'Victoria is named after her dad,' Pamela explained. 'They're so close...'

'Victor,' Erica said, 'can I send for a doctor?'

He shook his head. 'No, I'll be okay. My breathing's better already and Pam and the baby need me. We'll be okay, but God knows what will happen next. We don't even know this little lad's father. She wouldn't tell us, said he wasn't in her life anymore.'

'Then let's go get Noah from my sergeant, and I want you to go home. It's four o'clock now, and it's going to be a long night for you. I don't think for a minute the little one will sleep through, and you are grieving for your daughter. We'll come and talk to you tomorrow, get your statements, and please don't remove that last text from your phone, Pamela.'

It was with a degree of surprise that Erica saw how full the briefing room was. They had seemingly waited for their return before going home, keen to find out what, if anything, had shown up on the CCTV.

She took them through it all, explained they would hopefully know more the following day after Tech Support had done their thing, but even if they couldn't enhance anything on the grainy and indistinct film, they knew how she transported the bodies from her car to their resting place.

'It's been a bad day in that we have nine deaths to investigate, but a good day in that we know more. Go home everybody, spend time with your families and I'll see you bright and early in the morning. Last one in gets the coffees.'

There was lots of clatter and conversation as they all drifted away, and Flick followed her into the office. 'Been a rough day. You got anything planned for tonight?'

'A long hot soak in the bath. A shower won't cut it tonight. I want to relax. The Super wants an update in the morning, so I'll have to get my head around that.'

'You heard anything about Beth?'

'Her mum rang while I was driving back here from the shop. She's doing okay so far, still sleeping a lot, but talking more when she's awake. I think we can start to feel more positive now. I'll make ten minutes tomorrow, to go and see her and have a few words with her parents. They must have been through hell, and they've never left her alone.'

'You didn't expect her to survive, did you?'

Erica shook her head. 'No, I thought she would be dead before the ambulance reached the hospital. Those paramedics... what can I say? And there was a lot of blood. She was well and truly battered. We kind of expect the occasional roughing up when we're in this job, but this was nothing to do with her job, it was her psychopathic ex.'

Flick handed over a large white envelope she was holding. 'We've all signed this card for her, only needs your signature, boss. Can you take it tomorrow? We talked about sending some flowers, but they don't allow them, do they?'

'They don't, and it's no good sending fruit, she can't eat yet, her face is too swollen and she is having pain in her mouth, I believe. I'll pick up some magazines for her. She'll love getting the card. Come on, let's get off home.'

They walked down to the car park together.

Flick clicked her key fob. 'We're doing the WEA and Starlite membership listings tomorrow?'

'We are, so don't throw a sickie.'

Flick laughed. 'As if. I tried to make a start on them today. Night, boss. See you tomorrow.'

27

It was their salad night, and neither wife looked particularly enthusiastic about it. Frannie moved her lettuce around her plate, trying to make it look as though she'd eaten some of it, and Erica stabbed it with her fork, and loaded several prawns on to the prongs so she didn't have to taste the lettuce.

'Tell me again why we decided to have a weekly meal of salad,' Frannie said.

'Because we didn't want to put on weight.'

'Is it working?'

'No, but that's possibly down to Haribos.'

'So we could have chips with our salad?'

'We could.'

'And steak?'

'We could.'

'And swap the lettuce stuff for peas?'

Erica looked at her partner. 'We could, but I think you've cancelled out the whole salad evening bit.'

'You're right. Chips, steak and peas sounds nothing like prawn salad. I really don't like salad.'

'Let's discuss this properly. Why don't you like salad?' Erica waved her fork towards Frannie, a fork already spearing her next mouthful of lettuce.

'It's green.'

'Not all of it. Tomatoes are red.'

'I don't like red stuff either.'

Erica sighed. 'Look, be a good girl and eat it all up and you can have a bar of chocolate afterwards.'

Frannie smiled and punched the air. 'Yes! Result!' She ate a little more enthusiastically, and washed almost every mouthful down with wine. 'What are we doing tonight? I have some notes to write up but they'll only take me quarter of an hour or so. We could go to the cinema for a late showing.'

Erica shook her head. 'Best not, I want to get off early in the morning. I feel as though we're getting close to cracking this, so close I can almost taste it.'

Frannie stopped loading her fork. 'What? Have I missed something? It was only last night that you were using the phrase headless chickens. Has something happened?'

'It has. We know how she moves the bodies now, she was caught on CCTV last night.'

Erica stood and carried her plate and cutlery to the dishwasher. 'But let's not talk about it tonight. I go over it all day long, and it's not fair if I bring it home.'

Frannie said nothing, picked up her plate and rinsed it before stacking it in the dishwasher. Just for a second Erica wondered if she had upset Frannie by not telling her everything about the CCTV footage, but dismissed it from her mind. It was enough that it was constantly in her own head, without it being in Frannie's as well.

'Coffee?' Erica asked.

Frannie hesitated for a moment. 'No, I think I'll have another wine after I've caught up with these notes.'

Ouch, Erica thought, *So she's not too happy with me.*

.   .   .

They were in bed a few minutes after ten, although neither woman felt settled. With stressful jobs and a caseload that wouldn't stay at work because it buried deep into the brain, sleeping wasn't always easy.

'You awake?' Erica asked, and Frannie mumbled that she was.

'How often do you go to the gym?'

'Once or twice a week.'

Erica sat up and switched on the bedside lamp. 'Ever been to the Starlite?'

'I had a look at it in a flurry of getting fit after our Christmas pig-out, went once at the beginning of January, wasn't impressed so haven't been back. Why?'

'Just asking, really. So it's not a good gym?'

'It wasn't what I wanted. The one near my office is heaps better. I don't go often, but it's quite good. Better than the Starlite, anyway.'

'So you wouldn't know anybody who was acting suspicious at the Starlite?'

Frannie laughed. 'No, my love, I wouldn't. I don't know anybody at all, full stop.'

'Then you're rubbish, Frannie Johnson,' Erica grumbled, switching off the lamp and snuggling under the duvet. 'How can I send you in as my mole if you don't know anybody and aren't even a member?'

The Porter was losing the power it had showed at the height of the flooding. Named Porter because of its brackish colour it picked up from the hillsides of Derbyshire before pulsating out of the ground in Sheffield's hills, it was still a force to be reckoned with, and clearly a magnet for the woman who was currently putting the fear of the Almighty into Sheffield's residents.

Three officers had been left on duty for the night at various points on the river, and all had instructions to check in with each other hourly. They did so, working their way through the flasks of coffee they had brought with them, and the packs of sandwiches.

It was a long night, but not one of them dared to relax for even a second. There would be no more dead women on their watch. Fortunately, it was also a dry night, although cold, and they kept moving as much as they could. They were relieved at six o'clock and a second group of three officers took over. The first group had nothing to report, the second felt thankful.

A team from Forensics arrived at ten and searched the track leading from the newsagent's shop to the body-dump site, but found nothing. Slowly most of the crime scene tape was removed, leaving a small circular area around the body space. It would probably remain there until the winter gales took it, trailing it like a flag across the Ringinglow moors.

Erica arrived early and switched on her computer before removing her jacket. She grabbed a coffee and headed back to her desk, hearing the ping of an incoming email as she sat down. The email from the Tech people with the polished CCTV from the newsagent's shop arrived almost without fanfare until she saw the final sentence. Watch it through to the end!

She felt a small surge of anticipation and knew what had been bothering her. In the rush to get the grainy and inefficient film downloaded safely they had watched the arrival of the Fiesta, the removal of the suitcase and its disappearance over the grassed area, pulled by the killer. The woman. They hadn't watched her return.

Now there was no longer the fear they might lose the precious pictures by incorrect handling of such old equipment, the whole episode would be seen. She sat down at her desk, glancing around the main office to see who was in. Nobody. Had she really expected anybody to be in at six?

Her door opened and Flick said, 'Morning, boss.'

'Flick! Take your coat off, grab a coffee and come and watch this with me.'

They sat side by side and Erica clicked her mouse. The film opened two minutes before the arrival of the car, and they watched it through to where the killer dragged the suitcase up the grass incline. A second car pulled up behind the Fiesta after five minutes twenty seconds, but nobody got out. It remained for three minutes sixteen seconds, then pulled away and disappeared.

'I don't think that's connected,' Erica said slowly. 'They probably needed to answer the phone or something. If it was connected all we know is that it's a Corsa, I think, and we have no idea of its registration, although no doubt we can find it using ANPR. We'll check it out, I'll put the request in after we've finished watching this.'

They were sipping second cups of coffee by the time the killer returned with the suitcase.

'It's definitely a woman,' Flick said. 'She has a woman's walk. I know that sounds sexist, but it's true. We do walk differently. She's stepping carefully down from the edge of that grass onto the pavement. A man wouldn't do that.'

They watched as she opened the boot and stashed the suitcase inside it, then she took a cigarette from a packet in the top pocket of the black jacket she was wearing, lit it and climbed into the driving seat. There was a pause of over a minute, and the car moved. It did a U-turn across the width of the empty road and Erica clicked pause.

'Now we've got the bitch's number plate.' She scribbled down the number. 'ANPR can check this one as well. I know we're not going to be able to trace this to her, she's far too clever for that, but it will hopefully lead us to the general area where she stores it.'

They watched for a further five minutes, then the film ended.

The briefing room had filled up, and everybody seemed to be talking. They stopped as Erica entered, and she walked across to the whiteboard.

'Before we move on to today's activities, I'm going to see DS Machin. She's improving, and I don't think it will be long before they let her go home. I think they're keeping a close eye on the head injury, but her other injuries are healing nicely, according to her mum. I'll be taking that enormous card to her, and I'll tell you later what she says.'

There was a smattering of applause at her news, and Erica turned to the whiteboard, attaching a picture of Victoria Urland.

'In the meantime, let's catch a killer. I have forwarded the CCTV from yesterday to all of you. Make it your first job to watch this, and I've already asked for ANPR help in tracking down the two vehicles you will see on screen. I don't think the Corsa is involved, but because I think that it doesn't mean I'm right.'

She looked around the room and spotted Ian. 'Ian picked up

a cigarette end at the scene which you will see the killer throw away. It has returned a positive DNA result, so the rain and damp didn't do too much damage. Unfortunately that DNA isn't on our database, but hopefully it will be used to convict her when we bring her in.'

They all drifted towards their computers, and silence descended as they watched the CCTV footage. It was hardly any clearer than when Erica had watched it in Winston's back room, and she saw one or two of her team pull their monitors closer, not wanting to miss one second.

Flick followed her into her office. 'Never been so quiet,' she joked.

'Yes, they all like a good movie. Is she getting careless?' The question was abrupt.

'She is. The only other CCTV we've found her on was that first one where she picked up Susie Roebuck, again on a main road. But I've always thought that pick-up was a spur-of-the-minute thing. I think Susie would have been abducted at some point, but she saw her on her own, waved at her and Susie recognised her or her car, and bang, Susie's dead.'

Erica looked at Flick. 'She's running out of options on the river. Isn't she? We've got crime scene tape all over the bloody place, intermittent police officers on duty and unless she's actually working for us she won't know when that is, and she's obviously OCD with the damn river. It has to be there where she leaves her bodies. She fixated on the Ls, now she's fixated on the Porter. I thought she was fixated on the gym, but it seems Victoria Urland was taken because she went to a local bonfire. Our job for today is to find out more about her, where this bonfire was, and who she was with.'

'Her parents didn't know?'

'Funnily enough, they thought they did. She told them she was going to a municipal bonfire with some friends, and she would check in frequently because it was the first time they had looked after baby Noah on their own. The only check-in was a text to say change of plan, she was going to a local bonfire instead. She gave them no details, so we're going to have to track down her friends. We'll go see her parents today, and take it from there. I've asked ANPR to contact Ian, and I'll tell him to ring us if anything significant comes in because of that. Fingers crossed he can tell us where the car's kept, but I'm not holding my breath.'

28

Flick grinned at her boss. 'This membership and WEA list is fading into the distance.'

'I know. I feel the membership list can't help, because all we needed was the attendance records, and we've done them. The WEA ones need checking because they refer to the twenty-fourteen killings, and if this woman would desist in her murderous ways for a couple of days, we wouldn't have to be distracted with a new addition to the case. My God, I sound a proper cow, don't I?'

'Yes.'

'You didn't have to agree, but I think I chose the wrong words. You know what I meant. We start to get a foothold, and we have to stop because there's a new death. It's why I'm going to see Beth. I need time out.'

'Can I check something? These attendance records. Everybody has to sign in to get through those double doors into the gym itself?'

'Yes. She was quite emphatic about it. They don't all sign out. The way she put it was that some of them are too knackered to lift the pen.'

'Okay. When are you going to see Beth?'

Erica glanced at her watch. 'I'll go now. If they say she's been moved out of HDU I'll use the warrant card and get in anyway. Do you want to come?'

For a brief moment there was a look of panic on Flick's face. 'No, I'm fine thanks. Don't like hospitals.'

Erica smiled at her stand-in sergeant. 'You might need to get used to them. It's part and parcel of the job.'

'I know, and it doesn't bother me if it's a result of some crime or other, but to go and visit people, not knowing what to talk about...' She gave a shudder. 'No, I'm going to the gym.'

'Starlite? Is there a reason?'

'Might join it.'

'What?'

'Don't panic.' Flick laughed. 'You can join for free for the first month, but then you either leave or pay for the pleasure. I thought I'd go and mingle, but can you hurry up and catch her because I don't actually want to get fit by using treadmills and suchlike. Does my police life insurance cover me for a heart attack while on duty?'

Beth's face was badly bruised. The bandage around her head had been reduced in size, and her eyes sparkled as Erica came into the room.

'I understand I owe everything to you,' Beth said. 'You sent in the cavalry.'

'You would have done it for me,' Erica said awkwardly.

'I wouldn't have needed to do it for you. Frannie isn't a psychopathic maniac, unlike the partner I chose. So stop being all shy and retiring, that's not like you. Thank you for what you did, Erica. He took me completely by surprise. I expected a ghost or a skeleton, but as soon as I released the lock on the door he started on me. I think he was drunk, but that's no excuse.'

'He was extremely drunk. We had officers out on the streets immediately, looking for him. They found him sat on the floor in a bus shelter, absolutely legless. It was drugs and alcohol. He was locked up by the time they'd wheeled you into surgery. Your mum and dad not here?'

'No. I'm being moved to a different ward today. It's not HDU, it's something one step down from that, but it means they can't be with me all the time. It's a relief really. I've told them to check out of that hotel and go home. Dad's been travelling backwards and forwards checking on things and feeding the budgie, and I can see they're both exhausted. They've said they're coming back tomorrow, so today I'll concentrate on my recovery. I want out of here, and I think possibly three more days, if I'm a good girl, will see me back at home.'

'Alone?' Erica asked, concerned that maybe Beth might need help.

'Alone. I've got a phone if I need help, and if you've charged Evan with attempted murder, as I expect you have, he's not going to get anywhere near me for a long time, is he?'

'If you want to come to us for a week or so, till you've got your sea legs back, so to speak, you're more than welcome.'

'No, I'll be fine, honestly. I can go to sleep when I want if I'm on my own, and they've warned me to expect that for a bit. The head injury was pretty bad apparently.'

Erica looked at Beth through tear-filled eyes. 'I thought you were dead.' She handed Beth the large white envelope she was clutching. 'And everybody who's signed this thought you wouldn't recover, but they're bloody glad you have.'

. . .

Flick parked in the gym car park and walked around checking number plates and black cars. Nothing matched the information they had obtained from the CCTV footage. She walked around to the front door, and pushed it open.

The girl on reception didn't have a name badge; Flick took that as a good sign that maybe she didn't normally work on reception and might not worry too much about client confidentiality.

'Hi, I'm thinking about taking up your offer of a free month to decide if it's the right gym for me.'

'That's fine. Fill in this form, and I'll process it for you.' She pushed across a basic type of form and Flick took it, moving to sit beside a small square table. She filled in her details, putting accountant in the box marked employment. She used her own name and address, reckoning they might check up on that.

She finished, headed back to the still-unnamed girl, and gave it to her. 'What do I do now?'

'I'll log these details into the computer and then I'll show you the facilities.'

Flick waited patiently, walking around the room and inspecting the certificates hanging on the wall. At the end of the reception desk were two large doors that she presumed led into the gym, but opposite the desk were further double doors that said The Coffee Pot in curly gold letters.

A coffee shop... she put that to the back of her mind as she was summoned by the receptionist.

'Are you here for a workout today?' She looked Flick up and down as if to say you're not wearing the correct gear.

'No,' Flick said. 'I don't have the right stuff, I thought I'd check I could join first, then go shopping. I'll be back tomorrow.'

'Okay, no problem. When you come tomorrow, you need to sign in. It's for health and safety purposes. This is the book, and it's always on the reception desk.'

Flick nodded her understanding.

'If you'd like to follow me.'

Flick went through the double doors leading into the gym, and looked around her. It was busy with both men and women working on the assorted pieces of equipment, and she decided there and then that unless they needed to infiltrate, she would never step foot inside these premises again. It had a massive resemblance to hard work.

'You can, of course, use any of the pieces of equipment, and if you want to book a personal trainer please check what time your preference is available. Anybody will talk you through the various sections of the gym, but I'm sure you must already know this, you look as though you've been working out before.'

Flick almost choked. 'Yes,' she lied, 'but I need a change of venue. I think you get stale by going to the same place all the time.'

'Oh, definitely,' the still-unnamed receptionist said.

They walked around for a further ten minutes, Flick having some pieces of equipment explained to her that sounded more like items of mediaeval torture. She was relieved when they headed for the exit doors, and she found herself back in the reception area.

'And that,' Flick said, pointing to The Coffee Pot, 'is presumably where most people have a drink after their session. Can I get one now?'

'Yes of course. Thank you for joining, and we'll see you tomorrow?'

'Definitely,' Flick said, and moved towards the signing-in book.

'Oh no,' the receptionist said, 'if you're only visiting the coffee shop, we don't ask you to sign in.'

'Really? I'm surprised. As you said, health and safety...'

'The Coffee Pot is a franchise. They have their own

regulations. It's well used, and I would say ninety per cent of our visitors go in before heading home. A couple of romances have blossomed in there.' She giggled.

'Thank you,' Flick responded, and walked through the double doors of the coffee shop.

Flick ordered a flat white and took out her notebook. She didn't want to forget anything of this strange afternoon, especially the bit about anybody visiting the coffee shop only, didn't have to sign in. Their killer could easily have got to know her victims simply by going for a coffee. She wouldn't have been on any attendance list, wouldn't necessarily have to be on the membership list. A perfect set-up.

She glanced around – eight customers, including herself, and this was mid-afternoon. Two people were tapping away on laptops, a man was reading a newspaper while enjoying a panini with his drink, and most of the others either had books or eReaders to occupy their minds. Flick liked to people-watch and spent a pleasant half hour in The Coffee Pot, before following the man with the newspaper out of the doors.

'My first time in that coffee shop,' she said chattily, 'seems nice. The coffee was good anyway.'

'It's excellent,' he responded. 'I use it most days, my office is only five minutes away. It seems to attract a lot of people who return to it, rather than first-timers. I bet you go back again.'

'Certainly will. I've joined the gym.'

He laughed. 'I've heard it's not the best of gyms, but it's certainly one of the better coffee shops. Maybe I'll see you again,' he said, as they reached the car park, and she took out her keys.

'That would be nice. My name's Flick.'

'Robert. I'm in most days.'

The smile was still on her face as she unlocked her car, but by the time she had driven out of the car park, Robert had disappeared.

Flick and Erica arrived back at the station at the same time. Flick was about to go through the doors when she spotted Erica's car. She waited until Erica sorted herself out and got out of the car, then waved.

Erica waved back, and inwardly thought how much she was getting used to working with Flick. She remembered she'd been to join Starlite Gym, and grinned. Flick didn't even like climbing the seven steps to get to the doors, she tended to take the disabled ramp, so the idea of her doing exercise in a gym was almost laughable. No, extremely laughable, she corrected herself. 'You don't look any slimmer,' she said as she reached Flick.

'Oy, I don't need to look any slimmer. Met a nice feller though.'

'In police time? That allowed?'

'No idea. He's probably married anyway. But I have got stuff to tell you. How's Beth?'

'Battered head to toe, but much livelier. She's sent her mum and dad back home, and she'll have been moved to her new ward by now. They came to do that, so I left. She's talking about being home in a couple of days, but maybe that's her talking and not her consultant. I don't know.'

'That's good. She capable of being on her own?'

'She says she is, so we'll have to hope she's right. Let's get a coffee, and you can fill me in on all this activity, and tell me when you're going again, to actually do some exercising.'

29

Erica stared out of her tiny office window while Flick made them coffees. She turned towards the younger woman and smiled. 'You're doing well.'

'What do you mean? I'm getting your coffee right?'

'No, I meant in general. You've stepped up to the plate under difficult circumstances, because Beth is extremely well liked. And you think outside the box. You came up with going to the gym, I didn't, and by the sound of it, it's paid off. You want a KitKat?'

'Thanks. I'd love one.' Flick reached across the desk, and slowly took off the wrappings. 'It's ages since I've had one of these.'

'I like them because I can fool myself into thinking they're low in calories, so it doesn't count. So, tell me about this feller, and about the gym.'

'The girl on reception, who shall be unnamed because she didn't have a badge on, was most helpful, possibly because she's not used to being on reception and hadn't been trained in being polite but reticent. I filled in a form, put accountant down as my employment – but put my proper name and address in case they checked. I somehow don't think they will, it's all about numbers there, I suspect. She then took me through those big double doors at the end of the reception desk.' Flick shuddered and Erica laughed.

'It was that bad?'

'Worse! There must have been ten people in the room, all beavering away at high speed on these machines, or laid on their backs picking up weights. Honest, boss, it took my breath away, the thought of actually doing any of it. And I had to get all enthusiastic about it, to keep her thinking I was ready to take my clothes off there and then and get stuck in. Never in a million years will I buy workout clothes. I would say it was about fifty–fifty, the ratio of men to women. I walked around with her, watching them all, and most of them looked in pain. What's that all about then? Why would you do that to yourself?'

Erica laughed. 'And this unnamed receptionist never suspected you were a blatant fraud?'

'Not for a minute. The more questions I asked, the more interest I showed, the more giddy she got at having hooked a new member. I was feeling fed up because it looked above board, everybody was there doing what they wanted to do to get fit, and, as you said, I was the only one who was a fraud.'

Erica sipped at her coffee, knowing she felt exactly the same as Flick. She knew Frannie enjoyed a workout but it certainly had never developed into an obsession, it was more a way of filling in time if she went into work early, or she used the gym as a de-stresser at the end of the day. With this case, her own exercise had been a mixture of wading and stumbling through flooding river waters, clambering up riverbank sides, and walking endless stretches of the river, seeking inspiration.

'So you're going back?'

'Possibly, but it might have to be more official because I don't think I can get away with walking around that coffee shop pretending I'm not an idiot who simply wants to talk to people because I'm lonely.' She grinned. 'You see, I managed to prove today in one fell swoop that the attendance record meant absolutely nothing.'

'What?'

'It seems that The Coffee Pot is a privately owned part of the gym, who pay rent to the gym I suspect, for the use of their premises. In other words, you have to sign in to go into the gym to comply with their strict health and safety rules, but obviously you don't have to sign in anywhere to go for a cup of coffee. Anybody can wander through that reception area and go for a drink. I did. I went to sign in because she'd explained about the importance of signing the book that was always on the desk, and she said no. If all I wanted was a coffee I went and ordered one. So I did. And met the lovely Robert.'

'Tell me more.'

'Not much more to tell. I ordered a coffee, did some people-watching with the eight others who were there, and left at the same time as Robert. We chatted as we walked down towards the car park, and he was saying his office is about five minutes away. He carried on and I went to my car. I got the impression that more people who aren't gym members use the coffee shop, than people who are, but this leaves it wide open, doesn't it? Our first four victims are all gym members, but our killer doesn't have to have any connection to the gym. She could have chatted to them in the coffee shop, and because she was a woman, possibly a personable woman who can put them at their ease, they grew to like her. And they'd get into her car without thinking twice about it.'

'Shit,' Erica said. 'Shit, shit, shit. Just when things felt as though they were getting clearer...'

'Sorry, boss.'

'Brilliant job, Flick. And I think you're reading it right. What time does the coffee shop close?'

'Opens at eight for breakfasts, closes at eight at night.'

Erica drifted into thought, and Flick finished her KitKat.

'Talk me through the people who were there,' Erica said, sitting higher in her chair as though she'd suddenly come alive. She brushed off a piece of chocolate from her white blouse.

'There were eight, as I said. I made the ninth, but I sat at a table on my own. There were too many empty tables for me to justify sitting with someone and starting up a conversation.' She took out her notebook before continuing. 'Okay, nobody was with anybody else. They were all on individual tables. One woman and one man were working on laptops, and both seemed on really good terms with the staff so I'm assuming they maybe do a lot of work in there. Robert was reading a paper, possibly *The Telegraph* because it was big, and having his lunch. A panini, but I don't know what was on it.'

'Epic fail then,' Erica said with a grin. 'Carry on.'

Three women were reading, one with a real book called *Resistance* – I've looked it up, it's by Patricia Dixon – and two with Kindles. Other brands are available.' She spluttered with laughter before returning to her notebook. 'I don't know what the Kindle readers were reading. The remaining two were men. One was on his own phone texting and sighing, and the other sat looking fed up and drinking his coffee. He left first, after about ten minutes. I had a coffee, but I promise my Kindle never left my bag.'

'So you sat and surveyed them?' Erica kept her face straight.

'I did. Dragged my coffee out a bit, it was cold by the time I got up to follow Robert.'

'Might have looked less suspicious if you'd taken out your Kindle. Only saying...'

. . .

The report from Ivor referencing the autopsy performed on Victoria Urland was still waiting in Erica's inbox, and she finally clicked on it to open it.

It was much the same as the others; strangled by a ligature, once again a pair of tights being used for something they were never intended to be used for. Propofol was present, this time in a slightly larger quantity, and the deceased had given birth within the last four weeks. She thought of the tiny baby whose grandparents had brought him into the station to tell them his mummy hadn't arrived home from a bonfire, and she felt grief. A little boy never knowing his mummy, grandparents having to start raising a child when they were at the age when they could expect to have the benefits of a grandchild, someone to love, play with, spoil rotten, and return home to his mummy at the end of it. Their lives would change immeasurably.

Little Noah Urland would live with photographs of Victoria, and not her arms wrapped around him constantly.

The time of death had been estimated at eight to ten o'clock that bonfire evening, and Erica wondered why she should be in the killer's car at that time. Surely the bonfire wasn't over? Even ten was an early hour for an adult attended bonfire to finish. It was a priority they tracked down the change of plan she had mentioned in the text to her mother.

Erica pushed her chair away from her desk, but after checking her watch decided not to bother the Urlands with a visit; time was getting on, and with the responsibilities associated with a new baby, it wouldn't be fair on them. She picked up the phone and checked in with Noah's harassed-sounding grandmother, and arranged for a visit the following morning.

.   .   .

Flick had gone home, Ian was still at his desk, and a couple of others were near the photocopier. Erica glanced around the large room, and told everybody to go home.

'Ian, your wife will forget what you look like.'

'She might do, boss,' Ian said. 'Her mum's had a nasty fall, so she's gone to look after her till she's a bit more mobile. I'm okay, nothing to rush home for, and I'm picking up fish and chips for my tea. Besides, I'm ferreting around in the WEA class listings, and when I get to a point where I'm comfortable stopping, I promise I will. Now you go home.'

'I am. I saw Beth today, she's doing okay. Still on heavy medication for the headaches, but they've moved her from high dependency so she's thinking in terms of getting home in a couple of days. I'm not convinced...'

'Don't worry, they'll not let her go until it's the right time. Especially with head injuries. Her ribs okay?'

'She says they're fine unless she moves or breathes.'

'He really meant it, didn't he? Bastard.'

'That's one word of many I've used about him, Ian. I'm going home now, and tomorrow Flick and I are going to see the Urlands. We need to know which bonfire Victoria went to, instead of the one she was supposed to be attending. They may think they don't know where she went, but we may be able to jog something in their memories. We have to try, anyway. You'll be in charge of here, contact me if anything crops up.'

'I will, boss.' He swung back round to face his monitor. 'Oh, by the way, I've done it.'

'Done what?'

'Put in for my sergeant's exams. Couldn't take the bullying any longer.'

She scuffed him across the back of his head. 'Bullying? You ain't seen nothing yet. And well done, you do the job, it should be official and recognised. Don't back out or you'll really find out what bullying means.'

Erica drove home lost in a world of her own. With three sergeants on the books, things would have to change. She wouldn't be able to pretend she had three and didn't realise, her superiors would be planning transfers as soon as Ian passed his exams. She guessed it would be some time before Beth returned to work, and therefore Flick was okay for now, but by the time Ian received his promotion Erica would have issues to deal with that she really didn't want.

She pulled up outside her home, and saw that Frannie's red Audi was already parked on the drive. She momentarily forgot her problems and her smile lit up her face. This woman was getting her through this bloody awful case, and she didn't know what she would do without her.

Erica sat for a moment, then switched off her engine, locked the car and headed for the front door.

Frannie opened both the door and her arms.

30

Erica woke and checked her phone. 06:59. She silenced the alarm as soon as it rang at 07:00 and put a foot out of bed. She almost brought it back into bed, but instead slipped her feet into the fleecy slippers that had seen better days but still served a purpose. It felt icy in the bedroom and she knew it would be a good fifteen minutes before it became liveable. Maybe they should change the automatic settings for the central heating, these days a seven o'clock fire-up was far too late.

She sipped at her coffee with a sense of relief that there had been no early call-out, and she thought back to the previous day's conversation with Flick about the café. Her decision to make Flick acting DS until the return of Beth had been made with her fingers crossed, but the younger woman had certainly stepped up to the mark. She was proving to be intuitive, and had no fear of acting outside the box. Joining the gym, while creating laughter between them, had been inspirational. Erica grinned to herself as she tried to think of ways of sending Flick to the gym to work out, and do some surveillance.

Frannie entered the kitchen as Erica was finishing her coffee.

They exchanged a smile and a good morning kiss, and Erica grabbed her car keys and bag before shouting bye.

The journey into work was uneventful and she was surprised to see Flick's car already there.

The briefing room was unusually quiet; most of her team were immersed in their computers, and she smiled at how easy they were to manage. They simply did it. They discussed amongst themselves who was doing what, and it happened.

Flick waved and stood. She followed Erica into the DI's office, and waited until Erica had removed her coat before sitting down.

Erica followed her actions, and they sat looking at each other across the desk.

'So. You solved it yet?' Erica asked, keeping her face straight.

'Yes. It's Ian.'

'That's interesting. He's a man.'

'But if we arrest him, it makes our clear-up rate look good.'

'Has he agreed?'

'Not yet. Give me chance to get out the handcuffs.'

'Sergeant! He's a married man!'

They laughed. 'Seriously,' Flick said, 'I think I should take my laptop and go write a book or something in that café. Observe definitely, but maybe chat if I can get away with it. I'm sure Robert will be in, and he might be a bit forthcoming.'

'Or you could put Lycra on and go and do a workout,' Erica said, once again stopping the smile.

'Ah, but it's not about the gym, is it?' Flick was quick to point out. Very quick. 'I'm sure it's that café. We've checked alibis for everybody who attended the gym on the relevant evenings, and they're all clear. I'm sure we're onto something with The Coffee Pot now we've found out it's there. I think it's where she meets her victims, and we need to know if any of the four girls used that café. That's what I'm doing today – if that's good with you?'

'It's nice that you've asked. You got a plot for this book then?'

'It's a police procedural.'

'Oh good. Not much research needed for it. Give me a minute.' Erica picked up her phone and dialled the safe house where Katie and Becky were still ensconced.

She spoke to a sleepy Becky and asked the relevant questions about the gym and the café, then quietly disconnected after reassuring Becky that they were close to a conclusion. Erica lifted her head and looked at Flick.

'It seems all four of them used the café regularly. Take yourself off down there for a few hours, but you can't make yourself known to the owners. One of them might be the killer so I suggest you pay particular attention to them. If they start to make noises about you moving on, you'll have to do that, but stick it out as long as you can. Keep drinking and eating, then they can't really ask you to leave. And save your receipts, I'll authorise them. I'm going out to the safe house, have a chat with our two girls and see if they remember anything. I'll also ask the families of Imogen, Tanya and Victoria if they knew whether their daughters used the café.'

Flick stood. 'Okay, boss. I'm going to set up my book that I'm writing, so I don't look like a complete amateur when I get there.'

'You've brought your laptop?'

'Certainly have. I couldn't sleep for thinking about that damn café, so I knew I'd give it a shot for an hour today, but now I've got permission...'

Erica laughed. 'Go for it. Contact me by text if you need to, don't blow your cover by ringing me. Let's hope the receptionist is a different one.'

'It doesn't matter. I don't need to go into the gym. There's a door out of the café directly onto the street, so I'll go in that one.'

'So there's two ways in?'

Flick pulled a piece of paper towards her and swiftly drew a sketch of the reception area, the double doors into the café, then a bubble-shaped space representing the café with the doors leading out onto the main road. 'Ideal for any would-be murderer, isn't it? Nobody in the gym knows she's there if she came in off the road. And she can pull up outside like a good Samaritan if somebody comes out and fiddles with an umbrella, or stops to put the hood up on their jacket. Dreadful weather, want a lift home, Tanya? You can see it, can't you.'

Erica nodded. 'You can. Let's go and brief the team on what's happening. I'll put Will on to getting some information about the café and its employees, see who owns it, he's good at background digging.'

The briefing took longer than Erica thought it would. As the explanation of the café took hold in the minds of her team, the questions flowed and she could feel a sense of excitement that everybody thought it was a major step forward.

'So that's it,' she said finally. 'Flick will be unavailable once she leaves here, I'm going to see the families of our girls, plus going to the safe house. Does everybody know what they're doing?'

Sam held up a hand.

'Sam we're not in school.' Erica smiled. She liked the good-looking young officer; if he retained the enthusiasm he unfailingly showed, he would go far in his career.

He waved a piece of paper and pointed to the whiteboard. 'Can I?'

She nodded and he walked to the front, attaching the two sheets of copy paper that had been stuck together with Sellotape.

'I did this last night. The ANPR could only track that black car so far, then it disappeared, so I took the last-known recognition of it, and used several websites to track down garages and lock-ups within half a mile of that last sighting. If it's okay, boss, I'd like to take a car and go out searching. I know it's a long shot, and I won't give it more than a day because of that, but...'

'But nothing, Sam.' She walked over to join the PC. 'And well done. Seems we're all doing lots of homework on this one.'

She looked at his diagrams, his annotations and little speech bubbles. 'What's this star?'

'That's the last point it was seen by the ANPR camera. There's no further sightings at any point during the night, and we know she changes number plates so there's no point in following that. On the two CCTVs we've caught her on, it's showed the same car but with two different registration plates. I suspect she's got a little stash of them in the garage with the car.'

Erica nodded. 'I agree that it's in a garage somewhere. We've made enough appeals about this car for somebody to have come forward if it's on a road or in a car park somewhere. She takes a hell of a risk being out and about with it in this day of the police being able to check insurance, tax and everything on the spot.'

'She chooses her time, boss. Between eight and nine the ordinary copper on the beat is reasonably quiet. Any later and we start to get the idiots roaming at large, tanked up on beer, but the autopsy reports place death at eight to ten at night, don't they? It's almost as if she understands the police system. Or she's in the police.'

'Okay,' Erica said, 'I can rule Flick out. She's not fit enough to wheel an empty suitcase, never mind one with a body inside.'

Everybody laughed, and Flick grinned while holding up a finger.

'Sam, bring your bit of paper and come talk to me.' Erica left the room.

Sam straightened his carefully drawn diagram, and pushed it across Erica's desk. She looked at it, letting her fingers trace the various routes and buildings on it. 'Is it accurate?'

'As accurate as I can make it. I didn't have access to the council's site from home, so I did the best I could with Google maps and stuff. Why?'

'I don't want you going alone. We know, we've seen at first hand, how dangerous this woman is. See what Mike's doing, and if he can postpone it. He's a big lad, you should both be okay. And well done on this, you must have been working on this most of the night.'

'I was. But it's got to be done. It's the only lead we've got regarding this car.'

She handed the chart back to him. 'Leave a photocopy of this with me before you go. If she does get the pair of you, I'll need to know where to start looking for your bodies.'

'Thanks, boss,' he said, standing. 'You're all heart.'

She could see Flick beavering away on her laptop, Sam and Mike deep in conversation with their heads bent over Sam's diagram, Will tapping away on his computer and she knew she couldn't ask for a better team. This case had got to all of them, touched them deeply, and she knew it was because of the ages of the girls. Dead before they had chance to show their full potential, one of them leaving a tiny baby to be brought up by grandparents – it had been the hardest case they had worked on together, and by far the most difficult with the spectre of the twenty-fourteen murders hanging over everything like a pall.

They were a young team and most of them hadn't been around five years earlier, and yet all of them now knew as much as she did about those murders after spending hours going through case notes. They had all made it a priority that they knew of the link that connected the five-year-distant deaths.

Erica saw Flick check her watch, close her laptop and stand, before walking across to where Sam and Mike were at the photocopier, making the requested copy for her. She saw Flick speak to them, clearly asking a question because Sam nodded enthusiastically in reply, and they made an extra copy and handed it to her.

Flick walked back to her desk, took a sip of water and sat down for a couple of minutes while she went over the hand-drawn diagram. After rummaging in her drawer for a pencil, she carefully traced around buildings and roads, then started up her computer and typed something in. She scrolled the screen, took it back to the beginning, entered something else and punched the air. Then she stood and headed for Erica's office.

'Do you know,' Flick said, 'how close this area is to The Coffee Pot?'

31

Erica walked through the door into Beth's room and felt a burst of delight to see her sitting in the chair by the bed. She was still having fluids put into her, so remained attached to a drip, but everything apart from the bandage around her head appeared fairly normal.

'That's a sight for sore eyes,' she said, and handed over a couple of magazines. 'Your face looks so much better, the swelling's almost gone.'

'That's only temporary,' Beth said ruefully. 'He didn't manage to kick out any of my teeth, but he's loosened two so much I'm going to have them taken out because they'll drop out eventually if I don't, and cause me no end of aches and pains. I can have implants put in, but I need to wait before tackling that.'

'And your head injury?'

'It's doing well. The doctor will let me know tomorrow if I can go home. This is my last fluid IV, so all's good.'

'Okay, don't forget my offer of coming to stay with us for a few days until you're more able to get your own meals and suchlike. We'd love to have you. I've spoken to Frannie about it, and she didn't hesitate to say yes.'

'I know. She said so.'

'She's been to see you?'

'She has. She didn't say?'

'No, but I'm not surprised. She's always at the hospital. She has some really strange clients that frequently require hospitalisation after they've walked into a wardrobe door, or the kitchen door. You understand?'

Beth smiled. 'I do. She didn't stay long, brought me some Maltesers because I don't need to chew them, and repeated your offer. But fill me in on the case. Are you any closer to a result?'

Sam drove, and he and Mike headed towards where the last camera had identified the Fiesta as passing it. Sam took the first turn left after that point, and found himself on a narrow cobbled street, so indicative of that area of Sheffield. He drove slowly, and Mike did most of the observation, his head swivelling as he checked the side streets and alleyways that led off the road they were on. They reached the end and Sam stopped, judging which way to go next at the T-junction.

'Left?' Mike suggested. 'We can always do a second drive round, and take the right turns, we've got all day.'

With a brief nod of agreement, Sam quickly indicated left and pulled out. They followed the same routine until Mike spotted the row of garages they had been seeking. They drove down the narrow access road, and pulled up as the space widened to allow cars manoeuvrability. They climbed out of the squad car and walked towards the last garage in the row of seven. Much to their surprise the garage door slid up, but it was empty apart from a sleeping bag, a blanket, and a pillow. A small candle stood inside a grimy glass jar.

'Bijou residence,' Mike muttered, but nevertheless made sure the door was closed firmly. This garage was shelter for some poor bugger down on their luck. They walked back towards the entrance to the site, but none of the other six garages were unlocked. Two had holes in the doors through which they could see, but neither of them was home to a car, merely used as storage lock-ups.

Nobody was around for them to hold any sort of conversation with, so they headed back to the car, and drove out, following their left-turn rule.

Mike was ticking off their route by using a biro to draw along the roads they had already covered, and by one o'clock they were hungry. Their final left turn had brought them out on to the main road two hundred yards higher than the Starlite Gym, and The Coffee Pot where they knew Flick would be sitting writing her book.

'We could go in there.' Mike nodded towards the café.

'Think she'd be mad?'

'We'll not talk to her. Don't want to blow her cover, but surely six eyes are better than two. Come on. Let's go and see if they do chips.'

Flick saw her colleagues walk through the door and froze, but they ignored her and chose a table at the opposite side of the room. She realised they weren't going to acknowledge her, and breathed a sigh of relief.

Nobody had disturbed her for the two hours she had been sitting there, and she had actually enjoyed writing the book that had started out as a joke. She knew she would wipe it once the exercise was over, but it had given her a reason to do some typing, then stop and stare around the room as if seeking inspiration. In actuality, she had been people-watching, wanting to know who had come in, who had gone out, and who had been there as long as she had.

Robert had come in, enjoyed a coffee, smiled at her and left, so that didn't help at all.

She had used her phone to take photos when it was safe to do so without being spotted, and she had managed to capture almost everyone who had entered. She had definitely photographed every woman.

Sam and Mike stayed around half an hour, then left without even looking in her direction. *Good lads*, she thought, *good lads*.

The waitress came across to take her empty cup away, and Flick asked for a cheese and tomato toastie along with a pot of tea. The coffee was making her head buzz.

It was delivered to her table ten minutes later, and the waitress pulled out a chair. 'You a student?'

Flick swallowed. 'No, I'm an author.'

'I said you were! We saw you in here yesterday, so you must have enjoyed it to come back again today. What do you write?'

'Murder.'

'Oh my God, that's awesome. How many have you had published?'

'This is my first book.' Flick was thinking on her feet, eager to keep the conversation going. 'I've taken a year's sabbatical from work to see if I can do it. If I can't, I go back to my job. In accountancy.'

'I'm so envious. I do a bit of writing.'

Flick's heart sank. *Please don't ask for advice.*

'Will you be in again?' The waitress was smiling at her.

'I certainly will. Nobody has bothered me, I've been able to crack on with the book, and the food is excellent.'

'Maybe we can talk again.' She stood. 'I work every weekday until about seven, but not weekends.'

Flick smiled at her. 'I'd like that. You enjoy crime books?'

'Love them. Will you be here tomorrow?'

'I will. Let's make time for a chat when you get your break.'

. . .

Mike and Sam continued checking garage sites in the area but saw no sign of a black old-style Fiesta. They had found three garages unlocked but nothing in them, and it was only when they decided to call it a day that Sam suggested they go round to the garage with the sleeping bag in it. They had spoken to only four people, and nobody had known anything about a black Fiesta in the area.

'It's not only about the car, I'd like to check they're okay, whoever it is. It's crap having to sleep in a garage,' Sam explained.

He drove down the narrow entrance, made more difficult by the approaching darkness, and pulled up at the end garage.

'Do we knock?' Sam asked.

'It's their home, so I suppose we do,' Mike said. 'I can't believe we're having this conversation. Come on, let's see what he or she has to say.'

Sam tapped on the door. 'Hello! Police. Can we have a quick word, please? You're not in any trouble.'

There was silence, so Sam knocked again, this time a little louder.

Mike reached down to the handle and tugged. It lifted slowly and a frightened face peered out from the depths of the sleeping bag. The candle flickered but protected by the jar, didn't go out.

It was a young face, and Sam guessed at no more than seventeen. 'Hi,' Sam said. 'Can we come in?' He felt foolish.

The boy nodded without speaking.

'Only a couple of questions, lad,' Mike said, 'then we'll be on our way. You okay in here?'

Once again the boy nodded.

'You got a name?' Sam kept his voice low.

'Adam.'

'Okay, Adam. You might have seen us driving around this area all day, but we're only looking for a car, and my guess is you don't have one.'

This time the boy shook his head.

'You hungry?'

'Yes.'

Mike stood. 'I'll be back in quarter of an hour. McDonald's?'

Adam's face changed from bewilderment to shock. 'Please.'

Sam was sitting on the end of the sleeping bag when Mike returned, carrying three Big Mac meals, and three coffees.

He could see that Sam and Adam had progressed to talking, so busied himself sorting out the food.

'When did you last eat, Adam?'

'Yesterday. Somebody brought me a sandwich.' Adam looked up as Mike handed him the Big Mac meal, a large coffee and an apple pie. 'Thanks,' Adam said quietly.

'Let's eat while it's still hot,' Mike said, 'and then we'll talk.'

Adam, it transpired, had lived at home until he was sixteen. His mother had then moved a boyfriend in, and they simply didn't get on. Adam left without telling anyone he was going, and he hadn't been back.

'And you sleep here every night?'

'I've been here for about three months. I'm not going back to hers.' His defensiveness showed.

'We're not asking you to, pal,' Sam said. 'But there's better places than this to sleep. You want us to look at getting you into a hostel?'

'No, I'm fine here.'

'Winter's coming. The last three months were a picnic compared to the bad weather still to come before next April or May.'

Adam shrugged. 'I'll be fine. I sometimes earn a few quid, and then I eat.'

'How do you earn a few quid? Drugs?'

He shook his head. 'Not on your life. Don't touch 'em. No, I busk. I earn a bit till I get moved on.' He nodded towards the back corner of the garage. 'That's my guitar.'

Mike stood and walked over to the instrument. It was in the shadows, in its case. He opened it and looked at it. 'Nice one.'

'It is. My granddad bought it me a couple of years ago, just before he died. I brought a few clothes and that with me when I left. And twenty quid out of my mother's purse. I got moved on quick today, so only got about a pound. I'll try again tomorrow.' Adam finished the last of his fries, and took a sip of the still-hot coffee. 'This is good.' He reached across and picked up the apple pie. 'My mum used to make apple pie before she met the wanker.'

'That what you call him?'

'Not to his face. That's his occupation. I left when nobody was in the house, because he'd hammered me the night before and I'm not big enough to tackle him. I had a black eye, and a massive red ear. Bruises all over. I decided next time he might kill me, so I was out of it. I'm okay in here.' He looked around his garage. 'I'll have to try to find a padlock or summat for it, though, if coppers are going to come visiting.' He smiled for the first time.

'I might check on you occasionally,' Sam said, 'but you're old enough to make your own decisions so we won't hassle you. This is my card. Ring if you're in trouble, or simply ring. Now, we need to talk to you about a car. As you're in this area, you might see things we can't see. We can't be here all the time. This is a picture of the car we've been looking for.' He held out the picture of the Fiesta and Adam looked at it while eating the scalding-hot apple pie. He handed back the picture.

'No, sorry, I've not seen it, but I'll look out for it.'

32

Adam froze in mid-bite. The two police officers had left him their apple pies so he had something to eat next morning, and he had saved the dregs of his coffee to slake his thirst, but he'd never had a visitor at seven in the morning before. This didn't feel good.

'It's only me, Adam,' Sam said. 'You awake?'

Adam breathed a sigh of relief. His fear was that Wanker would track him down one day.

'Yeah,' he said. 'Having breakfast. Sorry I can't offer you any.'

Sam laughed. 'It's a good job I called and got us a bacon sandwich and a cup of tea each then, isn't it? Think you can manage one?' He held up the carrier bag he was holding.

'I'll try.' Adam grinned, and stuffed the final piece of apple pie into his mouth. 'Your mate not here?'

'No, we don't start till eight this morning, worked late last night. I've brought you a couple of bits to make life easier for you while you're here. If you do move to a flat or hostel or something, pass them on to somebody else.'

Adam bit into the bacon sandwich, his face lighting up. 'God, this is good.'

Sam took a bite of his, and lowered himself to the sleeping bag. 'You don't cater for visitors, do you,' he joked.

'Don't want visitors. I'm okay on my own. What you brought me?'

'An old but serviceable garden chair, a rug to put under this,' he said, patting the sleeping bag, 'so it's warmer at night, and a couple more blankets. Oh and a cooker.'

Adam blinked. 'A cooker?'

'Yes. We used to go camping, so I asked Mum if we'd any stuff left. I spent an hour sorting out the loft last night. Not only a cooker, I found a bag full of gas canisters in the shed, so try not to blow the garages up, yes? And Mum's sent you some tins of soup, beans, that sort of stuff, some white candles, matches and a tin opener. And a plate and a dish. And a knife, fork and spoon. I've packed most of it into a big plastic box to stop it rotting, so you should be okay for a bit till you can earn some more with your guitar.'

'Why? Why are you doing this?'

'Because I can. You're in need of help, it's what I do in my job, and you're not a run-of-the-mill yob who's out to make a bob or two through the drugs route. And I felt uncomfortable leaving you here last night, especially when the rain started.' He looked around. 'Seems dry enough in here though. Has it been okay through all this bad weather?'

'Yeah. No leaks. This car you're looking for. They done something bad?'

'Do you know about the five women who've been killed and left by the river over the past couple of weeks?'

'Kind of. Seen it on newspaper headlines.'

'It's connected with that. We're following all and any leads, so keep your eyes open. Don't approach the driver, ring either me or Mike.'

They finished their breakfasts, and Sam stood to empty the

car of the promised booty. When he'd finished he handed Adam a padlock. 'I'll keep one key,' he said, 'in case you become ill or anything, but I promise we'll only come as visitors, maybe bring you the odd beefburger. Lock up when you go out, and nobody will make off with your stuff. I'm going to work now. Don't forget, ring if you've any problems, or if you see that car.' He took out his wallet and handed Adam a twenty-pound note. 'And don't be hungry.'

He bent to lift the door, and straightened into a squally rain. 'You'll not be busking today. Bye, Adam.'

'Bye, Sam. And that car... first garage as you come on to this site. But she'll not be there yet, she usually only takes it out evening time.'

Sam waited in the car park at the station until Mike arrived, then spoke to him before they walked upstairs to join the other members of the team. Sam couldn't see any way around involving Adam, and he knew Adam had recognised that when he had given him the location of the car.

'I come from an area where we don't trust the police,' had been his simple explanation, 'but you brought me all this to make sure I was warm and safe. You didn't need to do that. That bird has helped me as well, the one who owns that car. She brought me the blanket, sleeping bag and pillow, and she always brings me some food when she comes for the car.'

And so the eight o'clock briefing went by without any input of any significance from Mike and Sam. They merely confirmed they had used a lot of petrol driving around the garage sites, with no sighting or information about the car.

. . .

Flick talked through her day, explained she would be meeting the waitress for a chat, using her new status as author to get the girl talking, and would try to bring in the issue of any women who visited the café, and made themselves friendly with the other female customers. She said she would give it one more day to try to get the information they needed. She confirmed she had photographs of all females who had been in the café the previous day.

Mike and Sam followed Erica to her office and asked to speak to her. She liked these two officers, had observed how well they worked together, yet had recognised a certain amount of reticence as they had given their report in the briefing. She waited, knowing the little mystery was about to be solved.

Sam took the lead, explaining how they had met Adam in the first place, their subsequent revisit to show him the picture of the car and to leave their telephone numbers, alongside feeding the lad.

'And he is safe?' she asked.

'He is,' Sam confirmed. 'I wrecked our loft last night and took him some stuff and a bacon sandwich to make life more bearable this morning. He suddenly seemed to find some trust, possibly because we didn't hassle him about anything, and told him to ring us if he was in trouble. He's a nice lad, boss, but happier living in an empty garage than living at home with his mum and...' Sam stopped himself from continuing.

'His mum and?'

Sam sighed. 'Wanker the boyfriend. Adam's name for him, not ours.'

'Okay. Is that all?'

'No! I gave him a padlock to make sure he could lock his stuff in the garage, and told him I'd keep one key in case he was ever taken ill. I kind of feel responsible for him. It seemed to open him up, and he said the car we were looking for was inside the first garage on the site.'

Erica stood. 'Did you check?'

'We checked all the garages yesterday, boss,' Mike said. 'It's how we found Adam. He wasn't there when we checked. But it was obvious somebody homeless was using it, so we went back later to see if they were anywhere about. He was. But when we were first there we found Adam's place unlocked, two other garages with damaged doors that we could see into, and the other five were secure and solid. We showed Adam the picture of the car, and asked him to keep his eyes peeled for it, to ring one of us if he saw it. It was only Sam taking him his breakfast and the other stuff he's taken that made him realise we were the good guys, I think, and he said where the car was.'

Erica sat, deep in thought. 'Sit down, lads. We have to think this one through.'

They sat and waited.

A few minutes later Erica picked up her phone, looked at it, then replaced the receiver. Then she picked it up again. Replaced it again.

'Look,' she said. 'We have a problem.'

'That's what we thought,' Sam said. 'I think your problem is the one I thought about before haring off down to that garage when Adam gave me the information. If we send Forensics in, or even a lowly copper single-handed, and she sees us, we've blown it.'

'You didn't go near it?'

'No, didn't even look at it when I drove past. I did tell Adam not to go near it, as well. However, he did say that she only goes in the evening. Anytime from five onwards, he said. And not every night. Whenever she does, she takes him some food. I didn't say anything out there in the briefing because I hadn't had chance to tell you, didn't want to second-guess how you would act.'

She nodded. 'I realise that. The truth is I don't know what to do. I need to see the place for myself, but again if she turns up... can we get surveillance there?'

'Not easily. It's an access road of hard-packed earth, surrounded by trees and grass. Nowhere to hide, no convenient buildings we could wait in – except for Adam's garage. I think he trusts us now, but...'

'I don't want to use his place,' she said quickly. 'I want everything to appear normal to her until she gets in that car. I don't want any slip-ups when we catch this evil bitch. I want her firmly linked to that car by actually being in it, and presumably she won't be in it before she takes some food to Adam. Do you think he would be amenable to having an alarm he can press to tell us she's left him? We can have surveillance outside on the street that can move in when she gets to her own garage. He can press the alarm to notify us the second she leaves him.'

'Maybe. We can ask him. I don't think he'll be busking today, it's too wet, so we can pop down and see him. You don't want to interview him?'

'One day, but let's get her first. He's a nice lad?'

'Seems to be. Around sixteen or seventeen, that's all, plays the guitar and earns a few quid by busking until he's moved on. He didn't bother telling anybody he was leaving, his mother's boyfriend, Wanker as he calls him, beat him up so he left the next morning with a few clothes, a guitar his granddad bought him, and twenty quid from his mother's purse. He looked terrified when we first opened up his door,' Mike said.

'I'm glad you did. And well done, you two, for looking after him. He doesn't want to go into a hostel?'

'No. I got the impression he was scared he could be tracked down there. He's okay in this garage, but it's bloody cold.'

'And has Adam only been having contact with this woman since this spree started. Two weeks or so?'

'No, that's the strange thing. She appeared on the first night he went to the garage. It was a hot night in July, and he left the bottom of the door open slightly, She pulled it up and saw him. She's been regularly ever since. Getting the car in safe working order? It would hardly make a speedy getaway vehicle if it broke down, would it. I think she's been working on it so it didn't let her down, and now she only has to go and change the number plates and she's good to go.'

Erica sighed. 'And the nightmare is, when does she feel she's good to go again?'

33

F lick ordered a coffee and chose the table with the best view of The Coffee Pot's front door. It was busier this morning, and tables seemed to have two at each one, rather than the solitary aspect presented the previous day.

She took her phone out of its case and stood it on a small stand she had borrowed from her younger brother, who seemed to have every gadget ever invented by man. She focused it on the door, and hoped it wouldn't be obvious that she was taking photographs of anybody who entered the café.

Her first job was to send a quick email to Erica explaining where she was – she hadn't wanted to intrude on the meeting that had been happening with Sam and Mike, in Erica's office, but hoped that they had something helpful to the case to pass on.

The door opened and she clicked her phone. Tonight she would put all the pictures from both days on a sheet, then hand them around at the next briefing. She looked up as the waitress approached with her coffee.

'I can take a break in ten minutes,' she said, 'before the

eleven o'clock rush starts. Have you time to talk to me? My name's Georgia Knight, by the way.'

'Flick, easier to say than Felicity,' Flick said with a smile. 'I'm here for a few hours, so any time is good with me.'

The door opened and Flick felt mildly panicked because it was a woman and she daren't press her phone with Georgia standing by her side, but fortunately Georgia moved back to the servery in time for Flick to swivel the phone slightly and capture the image. She moved it back to position and opened up the document she had spent the previous day composing.

Her evening after work had been spent online mixing with various authors on book clubs accessed through Facebook. She had read through their many humorous anecdotes about an author's life: missed deadlines, earning little but knowing they had to do it because they had to do it, and she listened to authors such as Stephen King who had made YouTube videos of their working lives. It had been an exercise that had surprised her.

She had imagined, without really giving any thought to it, that you had an idea for a story, you made a few notes and you sat down and wrote it. It seemed that wasn't the case, and Georgia was about to sit down with her and ask questions about writing that Flick had only discovered the previous evening. She felt nervous. She wasn't particularly good at this undercover stuff, and realised belatedly that she should have picked a different persona for her first stab at infiltration of the ungodly. She stifled a giggle. It was nerves.

She didn't need to be nervous. Georgia brought a coffee with her and sat down beside her. She looked into Flick's face, holding her gaze.

'Is it part of your research for this book that you're taking photographs,' she asked quietly, 'or are you not really a writer?'

Flick had only seconds to think about her answer, and she carefully pulled out her warrant card. She showed it to Georgia who nodded.

'Okay,' the waitress said. 'We'll keep our voices low. I actually thought yesterday you looked like a policewoman, but I gave you the benefit of the doubt. Why are you here? The dead river women?'

The dead river women. Flick hadn't heard them referred to in that way before, and she wondered if that was how the population of Sheffield thought of them. To anybody who wasn't directly involved with the deaths, she supposed it was natural to lump them all together. Or was it how this particular waitress thought of them? She would have known them all, or at least the first four...

Flick gave a small nod. 'Yes. We have several leads we're following up, and I'm sorry I had to deceive you, but I would have gained nothing by coming here in my official capacity. I am taking photographs, but I can tell you it's not the men we're interested in. This gym, and as a result of the connection to the gym, The Coffee Pot, feature high on the list of follow-ups for us.'

Georgia grinned, but kept her voice low. 'This is much more exciting than writing a novel. This is real life. Maybe I can help because I know most of our customers. I was flummoxed by you because I didn't know you.'

'Tomorrow I'll have a printout of everybody I've snapped over yesterday and today, so I'll pop down in my official capacity, and sit with you for a while until we've identified as many as possible. I'll clear it with your boss tomorrow, so don't worry about having to wait for your break.'

'Huh, she'll be chuffed.' Georgia laughed.

'Doesn't really matter how she feels. It's police business whether I'm being a pretend author or a real detective sergeant. I'm staying for a few hours, but I'd appreciate you keeping my author thing going.' Flick took out the picture of the car. 'Does this look familiar? Have you seen this car anywhere in this area? Picking anybody up?'

Georgia took the picture from her. She studied it for a few seconds, then shook her head. 'I thought I did, but the one I've seen has a different number plate, so sorry, no I don't know this one.'

'You remember number plates?' Flick's eyes widened at the thought that anybody could remember number plates. She struggled to recall her own, never mind strangers' ones.

Georgia smiled. 'Don't think I've got a superbrain, please. The one I remember, and I don't remember all of it, has my initials and my year of birth on it. It starts off GK01. There's three other letters after that but I can't remember them. But this car can't be the one I'm thinking of, because this is different altogether.'

'How do you know the one you can remember? Does it park around here?'

'I've seen it in the gym car park. I used to go and sit out there during the summer to read, while I had my evening break. If we do the late shift, we get a break around six.'

Flick felt a lurch of excitement. 'And you never saw anyone in it?'

'I once saw it pull up outside in pouring rain and the driver offered a lift but Iola shook her head and the car drove away.'

'Iola?'

'Gym member. Sorry I don't know her other name, but her first name is spelt IOLA. It's quite unusual so you can probably track it down pretty easily. She's a customer here, but only when she visits the gym.'

The café door opened and Flick leaned forward slightly to snap the woman as she entered. She paused in the doorway to shake her umbrella before heading for the counter.

'It's starting to get busy,' Georgia said. 'I'd best get back to work. I'll see you tomorrow with your photos?'

'You will. You have a phone number in case anything happens to prevent it?'

Georgia scribbled her number on Flick's notebook, and stood. 'And might I say, Flick, I'll never become an author by talking to you.' She laughed and headed back behind the servery.

Erica had filled her Super in on all developments, and he had agreed with her that they needed to tread carefully until the suspect was in custody. After the hour-long conversation in which she had shared everything her team had given to her, she returned to her own office, made a strong coffee, and pulled her phone towards her.

She stared at the rain pouring down her windows, and bleakly wondered if this was it for ever – torrential rain, unending sludge and wetness, rivers flooding. Maybe they would all buy boats in the future instead of cars...

She was about to disconnect when Frannie answered.

'Sorry, lovely. I was leaving a client's home when I heard my phone ring. I'm sitting in the car now, so I can talk. It's pissing it down again.'

'I know. I was thinking we might buy a boat.'

'Good idea. Can you row?'

'No, but I bet you can.' She laughed. 'And I'm good at putting on waders now, in case you overturn us.'

'Did you want something sensible, or shall I go boat shopping?'

'I wanted to hear your voice really. I needed to talk to somebody who has no connection to this case. I've spent an hour in with the Super, and I feel drained. He insisted on me crossing every i and dotting every t.'

'Now I know you're tired. That was ever so slightly the wrong way round. Good job I understand Erica-speak. Has something happened to need an hour with him?'

'It has. I'll maybe tell you tonight when I've thought it through again, and when my team start to report in. They're all over the place today. What time will you be home?'

Frannie hesitated. 'I was going to the gym...'

'Not the Starlite?' Erica knew the stress showed in her voice and that she was being irrational.

'No, not the Starlite. You know I don't use that one. This one near the office. And you really don't need to fret about me. I'm hardly in the young and beautiful category. And I've got my own car, so not likely to need a lift to anywhere, am I? It's sending you ever so slightly off kilter, this case, methinks.'

'Methinks so too.' Erica forced a laugh. 'I'll let you go. Try not to be too late home, I could do with a hug.'

'Then a hug you shall have, and I'll skip the gym. We'll have a pizza and watch a film and drink wine. That sound good?'

'Copious amounts?'

'You can't, but a full glass may be called for. You're in the middle of a case that seems to require your presence at all strange hours of the night, so I'm limiting you to one glass of wine, sipped slowly to make it last. I'll let you choose the film, though, to make up for it.'

Erica smiled as she disconnected. Her wife seemed to have the knack of making life simple. It usually involved wine, but she never let anything faze her, not even the most difficult of cases she had to deal with in her own job. Traumatised children, battered wives, even the occasional battered husband would be enough to flatten anyone, but she handled it, almost compartmentalised it so that it didn't impinge on her own life, but she never had a bad word to say about anyone. Erica knew their years together had been special, and she hoped they would have many more.

She turned on her computer and pulled up Google Earth. She wanted a close look at the garage site; there had to be some way of keeping observation on the comings and goings. She fiddled around for a while until she got the angle and clarity she wanted, and realised quickly that with such a narrow entrance, once the suspect was inside the garage site, a vehicle could easily be positioned across the entrance to block her exit by vehicle.

She identified Adam's garage from the description given to her by the two officers, and she wondered how they could make sure he was absolutely safe once the action started. If it started. First of all they had to know when she was there. There was no CCTV, nowhere to put cameras, and did she arrive in a car, or even by taxi? She would ask Sam to go find the lad, and ask if the suspect ever arrived in a different car before leaving in the Fiesta.

Erica took out two paracetamol from her drawer and swallowed them with the rapidly cooling coffee. This bloody case was one constant headache, and she doubted if paracetamol would help in any way.

34

A dam was eating a bowl of vegetable soup when he heard the knock on the garage door.

'Adam, it's Sam. You in?'

'I am.' He watched as the door slowly rose a few feet. Sam entered quickly, then pulled the door back down to the bottom, carefully balancing two takeaway coffees.

'Finish your soup, then we'll chat.' The police officer smiled. 'This is starting to look like a proper home.'

'Central heating's crap.' Adam grinned. 'Your mother's a lovely woman, by the way. Please thank her for me; she's sent loads of stuff that's easy for me to cook, or doesn't need cooking.'

Adam had brought in a few bricks he had scavenged from outside and created a raised plinth on which to stand the camping cooker. The rug was underneath the sleeping bag, an extra layer of protection against the cold that struck upwards with some brutality from the concrete floor.

'It was good sorting through it all after you'd gone. I think,' he hesitated, trying to find the right words, 'that what your mum and you have done is possibly the nicest thing anybody has ever done for me, and you don't even know me. I could be a real blagger, lying to you, into drugs, and you wouldn't know.'

Sam laughed. 'Credit me with some intelligence, Adam. Of course I'd know. Yes, I've been lucky to be blessed with the parents I have, but I've been in this job long enough to see the dark side and you're not part of it. You'll get yourself out of this, I know.'

'Started already.'

'Started what?'

'I've got a job. Begins next week. I nipped round to the shop for some milk and the feller who owns it was having a right bull and a cow with his cleaner. She walked out, and I jumped in. I'm going round there on Sunday at twelve, when he closes, and he's going to show me what he wants doing. You've done this,' Adam said, looking up at Sam.

'Me?'

'You and Mike. I was pretty down when you turned up.'

'Invading your space.' Sam laughed.

'Yeah. You did. But you bought me a McDonald's. You didn't have to do that. And then you turned up with the contents of your loft. And now you're here again with a warm drink, and I know you're checking on me, but I can take that.'

'I'm not checking on you, I'm here to ask something. And to tell you something.'

Adam sipped at his coffee. 'Oh?' His eyes searched Sam's face; he was instantly on his guard.

'Stop worrying. It's about the black car. At least, it's about its owner.'

'I've told you I don't know her name. She's never said it.'

'You say she doesn't arrive here to collect the car before five.' Sam glanced at his watch. 'It's not three yet, so I should be safe. It's important no police are here when she arrives. The car is of little use to us if its owner scarpers and we lose her. It's been damned hard work tracking her down, and we've only done that because we had the happy accident of finding you. Luck like that never happens twice, I can assure you. It doesn't usually happen once. So after this, I won't be able to contact you until we've got her. However, we will be in the area. I don't have details yet, but if she does come she'll probably bring you food. That's what she usually does?'

Adam nodded. 'Yes, then she goes down to her garage, gets out the car and disappears. In the summer she used to take it out for ten minutes, then come back and leave after a wave towards me. But this past couple of weeks she's kept it out for longer, and brings it back after I've nodded off. I don't hear her. The rain's drowned out all other sounds.'

'How does she get here? Does she have another car?'

'No idea. If she does, she leaves it out on the main road, because I only ever saw her walk up that alleyway to get to the garage. I used to think she maybe had a van or something that was too big to get down here, but I never saw anything. Sorry I can't help with that.'

'No problem. Now we come to the tricky part because I know you like her, but she's killed nine young women, Adam. She killed four in twenty-fourteen, then stopped for five years and now she's killed another five over the past couple of weeks. She's an extremely dangerous woman who wouldn't hesitate to kill you if she thought it was necessary. We're instigating surveillance as we speak, and the second she enters this site a large vehicle, probably a car recovery truck because that's something you would expect to see parked on a road rather than a car park, will move into position and block the exit. If she does come to see you first, the second she leaves here,' he swept his hand around the garage, 'I want you to press this.'

He handed Adam a small gadget. 'It's a simple alarm, but it will notify us of where she is. Make sure she has closed your door behind her before you press it. Act as you have always acted towards her, and we'll take care of everything else. And stay in here. I'll let you know as soon as we have her in the back of a police car. Do not respond to anyone then but Mike or me.'

Adam turned over the alarm, twisting it between his fingers.

'Press it now,' Sam said. 'We need to test it. We have someone outside with the receiver in place.'

Adam gave a small nervous laugh, and pressed down on the red button. Nothing audible happened, but after a few seconds Sam's phone rang. He spoke briefly, and turned to Adam.

'That's fine. So I'll disappear as soon as I've finished my coffee, and you'll be on your own. I know this sounds strange but we don't think she'll be here tonight because rain isn't forecast. However, we're back to gale conditions and torrential rain tomorrow, and that's when she usually operates. You okay with all of this? Say if you're not, and we can move you out of here and leave everything to chance.'

'You kidding? This is the best thing that's ever happened to me!'

'As soon as we have her we'll get you into the station for a statement, an identity parade probably...'

'It won't be in the papers, my name, will it?'

'No, I promise you that. Make sure you don't open your mouth to talk about it, because there's always somebody who'll have loose lips, believe me. I realise you don't want your family tracking you down.'

'I fucking don't.'

Sam realised that it was the first time he had heard Adam swear.

.   .   .

Sam walked out of the garage site and sat in his own car. Mike was in the passenger seat. 'Worked perfectly, that alarm. Adam okay?'

'He is. Wait while you see his garage now. A proper little home. Still freezing cold at night though. He'd warmed himself a tin of soup when I got there. I gave him the option of us putting him somewhere safe until it's over, or helping us as we've discussed with the boss. No contest. He wants to help.'

'Nice lad.'

'Yep. Wanker's certainly got a lot to answer for. Anyway, Adam's picked up a little cleaning job, so maybe the garage will be passed on to one of his mates in the near future. Hope so. It's going to be a long cold winter if not. I've explained to him that although we'll be here, we're not expecting her to come tonight because it's not raining, and it's not been forecast. He's on the alert for tomorrow night though.'

By eleven o'clock that night all surveillance vehicles had moved half a mile away from the area, leaving one newly arrived car containing Ian Thomas and Kev Ward to take the token overnight watch. No activity was expected, their OCD suspect liked the rain.

It was dry and slightly warmer than of late. A good autumn evening, reminiscent of bonfire nights he remembered from his youth, Ian thought. The sky wasn't quite the deep black they had been experiencing recently, the moon helping to wash the clouds with a paler blue hue. His thoughts drifted back over the case; there was a mild sense of anticipation that tomorrow would see the end. This woman, this killer, could have no idea how close they were, how fortuitous Sam's instinct to go back and talk to the resident of the garage would prove to be. When this was all over, Ian would like to go and shake the young lad's hand.

Ian leaned against the car sipping at the coffee he had collected from the late-night burger van, contemplating his proposed career move. He hadn't wanted to do it, but it would mean more money...

His phone rang and he saw 'Boss' on the screen.

'Boss?'

'Only checking in, Ian. Everything quiet?'

'It is. Go to sleep. We've a busy day tomorrow.'

'I'm still at work. Rereading reports, linking one thing with another...'

'And?'

'And nothing. I've had a bollocking from the wife for still being here, so I thought I'd check everything was quiet, then go home. Frannie's gone to bed because she's got an early start tomorrow, so it's Horlicks and bed. Sweet dreams, boys. See you tomorrow afternoon.'

Ian disconnected and shook his head. No wonder Frannie had been pissed off, still in the office at nearly midnight. He took out a cigarette and lit it. It really was a peaceful night. They had a full view of the opening to the garage site, and an equally full view of any traffic using the road on which they were currently parked.

He let his eyes roam, saw nothing to cause him any concern so dropped the last of the cigarette into the dregs in the bottom of his coffee cup. He collected Kev's and walked back to the burger van to deposit the two cups into the litter bin.

'On surveillance then?' the burger van owner asked.

Ian grinned, and walked back towards Kev. 'So much for being bloody undercover,' he grumbled, as he slid back behind the steering wheel. 'Even the burger bloke knows we're police.'

. . .

Flick spent most of her evening at home collating all the pictures she had taken at The Coffee Pot. She was surprised to see that there were thirty-four pictures, spread over five sheets of paper. She left a small block under each one for any names to be added that Georgia might be able to provide, then Flick emailed it to her police address. She would print them out before the briefing, and distribute them around.

She read through the plan for the following day that Erica had started before bringing her in on the finer details, and knew it was a good plan. That it relied on rain was a minor problem. If the weather didn't follow the forecast, it would one day before much longer; that was a given in South Yorkshire. She moved to close down her computer, then stopped herself. She'd had a couple of additional thoughts about the following day and had included them in her own copy. She decided to send it to Erica, along with her rogues gallery of café visitors.

Clicking send, Flick finally closed down the laptop and headed for bed.

35

Erica walked into the kitchen as Frannie was leaving. They exchanged a brief kiss, and Frannie zipped her coat.

'You got a late start?'

'I've *taken* a late start.' Erica smiled. 'I didn't get in till midnight, and it's another late one tonight probably.'

'Oh? I might go with the others for a meal then, if you're not going to be here.'

'It's this case,' Erica said in a half-hearted fashion, swinging her arm around as if to include the whole world in the statement. 'I'll be bloody glad when it's over.'

'So will I,' Frannie said as she went out into the hallway. 'Don't work too hard, and I'll see you tonight at some ungodly hour. Love you.'

Erica heard the front door close, and she poured herself a coffee, sank down at the table and dropped her head onto her arms. She was tired, she was scared they had it wrong and their plans for the surveillance wouldn't lead to anything, and she needed this case to be done with.

'Alexa, play Radio Two,' she called, and the little round box responded. She listened to the eight o'clock news, and a Billy

Joel track filled the room. 'I am an innocent woman,' she sang along, changing his words slightly, then sipped at her coffee. She would work from home until the two o'clock briefing, going over everything one more time to make sure there would be no slip-ups if the killer did take advantage of the promised rain. The longer-range forecast said hardly any precipitation over the next two weeks, so if nothing happened tonight it gave them breathing space if she followed her routine, but experience told her murderers rarely followed rules.

Showered and dressed in jeans and a thick jumper, Erica settled herself in the lounge with her laptop. She opened Flick's email first, and smiled. She knew it would be some carefully thought addition to the evening's stakeout, and she read through the highlighted parts Flick had included, nodding as she agreed with them.

She clicked on the file labelled 'Coffee Pot visitors', and carefully scrolled through all the pictures. She recognised two; Jenna in her wheelchair with Danny helping her manoeuvre around the tables. The rest she didn't know. It did occur to her that the owner and Georgia Knight knew everyone, and everyone who was a regular would know them... would customers accept a lift from either one of them? Too damn right they would.

She picked up her phone and Flick answered immediately.

'Hi, boss. Thought you'd still be in bed.'

'I feel as if I should be. I've opened your email and the amendments are good. I'm looking at your pictures. I know two of them. The girl in the wheelchair and the feller with her are two people we've already interviewed. They were with Susie Roebuck and Clare Vincent at the theatre that night. They're uni students. Did you have concerns, as I do, that Georgia and the owner of the café know everybody? Customers would accept a lift from them.'

Flick laughed. 'You're a mind reader, boss. I'm checking both of them as we speak. When I've got some information I'll contact you.'

'Oh, God. Sorry,' Erica said, ruffling her hair. 'I should have known you'd be on it. Maybe I should go back to bed,' she ended with a laugh.

'I'm heading to The Coffee Pot to talk to Georgia officially, get her to go through these pictures and see who she can identify. Her boss is a proper tartar, times them to the minute on a break, so she's going to be really chuffed when I turn up and say I need Georgia until I'm done. Quite looking forward to throwing my weight around. Hate bullies.'

'Go you,' Erica responded, and they disconnected.

Immediately the phone pealed out. Beth.

'Hi! You okay?'

'I'm scared.' There was a tremor in Beth's voice.

'Why?' Erica tried to make her voice calm.

'I can go home. I'm packed, about to ring a taxi, and I'm scared of going home.'

'I'm on my way. I'll be there in ten minutes, walk down to the Huntsman entrance and wait for me. You got all your medications?'

'I have. I'm literally sat in my chair shaking, looking for some courage. They've stripped my bed, and I suddenly realised there's only me.'

'No, we have a spare room as you know. Stay as long as you want. See you in ten.'

She grabbed her coat, put on her boots, and opened the door. The rain was torrential; she looked up to the heavens and said, 'Thank you, God.'

. . .

Beth seemed shrunken. The bandage around her head had been replaced by a large piece of gauze, and her fingers were still strapped together, although healing, she had said. Erica fastened her friend's seat belt, and they drove home with the windscreen wipers on at full speed.

'Hasn't it stopped raining at all?' Beth said.

'It has, but when you hear what I've to say, I'd like you to do a little rain dance as your contribution to today's activities,' Erica said with a smile, trying to raise an answering one on Beth's face. It didn't work.

'You need it to rain?'

'We do. When you've had a rest and something to eat, I'll tell you all about it. I'm going to have to leave you, because I'm doing today's briefing at two, then I'm out until probably the early hours of tomorrow, but Frannie won't be in too late. She's going for a meal with her colleagues because she knows I won't be home, and I don't really want to mess her about and ask her to come home instead. Is that okay?'

'It's fine. I'll probably have an early night anyway. Have you told Frannie I'm here?'

'I've not spoken to her, but I've sent a text and she's responded. Don't worry, she's not going to be surprised to see you.'

Erica left shortly after one, leaving Beth curled up on the sofa, sleeping. She took with her a list of items Beth needed from her home, and called in there before heading into work.

The briefing room was packed, and Erica noticed everyone at some point glance towards the window, checking it was still raining. Erica was no longer worried about that – it seemed it was going to rain almost non-stop for two days, and she knew this woman wouldn't pass up a blatant abduction offering like that night was proving to be.

Erica was aware she was nervous. Suppose they had it wrong. The evidence showed the small black car was right in the thick of this spree killing, and in her mind it almost felt like they were arresting a car. They had no idea of the identity of the driver, everything was a guess based on rainfall levels, and the damn river seemed to be complicit in everything that had happened or might happen that night if they didn't get this right.

They had no evidence that what had been inside that suitcase was a body – it could have been somebody fly-tipping into the river to get rid of rubbish. It could be pure coincidence that a body had been found in the same spot.

Erica felt sick at all the what-ifs cascading through her brain. She knew she was going out on a limb, had no idea what the repercussions would be if she got it wrong and they ended up with a riverside corpse yet again, and as she watched the bustle of them meeting up with their partners for the operation, she shivered.

She had opted to go in the car rescue truck. They would be the first to know that the killer had left Adam – again supposition that the killer would follow her normal routine, then bring him a McDonald's – and the truck would immediately pull across to block off the garage entrance and exit. Nobody would go in or out in a vehicle. Once that was in place the entire team would move and Erica would lead them in to arrest the woman.

The team of eight people were in place. Erica had refused the offer of armed backup, purely because at no point had firearms been in the equation. Every one of the nine deaths had been by manual strangulation with tights and she had no reason to believe the modus operandi would change at any point.

She hoped.

Erica and Flick climbed into the truck first, and eased uncomfortably behind the two front seats. The driver had placed a blanket on the floor, but it added nothing to their comfort.

Will Bramwell and Kev Ward were in the front. It would raise no strange glances in their direction if both front seats were filled by men. Erica had made it clear that as boss, she wanted to be first onto that garage site, this case had haunted her for far too long.

By four o'clock all cars were in position. Every one checked in at intermittent times and yet the occupants of the rescue truck couldn't see anyone. The plan had worked so far.

By five o'clock Erica and Flick were stiff and sore. They were threatening Will and Kev with gagging them if they didn't shut up arguing over whether Sheffield Wednesday or Sheffield United was the best team in the city, but that seemed to have no effect at all.

'I need a wee,' Flick announced. 'I shouldn't have had that last coffee.'

'No you shouldn't,' Erica responded. 'Rule number one for surveillance is don't drink for a week beforehand. You'll be hours before you can get to a toilet.'

Flick sighed and didn't answer.

The rain battered on the windscreen and appeared to be

getting heavier. Erica could only imagine what the Porter must be like; she knew it would once again be in full spate, and this woman wouldn't let that go. Perfect conditions for murder, for continuing what she believed to be her anonymity with regard to this crime. And anonymous she was, for the moment. Her one flaw was she needed this little black car that they had under their own watchful eyes.

Sam and Mike checked in to say all was quiet, but while Sam was speaking he said, 'Hang on a minute. Car pulling up about two hundred yards away.'

There was silence in the truck while they held their breaths, waiting and hoping this was what they had been praying for.

'Boss? You there?' Sam sounded tinny, but she could hear something in his voice. Excitement?

'Go ahead, Sam.'

'It's stopped. Somebody's getting out. We'll hold back until we see where they're going.'

'Over.'

For a minute nobody spoke, then the radio crackled once more.

'Boss, they've turned left and are heading up the road towards you. We're not close enough to read the reg yet, will do that as soon as we get to it. We're driving up to it and parking behind it in one minute. Think it's either an Audi or a VW. This damn rain isn't helping. Do you have sight of the person yet?'

'We do, Sam. Get that reg checked ASAP, I'd like to know who we're arresting. This bloody rain's brought her here, but it's stopping us seeing much. She's carrying a carrier bag. Let's hope it's got Adam's tea in it.'

There was an air of expectancy inside the cab, and they waited. They could see little, and Erica told Will not to use the wipers. If they couldn't see out, the killer couldn't see in.

The figure reached the garage site and paused to look around before entering and disappearing.

Still they waited. They jumped when the radio crackled. 'Boss, we've got the reg and confirmation of the owner of this red Audi,' Sam said. 'It's a Francesca Johnson.'

36

F lick stared in horror at Erica. Her morning with Georgia had led her to think Georgia could be the prime suspect, and she had taken great care not to reveal any of the evening's activities to the waitress.

Suddenly Erica moved. 'Flick, I need to get out.' Kev jumped down from the truck, giving Erica egress. She almost fell out, moved across to the grassed area and vomited. Her stomach heaved and heaved until it was empty. Flick handed her a cloth she had grabbed from inside the truck.

'Boss, you can't have anything to do with this now,' she said urgently. 'Wipe your face with this and go and sit in Mike and Sam's car. We'll deal with whatever has to be done.'

The beep of the alarm they had given to Adam sounded inside the cab, and Erica moved before anyone could stop her. She grabbed the radio in Kev's hand and called, 'Go, go, go,' the agreed signal. She handed it back to Kev and ran across the road, followed by a panicked Flick. Erica heard the engine growl as it started, and knew Will was moving the truck across the entrance.

Erica reached it and ran up the muddy roadway, closely

followed by Flick and a mystified Kev. Erica knew the name Francesca Johnson meant nothing to him.

Ian, Sam and Mike were there within thirty seconds. The plan had worked perfectly, although only Ian and Flick wondered how the hell they were going to stop their boss from committing all sorts of fuck-ups over the next few minutes.

The Fiesta reversed out of the garage, and Frannie swivelled her head to look out of the back window.

She had a choice. She could put her foot hard down and slam the love of her life into that brick wall, or she could stop the car, get out and kiss her for the last time.

Neither option suited Flick. She picked up a huge rock, ran towards the car and slammed it against the driver window. It was enough to shock Frannie, who was a second too late in stopping Flick from opening the driver's door.

Ian had reached the car as well, and calmly leaned in and switched off the engine. 'Out,' he said.

'No.'

'No? You want me to get you out physically? And you'll be on this muddy wet floor in about ten seconds if I do, and you won't be getting up in a rush. Don't piss me about, Frannie, get out the fucking car.'

'I want to speak to Erica.'

Flick reached inside the car, pulled off the black knitted beanie and grabbed a chunk of Frannie's hair.

'As my colleague said, Frannie, get out the fucking car,' and Flick pulled with all her might. Frannie tumbled out, screaming, landing in the mud.

'The charge of resisting arrest will be nothing compared to

the charges you've got coming,' Ian said, and placed his foot in the middle of her back. 'Hands behind you.' He snapped the handcuffs on as she conceded defeat.

Erica hadn't moved. She stared as they got Frannie out of the car, watched as she was handcuffed and hauled upright, and then as Flick and Ian walked her back down to where the truck was blocking the exit. Ian's car had been designated the one to transport the killer back to the station, so Flick went with him. Sam and Mike stayed with Erica, now fully understanding what had gone so dramatically awry.

'Boss,' Sam said, 'I'm not going to say much because I don't know what to say, but can I take you to Adam. I think you need a cup of sweet tea or something. You're in shock. Please.'

She looked at Sam, not really seeing him, but nodded. She knew Forensics were on call to move in and get the car onto the rescue truck, but it was no concern of hers now. The second she heard Sam say the name Francesca Johnson she had known it was no longer anything to do with her.

Sam gently held her arm and steered her towards the top garage, where Adam had already raised the door slightly.

Sam introduced them and asked Adam if he would mind making Erica a cup of tea. Adam didn't query anything, simply lifted the heavy bottle of water and poured it into his kettle.

Will reversed the truck down the narrow roadway with six inches to spare either side, then clambered out once the truck was fully in the garage clearing. He remained with the car until Forensics arrived. When they did, they didn't take long, briefly checking it over, taking photographs and supervising it being loaded onto the truck. Once that was done they moved inside

ANITA WALLER

the garage. There was a small generator humming quietly in the background, and an old fridge plugged into a socket. Once the fridge was opened it was obvious it was there primarily for the tiny freezer top box. Inside that were nine sealed plastic bags, each containing the tip of a little finger. Names were written on the front to identify their previous owners. The normal part of the fridge contained a box of vials labelled Propofol, all full and unopened.

Kev had stayed behind once Will had driven off, and he walked up to the top garage, knowing his boss, along with Mike and Sam, were there. He stood outside for a moment, unsure how to handle the situation. Then he knocked on the door and shouted out Mike's name.

The door lifted and Kev looked inside. His DI was clearly in shock, clutching on to a mug of tea. She was sitting on the garden chair, Sam and Adam sitting on the sleeping bag.

'Boss,' he said gently, 'you still in charge?'

She shook her head as if clearing her thoughts, and looked at the young man in front of her.

'I suppose I am until I get back to the station. Then they'll send me home so fast my feet won't touch the ground. You need me for something, Kev?'

'No, boss, only information for you. The car has gone, Will's taken that straight to Forensics, but the team are inside the garage. I believe they've now locked up the case so tight...' He paused, wondering how to make the find sound not so horrific. He couldn't think of any way to soften it so carried on. 'In the corner of the garage is a small generator and there's an old fridge plugged into it. One of the old kind with a little freezer top box. Inside that top box they've found nine plastic bags each containing the tip of a little finger. They've also found her stash of Propofol.'

. . .

Erica felt her stomach churn once again, and she took several sips of the tea, hoping to distract it from wanting to splatter yet more stomach contents over the floor of Adam's garage.

'Thank you, Kev.' Her voice shook as she spoke, and she felt a tear trickle down her cheek. She wiped it away. No weakness in front of her team.

But they could see the weakness, feel her pain.

She handed Adam the almost-empty cup and smiled at him. 'You're an exceptional young man, Adam, and I'll make sure you get some recompense for the help you've given us today. I know you have Sam and Mike's numbers, but this one is mine. If you need anything, ring it.' She handed him her card and stood. 'I have to go back to the station, Mike, and speak to the Super.'

Mike nodded, and all the police officers shook Adam's hand before leaving his garage. Erica stopped as they approached the garage that had held the Fiesta and one of the Forensics team saw her peering in. 'Ma'am? You okay?'

'I am, but I needed to see the layout inside.' *Needed to see where my wife must have spent so much of her time.*

Mike put his arm around her shoulder and gently steered her away. 'Come on, boss. Let's get you sorted. You can leave this to others now.'

The briefing room held many people, but it was quiet. After such a successful result as this case had given, there would have normally been raucous laughter and jubilation, but a boss such as Erica, a much-admired DI, to be right at the heart of that result meant no celebrations.

She walked in, flanked by Mike and Sam, and everyone stopped what they were doing and turned towards her.

'Thank you, everybody,' she began. 'As you all know we appear to have everything we need for a conviction in this case, and we must make sure our paperwork is spot on. I probably won't be here for a bit, my life is too closely tied to the killer's life.' She tried to swallow the lump in her throat. 'I'm relying on you to get it right, so don't let me down.'

She turned and walked towards the door, afraid to say any more. She couldn't let them see tears.

The applause began before she had gone three steps, and for a split second she hesitated, then carried on outside the room and down the corridor towards the lift. The applause was still there as the lift carried her to the ground floor.

Erica arrived home to find Beth on the sofa, reading. 'Are you okay?'

'I am.' Beth looked puzzled. 'I didn't expect you home until much later than this. It's been lovely to relax without having constant temperature and blood pressure checks. I had a lovely long shower...'

Erica finally let the tears flow.

'Oh my God! What's wrong? What's happened? You didn't catch her?'

Erica sank into the armchair, and reached across for the box of tissues. She dried her face, attempted to stop it getting wet again unsuccessfully, and Beth stood carefully and walked over to her. 'I can't hug you,' she said, 'but it looks as though you need one. I can make us a hot drink, and I can certainly pour us a brandy if you've got any.'

Erica nodded and pointed to a sideboard at the back of the room.

A minute later they both cradled a brandy glass filled with more than a single brandy, and Beth waited.

'Drink that, and talk when you can.'

. . .

Erica sipped at the brandy, feeling it hit her stomach and hoping it wouldn't cause her to race to the toilet for another bout of vomiting. She didn't know how to talk about the afternoon's events, didn't know how to react to her Super's words of internal investigations and garden leave for the foreseeable future.

It was the worry etched on Beth's face that made Erica start to talk and once she had started she couldn't stop.

'It's Frannie. Frannie is our killer. Honest to God, Beth, nothing in our life would ever have led me to see that. I've been going over and over things in my mind and although I've not looked in my journal yet, I know now, with hindsight, that her late-night meetings are all going to coincide with the murders of these girls.'

'You keep a journal?'

'I do. It's so I don't forget things, and it winds me down filling it in for half an hour at the end of each day. I make a note of mainly nice things that happen, or plans we've made, and we always jotted late meetings in it so the other one could check if we weren't home. My journal will probably be a big part of the evidence against her. Shit, Beth, it was awful this afternoon. I only knew of her identity seconds before we got to her. She parked her car near to where Sam and Mike were on surveillance, and they rang in the number plate for an ID check. She'd already turned into the garage site when they radioed to say it was a Francesca Johnson. The name didn't click with either of them, and it was raining so hard we hadn't been able to see much, so I hadn't recognised her. She was dressed in black, hood almost covering her face. The shock hit me and I almost fell out of the truck to be sick. I was the first into the garage site and she was reversing the Fiesta out of the garage. Her face, Beth. I could see it on her face she was going to reverse into me and kill me.'

37

They hadn't allowed Frannie to wash. The mud was all over her face, her clothes, in her hair, but they removed the handcuffs once she was safely in the interview room. Her night in the cells hadn't removed the smirk from her face, nor the cockiness from her attitude.

Frannie smiled when they asked if she needed a solicitor. She said she didn't need one, the case would only be going to court for sentencing. She continued to smile when they cautioned her.

They left her sitting on the hard straight back chair for ninety minutes, then Flick entered the room accompanied by Ian. Originally DCI Chambers, an officer from a neighbouring station brought in specially to oversee the case in Erica's absence, had said he would do the preliminary interview, but after speaking with Flick had decided she should do it, in view of her closeness to the case. He would observe from the viewing room, stepping in if he felt it necessary.

Flick logged everybody in for the tape, and then opened her file.

'Can I say something?' Frannie asked.

'Yes, but remember you are still under caution. And please be aware we can get you a solicitor if you should decide you do need one.' Whatever this woman had done, Flick felt uncomfortable that she hadn't wanted or requested legal representation.

'I know. I really only want to say I have done everything you are about to accuse me of, that my wife had absolutely no idea, and no reason to believe the woman she was chasing was me.'

'Thank you. That will be noted.' Flick wanted to say 'we know that, you stupid cow', but refrained. She took the picture of Susanna Roebuck out of her file and pushed it across to Frannie.

'This is Susanna Roebuck, where we recovered her body. This isn't where you left the body. Can you tell us anything more about this?'

'Yes. I picked Susie up outside the university theatre. It was raining really heavily, and I told her to jump in the car, I'd give her a lift. She said she was waiting for Clare, her friend, so could we hang on a minute, and she got in the front seat. I injected her immediately with Propofol and drove away. I couldn't kill two people at once, I didn't have a second syringe.'

'You knew Susie prior to that night?'

'Yes, I used to chat to them both after they'd been to the gym. In The Coffee Pot. We got on really well, especially after I told them I had a wife. They were in a relationship, you know.'

'What happened after you'd injected Susie?'

She passed out almost immediately. It was a dreadful night, and I wanted to get as close to the River Porter as I could. That was the place I had chosen to honour their beauty.'

'Go on.'

'I drove her to the pocket park and left the car in the car park. I strangled her there, in the car, because there was nobody about. I carried her to the pocket park steps, and undressed her there, rested her against one of the uprights for the railings. I carved a V into her hand and snipped off the tip of her little finger. The river was so noisy, like a great roar. My lovely little summertime Porter certainly had her winter head on that night. I posed her, beautiful Susie, so that everyone could see what I could see. Her nakedness was her beauty. I bent to collect her clothes to put them in the bag with her little fingertip, and she slipped sideways and into the river. I followed her to try to get her back, but she'd gone, downriver. I climbed out wet through, gathered everything together and went back to my car. It was extremely disappointing.'

Flick suppressed the shudder. 'I bet it was. What did you do once you'd returned to the car?'

'I got in and closed my eyes for five minutes. Relived it, so to speak. It's a massive turn-on, being with a beautiful young dead body, you know. Then I got out, went in the boot, and found a dry pair of jeans and jumper. It was a struggle getting changed in the car, but I couldn't go home to Erica wet through.'

'And what was the colour of the dry jumper?'

For the first time Frannie looked surprised. 'Red, I think.' She reached across and pulled the picture of Susie towards her, and Flick deftly pulled it back, removing it from her gaze.

She took out the picture of Clare Vincent, and once again Frannie smiled, reliving the moment in her mind.

'The lovely Clare.'

Flick replaced the picture in her folder.

They went through the full gallery of victims with Frannie, finishing with Victoria Urland.

Flick was feeling sick. The depravity of the woman was obviously being allowed out for the world to see; she could finally be herself, instead of having to pretend to be a career woman with social services, the wife of a senior police officer, and a woman to be admired and respected.

'Victoria Urland,' Flick said, and briefly waved the picture in front of Frannie.

'Ah, beautiful mummy Vic,' she said. 'She still had her pregnancy roundness. I knew what time she was going to her bonfire so I was conveniently outside her parents' house to pick her up. She'd been in The Coffee Pot the day before, with the baby, and we'd chatted. As far as she was concerned, it wasn't pre-planned. I offered to drop her off at the civic bonfire, told her I was going to a friend's bonfire. I think she fancied me, and she jumped at the offer of a change of venue. She was dead within half an hour.'

Flick could see Ian's hands clenched, his knuckles white. He was reaching boiling point.

Ian spoke for the first time. 'Did you touch them?'

'What?'

'Don't act innocent. Did you touch them?'

Frannie laughed at his discomfort and aggression. 'You can't raise an orgasm in a dead body, Ian.'

Ian stood and slammed his hand down on the table. Flick touched his arm, and he slowly returned to his seat.

'Answer DC Thomas's question, please.'

'Maybe,' Frannie smirked. 'They were all so beautiful...'

Flick took a deep breath; like Ian, she was struggling to control her temper. She actually wanted to grab this woman again by the hair, and slam her face into the tabletop. Instead, she said, 'Propofol. We found your stash. Where did you get it from?'

'An American website. You can get anything from the States. But you know that already, don't you, you'll have checked the vials from the fridge, without a doubt.'

. . .

Flick gathered up her file and both officers stood.

'Is that it?' Frannie asked.

'No. Interview suspended. DS Ardern and DC Thomas leaving the room.' She switched off the tape.

Leaning slightly towards a bewildered-looking Frannie, she said, 'We'll be back for you later to talk about the others. Probably tomorrow. We'll maybe let you have a shower after that.'

The tension in the briefing room was palpable. Nobody wanted to go home, nobody could raise a smile, and when Flick and Ian walked in all talk stopped.

Flick moved to the front and turned to face the team. 'She's admitting to everything. We've only covered our five girls so far, but she's given us everything we've asked, and this one isn't going in front of any jury. She's refused legal representation. We have to get our heads around the twenty-fourteen questions now, so that's it for tonight. Thank you, everybody. I realise it's hard to wind down after the events of yesterday, and I'll be speaking to the DI tonight. Eight o'clock tomorrow, everybody, and not a moment earlier.'

Without exception, every member of the team asked her to pass a message of support on to Erica, and Flick smiled through it, aching inside. What she was doing should have been Erica's job, she should have been the one to put this evil woman away for life. Instead, she was going to have to live with the stares and finger-pointing for the rest of her own life, and it simply wasn't fair. Nobody on the team had seen this coming at all.

Flick and Ian seated themelves across from Frannie. Ian spoke their names into the recorder and immediately Frannie spoke.

'There are four others.'

'We know. Leanne Fraser, Lucy Owen.' Flick hesitated as she glanced down at her notes.

'Laurel Price and the beautiful Lilith Baker-Jones.' Frannie smiled as she said the names.

Flick stared at her. 'You have no remorse? You killed nine women, all at the beginning of their lives, for what?'

Frannie shrugged. 'I can't help it. I've always known one day I would be caught and then my memories will have to be the only things I have left. I tried. I battled my feelings for two years before I killed Leanne Fraser. Give me my statement to sign, or whatever you need to do, and let's get it over with. I can spare Erica any court appearances. I'm settled; it's over for me.'

Flick closed her folder, and stood. 'Before we switch off, tell me the only thing that you've not touched on. Why did you wait five years? Why did you suppress these feelings that you say you have inside you, for five years, because I can tell you now, Frannie, you're going to face an awful lot of psychoanalysis before they decide whether you'll serve a prison sentence or whether you need to be somewhere more suitable for your particular proclivities. Either way, I'm sure they'll keep you isolated from the pretty young girls.'

Frannie heaved a sigh. 'That's fairly simple. What I'm going to say next is the last thing I'll say, because now is the time for me to take what's coming and to live with my thoughts. They'll find some medication to suppress what they will call "my urges", and likely as not stick me in some psychiatric unit until I die. I stopped the killing in twenty-fourteen because something happened to me that was so profound it changed me. It changed me for five years but my true self has surfaced again, and I've had to accept who I really am. The thing that changed me five years ago was I fell in love with intended victim number five.'

EPILOGUE

TWO MONTHS LATER

Erica sat on the bench and stared out to sea, wondering if it was safe to return to Sheffield. As soon as news had broken of the identity of the killer, her home had been inundated with press, and she had quickly driven Beth to her own house, gone back, packed a bag and escaped.

She hadn't had a destination in mind, and had pulled up, blinded by tears, in a layby in Derbyshire, wondering what the hell she was doing. She had rung her Super and explained the situation at home, trying to stifle sobs, and he had calmed her down.

'I have a cottage in Whitby, and we won't be going there until it's considerably warmer than this, Erica,' he said gently. 'We leave a key with a lady who fettles it for us, and I'll ring her to tell her you're on your way. She'll explain the heating and stuff, go and I don't want to see you again until the end of March. By then, I'm hoping this will all be over.' She had smiled at his Yorkshire use of the word fettle, and thanked him through her sobs.

And today Flick and Beth were coming to see her. They said

they were coming for fish and chips, but she knew they were only going to be there to check on her.

And then she saw them, walking and then running towards her. She stood, Flick held open her arms, and said, 'Group hug.'

They talked and talked, amidst copious amounts of vinegar and salt, and ate their fish and chips. Flick told her Becky Charlesworth and Katie Davids were back at uni, chastened by the experience but determined to do well in exams. It was as if the previous two months had blurred into non-existence, until the subject drifted to Frannie.

'When are you coming home?' Beth asked.

'I don't know. It's been the quietest Christmas I've ever had, but I bought a tiny foot-high tree to give a nod to the occasion, and sent myself a card. And read. Thank God I remembered to include my Kindle in the desperate bout of packing to get away. I'm off work until the end of March, as per the Super's orders, so I'll probably head back in a couple of weeks. Is all the paperwork completed on the case?' The question was thrown into the discussion with a degree of nonchalance.

'It's all wrapped up. In the end it's not even been that difficult. She's confessed to every murder, all nine of them. We don't have a definite date yet, but the Super seems to think it will be the end of March, so bear that in mind when you're setting your return-to-work date.'

'Did they find anything when they searched my house?'

'Not a thing. It seems that garage held everything they needed. She'd bagged up the clothes of each victim, and obviously we got the finger ends straight away from that freezer. She labelled everything – it was almost as if she'd planned for the day when she would be captured, almost as if she wanted that to happen so she could be stopped.'

'She's mentally fit for sentencing?'

'They haven't said she isn't. That's as much as we know.' Beth leaned back in her chair, and surveyed her empty plate. 'I'm stuffed. That's the biggest piece of cod I've ever had. It would have been enough without the chips and mushy peas.'

Erica looked at her sergeant's plate and smiled. 'You managed though. It's the Whitby air. Puts hairs on your chest.'

'I don't want hairs on my chest, thanks. Shall we order another cup of tea?'

'No, I'll get the bill and we'll go back to the cottage. It's really cosy, we can relax there and you can tell me how you two are getting on. And the rest of the team.'

It was only when they walked out to get in their car for the long journey back to Sheffield that Erica asked the question.

'Did Frannie say at any point why she stopped killing for five years?'

Beth and Flick shot a glance at each other and Flick answered. 'It was virtually the last thing I asked her. She said, "I fell in love with intended victim number five." I'm sorry, Erica, I wouldn't have told you that if you hadn't asked. We don't know who it was she fell in love with, but it certainly stopped her.'

Erica drew in a breath. 'It was me. I was intended victim number five.'

'But your name begins with E.' Beth frowned. 'We've been working on the assumption it was somebody else whose name began with L, and then she met you.'

'No, I met her through work. I had to talk to her about a case, and we fell in love instantly. I had to give my full name for a form we had to fill in, that first time we met. She knew my first name wasn't Erica, but she always called me that because I asked her to, told her everybody else did.'

'So what *is* your real first name?' Beth was frantically trying to work out if this information needed adding to the paperwork they had already signed off.

'If either of you laugh, I will personally see to it that you are sent back on traffic duty. Is that understood?'

They both nodded.

'My mother was a gardener. She loved shrubs. Erica is the genus for heather. I don't mind Erica. It's pretty. She also liked Lupinus. I refused to be called Lupin from the age of four.'

'Lupin?' both women echoed, staring at their boss.

They held in the laughter for five miles of their journey, and then Beth giggled. Flick knew why, and immediately pulled over, knowing this bit of information would never find its way onto the court papers.

Their laughter filled the night air, and they finally felt the words were right: case solved.

THE END

ACKNOWLEDGEMENTS

There are many people to thank for this book coming to fruition, and I have to start with Erica Cheetham, Beth Machin and Rebecca Charlesworth for the loan of their names. Thank you, ladies. Hope I did you proud.

When the idea for the book came to me, I didn't want any old nameless river, I wanted a Sheffield one, and believe me, we have plenty to pick from. I settled on the Porter because I knew nothing about it. On YouTube there are lots of videos by Patrick Dickenson who tracks our rivers, goes under the culverts, and generally spends most of his life wet through. I watched his two videos on the Porter and was hooked. I have since contacted him and he has sent me information about the best places to put dead bodies, and information about the access places. The man is a star, and I am truly grateful, Patrick, for your help.

I have to thank my publishers, and their team, for everything. Bloodhound Books, this is our seventeenth book together, who would ever have thought that? Massive thanks to Fred and Betsy, Tara, Heather, Alexina and the publicity team, and of course to my brilliant editor Morgen Bailey. She keeps me on the straight and narrow, and points out where I've been a little lacking. Or a lot lacking.

I have a beta-reading team who are second to none in the work they do for me. Huge thanks go to Marnie Harrison, Alyson Read, Sarah Hodgson, Tina Jackson and Denise Cutler, you're amazing. They read my book when it is at its most vulnerable, immediately after me typing THE END. They don't pull punches, they are an amazing team. Thank you, ladies.

And then I have an army of ARC readers. There are around forty people in my team, and all guarantee a review by launch day. They get their copy three weeks before anyone else, and it's a nail-biting time for me until their feedback starts trickling through. They are so supportive, a wonderful group of people.

And a final thank you to you, my readers. Without you it would all be pointless, and I love the way you give me your wholehearted support with every book I write. Thank you all.

Anita Waller
Sheffield 2020

A NOTE FROM THE PUBLISHER

Thank you for reading this book. If you enjoyed it please do consider leaving a review on Amazon to help others find it too.

We hate typos. All of our books have been rigorously edited and proofread, but sometimes mistakes do slip through. If you have spotted a typo, please do let us know and we can get it amended within hours.

info@bloodhoundbooks.com